All the best

E. Liz Bramich

E. Liz Bramich was born in Birmingham, educated at a local Grammar School and then took a B.Sc. in Zoology from the University of Leeds. A teaching career followed in Warwickshire and Lancashire. Married with two children, she now lives in Inverness.

E. Liz Bramich is also the author of *The Tyranny of Ichthus.*

Anyone for Carrot Cake?

E. Liz Bramich

This is a work of fiction. Names, characters, businesses, places, events, locales and incidents are either the products of the author's imagination or used in a fictitious manner. Any resemblance to actual persons, alive or deceased, or actual events is purely coincidental.

The views and opinions expressed in the novel are those of the characters only and do not reflect or represent the views and opinions held by the author.

Copyright © E.Liz Bramich 2018

CONTENTS

Chapter One. Frank Hector's early life	1
Chapter Two. Saturday 3 March	17
Chapter Three. Sunday 4 March	51
Chapter Four. Monday 5 March	73
Chapter Five I. Friday 2 March	93
Chapter Five II. Friday 2 March. At the Days'	101
Chapter Five III. Friday 2 March. At the Hectors'	121
Chapter Five IV. Friday 2 March. At the Days'	143
Chapter Five V. Friday 2 March. At the Hectors'	149
Chapter Five VI. Friday 2 March. Ate the Days'	163
Chapter Five VII. Friday 2 March.The Dinner Party	173
Chapter Five VIII .Friday 2 March	201
Chapter Five IX. Friday 2 March	253
Chapter Five X. The Drive Home	257
Chapter Five XI.	273
Chapter Five XII	283
Chapter Five XIII. At the Hectors'.	293
Epilogue. April.	307

CHAPTER ONE

Frank Hector's early life

'Oh God, help me, help me, HELP ME!'

The downtrodden wife of Big Frank looked heavenwards and pleaded, but help was never forthcoming, from God or from anyone else.

Young Frank Hector had done little to help his mother in her perpetual struggle to placate his brutal father, Big Frank. At first, it was because he was too little, too young and too weak but, ultimately, he was too uncaring.

He had had a miserable existence from his birth. Together with his mother and his sister, Sarah, he had been continually terrorised by the vicious, controlling activities of his father. He left the family home as soon as he was old enough.

Ali Hector, dowdy, tired and care-worn, scurried round the tiny scullery, in the miniscule cottage which she shared with her family, anxious to have her husband's dinner on the table upon his return from the pit. So exhausted was she, after her meagre lunch of thin, unappetising soup, that she had fallen asleep. Her husband, who kept her in a permanent state of terror, was due home and she was short of time and unprepared. Her frantic activity resembled that of a pale, golden hamster furiously pedalling on a wheel in its cage from which there was no escape. Listening intently by the open window, she could detect the *stomp, stomp, stomp* of his steel toe-capped boots on the hard, narrow footpath outside. It was a signal which always unnerved her as she anticipated with a trembling lip his inevitable entrance with his bellowing, rasping voice, loud in her ear,

'Where's mi dinner then, yer useless article? 'ope it's better than yer last effort'.

She endeavoured to escape his wrath and the inevitable slap around the head by not keeping him waiting.

With shaking hands she brought him a bowl of pork rib stew and in her nervousness she spilled some gravy onto the bare table top. He glared at her.

'Yer clumsy article! Get this mess wiped up!'

Mopping it up with her dishcloth with one hand and handing him a spoon with the other, she backed away out of his reach.

He spooned some of the thin, pale, fatty gravy and raised it to his nose, still streaked with the filth from the pit. He sniffed the contents of the spoon.

'What's this muck, yer givin' mi?'

He put the now tepid liquid into his mouth and immediately spat it out. With a swipe of his hand he swept the bowl and its contents across the kitchen smashing the bowl into tiny fragments. He roared at her,

'Get this bleedin' mess cleared up, yer faggot. I'm off t' t' Cock.'

He took two strides and cracked the side of her head with the flat of his hand.

'Mebbee, you'll tek more care, and get mi a proper dinner next time.'

This pale, wispy-haired, frail woman, who appeared to be perpetually ailing and anxious, was in awe and dread of her brutish, domineering husband to such a degree that she had developed a nervous tic and a stutter whenever he came near her and she would automatically turn her head away from him putting up her hands to protect herself. It was a futile gesture which made him laugh out loud. He referred to her as 'an excuse for a woman', and if that were the case, then it had been his actions and oppressive behaviour which had made her so. The perpetual, severe bruising to her body, manifested itself on her skin by a rainbow of colours, changing from blue to brown to yellow as the skin recovered. Her baggy dress and pinafore helped to keep them hidden from view, but such was his cruelty and arrogance that he did not care that the people in their community witnessed her blackened eyes. These badges, which he had bestowed on his wife made him proud to be the most feared male in the village and he hoped that his notoriety would spread to the districts beyond the village boundary.

Frank Hector Sr. had worked at the coal face in the deep pit at Low Ridge Mine. A powerful, bulldozer of a man, a hard worker, and a hard drinker, he was as hard as nails. Now employed by the colliery as the overman, he ruled his team down the mine with an iron fist. The treatment of his wife and children was no different. He was a controlling harrier who would brook no opposition. All who knew him were terrified of his callousness and his menacing manner. People in the vicinity steered clear of Big Frank Hector.

His wife and children's obedience was absolute. There were two children in the Hector household, a daughter, Sarah and Frank Jr. The boy resembled his mother in stature, much to the disgust of his father. Big Frank had no time for his weakling son, often referring to him as 'th' apology' and his treatment of young Frank was correspondingly harsh, both verbally and by the use of his broad, leather, buckled belt. He would claim that such severe discipline would make a man of him. Frank, like his mother, displayed his terror, whenever his father came near him, by uncontrollable twitching. This constant anguish left him with a tic in his cheek which manifested itself in times of anger, anxiety or stress. No-one ever questioned Big Frank's treatment of his family. It was none of their business and they kept their noses out of it.

As a toddler, little Frank had suffered a severe attack of chicken pox. So extreme was the infection that he was smothered from head to toe with red, itchy blisters, particularly on his scalp, face and genitals. This slight, emaciated boy, as a result of his scratching every scab within reach of his tiny fingers, suffered unsightly pock marks on his face and his genitals, and on all those areas of his body which bore the rash.

'Got nits as well as t' pox 'as 'e?' joked the unsympathetic Big Frank as he watched his young son scratch his head in an attempt to relieve the intense itchiness on his scalp.

Frank Jr's reluctance, on account of his wretched appearance, to venture far from home to play rough and tumble with his peers had caused him to find other interests. At school, he became engrossed in reading and music. His teacher unlocked in Frank a rare talent for performance which would have amazed his parents had they been sufficiently interested. He would devour any reading matter available to him at school for there was none to be had at home. Nor was there any music; Frank Sr. had had no time for such cultural pursuits, which he had considered unmanly, and so in order to rid his son of these habits, he beat little Frank all the more.

His sister, Sarah, was two years older; like her mother, she was pale and thin. She had left her childhood behind at the age of twelve years. To provide some amusement for herself in a home where none existed, she would invite Frank into her bed and display to him the physical changes that were happening to her body. He was intrigued to see hair sprouting in her armpits and between her legs. She invited him to touch her budding breasts and her nipples and watch them harden into tiny pink thimbles and she would open her legs wide and tell him to put his fingers in that place normally kept secret in her underwear, a hitherto, unexplored channel of her unadulterated innocence. It was an exciting experience for Sarah to educate her little brother and Frank Jnr. was grateful to her for sharing it with him.

Having witnessed his sister's metamorphosis from child to woman, he began to regard, with a renewed interest, the girls at his school and those who lived in the streets nearby. He became sensitive to the secret glances which passed between the girls and the boys and he became eager to catch any snippets of conversation relating to sexual matters and there were many for him to absorb. He availed himself of any opportunity to look, touch and learn about girls and their wily ways. He would hear from other boys, those who were more physically advanced and attractive than he was, about their sexual exploits with some of the more promiscuous girls. So far, outside the home, he had not participated in any such adventure himself.

Frank's initial experiences with girls had amounted to a series of secret, exciting, adventurous meetings, in which the investigation of each other's genitalia took place. The thrill he had had when he, while still pre-pubescent, was invited by a young girl in his class to her home where she took him into the poorly lit, under-stairs cubby-hole to look at her vulva with its initial, coarse growth of pubic hair and to feel her soft, wet inner parts had caused his trembling knees to grow weak with intoxicating excitement and there was a greatly surprising stiffening in his underpants. Such young girls often matured into the young sirens who would later taunt him about his 'little worm' but, in those early salad days, it had not prevented their enjoyment of his inexperienced stroking and his penetration of their juicy crevices with his sticky fingers. Some girls of his acquaintance were so avid for a sexual encounter that they would tolerate any male fondling their breasts and bottoms while still modestly covered by their shirts and skirts. He was able to witness such events when groups would convene, in the absence of parents, in one of their homes. He took the opportunity to watch their various behaviours and to listen to the moaning and grunting from each pair of wildly thrashing, sweaty bodies in their clumsy acts of intimacy and to smell the accompanying sweet scent of these illicit exploits. He experienced much enjoyment as a voyeur to the practices of the inexperienced young pleasure-seekers of his acquaintance.

One promiscuous girl, a pert young siren, named Carol, who lived two streets away from his home, was already at the tender age of thirteen well-endowed with the sort of shape which caused the boys to salivate. She was aware as she strutted along, her breasts thrust forward under her tight, bright red polyester jumper, with her tempting buttocks, trim and taut under her rather too short, tight skirt displaying her shapely legs, that she had something to offer to all-comers. She was well-known among the boys in his class for being easily available to any and to all of them. He would watch them go off in a group into the fields - into the long grass or sometimes into the local park where there were adequate hiding places among the bushes for their playtimes.

He accompanied the group on one occasion. It was a day in late summer, the autumn term at school having commenced earlier that week, when the sun shone down, brilliantly, from a cloudless, blue sky, and the temperature soon soared to the high seventies. The listless pupils had lolled, with heavy eyelids, over their desks in the hot, airless classroom as they listened to the constant hum of the flies and watched their continual collisions with the window panes in their persistent, relentless attempts to escape to freedom. The group of five, comprising Frank and Carol, another girl, Emma, and two other boys, made their way to Little Scarp Municipal Gardens where they were sure of some privacy among the shrubberies.

They made their way to a secluded area where, in spring, the heady perfume from the yellow *Azalea luteum* and the orange *Azalea fireworks* had permeated the air, acting like a sleep-inducing drug to those inhaling their scent. Now, in late summer, those wildly-coloured blooms had been replaced by dense, green foliage, whose security these young dabblers craved for their early sexual experiences. The flower beds had been planted out with French and African marigolds providing a garish sea of orange waves stirred up by the late summer breezes. Along the hedgerows, the multitude of the familiar, common *Crocosmia montbresia* displayed their long sword-like leaves and spikes of burnt-orange flowers. In the well-screened shrubbery, Frank watched, with fascination, the other boys take their turns with both girls, each boy doing to them whatever took their fancy. Frank's concentration unswerving, his eyes wide and mouth open, he observed Gary and Jason maintain erections with which they penetrated each gyrating girl in her turn. The girls lay adjacent to each other, their legs splayed wide in the air and he heard them squealing with delight at their bodies' response to this male attention.

Frank had been invited to join in the fun. He managed to get an erection of sorts in his puny pipe but he was the butt of ridicule from both the girls and boys alike when they observed his pathetic specimen. His self-confidence, little as it was, was reduced to zero. This would be the last time that he would participate in this particular group activity. The experience had taught him a valuable lesson about the nature of the female sex. He was determined that in any future liaison with a female, he would assume dominance. Women would only be tolerated on his terms. He nursed the belief that the female sex was intrinsically cruel and in any future relationships with the opposite sex, he would pre-empt their cruelty with some of his own.

He thought about the relationship between his own parents. What had caused his giant of a father to browbeat his tiny mother so? Frank could not imagine which of her behaviours had irritated his father so much that he resorted to frequent violence. But in his subconscious mind, young Frank had internalised the 'bullyboy' tactics of his father and they were stored away in a compartment in his brain for such time in the future when a member of the female sex, by her actions, unlocked the compartment and released the punitive contents.

The three victims of Big Frank – Ali, Frank and Sarah, sought solace in the church. They attended the Pentecostal Gospel mission in the village of Little Scarp in which they lived. Little Scarp did not live up to its name; it was, in fact, a large, populous mining village, a few miles east of the pit at Low Ridge where Big Frank was the overman. Amongst the workforce, the talk was that mining for coal was doomed, but Low Ridge pit was so productive that the men believed that work would be available for years to come. The air retained the constant stench of burning coal and the blackened buildings displayed the evidence of the sooty atmosphere. Further north, a few miles along the main road, was situated the affluent village of Higher Ridge. It was remarkable that two villages, so near geographically, could differ so – one in the valley from where the acrid, smoky fumes released from the fires of miners' cottages failed to escape and one on the side of the grassy, tree-lined hill where the prevailing breezes kept the air fresh and clean.

The Pentecostal Gospel mission was located on Canal Street, in a fine, solid, Victorian building, erected from red bricks, with sills and cornerstones, constructed from locally quarried stone, sadly dulled by the perennial, incessant outpouring of smoke from the multitude of chimneys in the vicinity. In this oasis, the Pastor, the Reverend Edward Pickering attended to the spiritual needs of his congregation. His other profession was that of a highly regarded Chartered Accountant in the nearby town of Broadclough where he resided in the most affluent district of the town with his wife and daughter. He spent most of his evenings away from Broadclough, either conducting services at the Mission or acting as Counsellor to the inmates at Pinchfold Castle Prison.

It was the Pastor who had initiated Frank into his first, enjoyable sexual experience. Until this event, Frank would allege, somewhat disingenuously, that he had had no knowledge of the intimate habits of the sexes. He had insisted to any inquisitor that he had been too intent on attempting to avoid confrontation with his father and a subsequent leathering across his backside. The Reverend Pickering had been aware of this small, weary family-group of mother and two children. His experience enabled his recognition of the total lack of self-confidence and self-esteem in the pock-marked young teenager. By research, he had discovered the boy's cultural leanings, not always present in the tough location inhabited by aggressive individuals. By probing, he discovered that there was a total lack of books in the Hector household. He found out that Frank enjoyed his music lessons at school. He detected that life at home was hard, indeed unbearable. He identified that their attendance at the Mission was an escape from reality rather than a belief in the Divine. The Pastor, having gained the trust of this attenuated family, would bring young Frank and his sister a regular supply of comics and other reading material, sweet treats, drinks and pocket money so that, slowly, the Pastor gained the boy's confidence. Frank began to believe that not all men were harsh and uncaring like his father. In Reverend Pickering, he believed he had found a man he could trust.

The Pastor was a frequent visitor to Pinchfold Castle Prison where he was a prison visitor, preacher and counsellor. It had come to his attention that there were certain young inmates - convicted rapists, who were in denial of their crimes. In conjunction with the warders, an experiment was devised which would be carried out by the Reverend Pickering during designated visits to inmates who were yet to be identified as potential subjects for investigation. In order to obtain a means of comparison with 'normal' males, he would seek permission among his parishioners to include them in the same experiment. The Reverend Pickering, because he was a revered cleric, was considered to have a hot line to the Almighty because he spoke in 'tongues', a feat practised by only the most sanctified of men. He was trusted by the God-fearing community to be the best person to conduct such research.

The Pastor selected his targets with some cunning. Attending the Mission were a number of youths whom he identified as worthy of consideration for his vile, sham experimentation. The boy, Frank, had been an obvious choice. He had reached puberty and he had personal needs which had not been met elsewhere. He was insecure and needed friends. The Pastor sought to identify other youths with similar dispositions.

The Pastor decided that the best plan of attack would be to approach each member individually. He proposed to each in turn that their participation would be rewarded with a fee as was the usual practice in all medical experiments. He determined that his payment of fees would be on a sliding scale, starting with an initial payment of £1 for the first test, increasing to £2 for subsequent tests, the timing of which the Pastor and his 'guinea pigs' would agree.

Young Frank showed immediate interest in his mentor's scheme. The Pastor had been good to him and now he could return the favours by joining the experiment and he would get some cash as well.

Young Frank had attended his first 'experiment' with the Pastor after the prayer meeting one Friday evening. The meeting took place in the Pastor's office at the back of the Mission building. It was a small, dingy room with a desk and two or three stand chairs. Frank was invited to enter. The Pastor still wore his priestly attire of a smart suit, a carefully ironed shirt, a dog-collar and his clerical gown. He removed the gown, the jacket and the dog-collar and carefully placed them on a coat hanger behind the closed door. He donned a white laboratory coat. He drew the blinds and switched on the single light bulb which dangled loosely from the open, green, plastic lampshade. He placed a one pound coin on the desk.

'Now, Frank, drop your trousers and under pants and we'll begin'.

Frank was instructed to drape himself across two stand chairs placed side-by-side adjacent to the desk. Frank was an obedient child. To challenge this odd request did not occur to him especially as his instructor was so revered in the community. The Pastor got close up to him and looked keenly at Frank's little, pock-marked penis.

'What a funny little fellow you have,' he remarked. 'What do you call it?' Frank blushed. He confessed that he had never called it by name. 'Well, you must give it a name, so that you'll always have a friend to play with,' said the Pastor.

The Pastor encouraged Frank to manipulate his penis in order to get an erection so that the experimenter could take measurements of its length and girth when fully erect, this being the purpose of the experiment: *The comparison of erectile function in young, convicted rapists with that of the 'normal' male.* Frank, with the helpful suggestions from the Pastor concerning how he should stroke and rub his floppy genitals, achieved the desired outcome.

'Congratulations Frank! Such splendid work for a first attempt. This is a good result. I am very pleased with your efforts. Here is your fee. Don't spend it all at once!' he joked as he chuckled to himself.

'S'cuse me, Sir. Please Sir."

'Yes, what is it, lad?'

'What's that badge on your jacket?'

'That badge is the sign of the fish. It's a badge which all we true believers wear.'

'Oh… can I get dressed now?'

'Yes, lad, and look sharp. It's getting late. Your mother'll be wondering where you've got to.'

Frank, still prone on the chairs, had been pleased with his performance. He had enjoyed the physical sensation. He also had £1 to spend. It would be double that next time and he had helped his good friend, the Pastor, in the pursuit of his commission. He left the Mission in good spirits and headed off to the shop in order to spend his money before his father could take it from him. Thus, young Frank Hector embarked upon his sexual journey. He named his friend, 'Eddie', in recognition of his new friend and mentor. What he could not have known was that these experiences in his formative years would lead to his destruction some thirty years on.

Meanwhile, the Reverend Edward Pickering, took a towel and wiped his sweaty brow and other parts of his anatomy, titivated his moustache and smoothed his damp, thinning hair, replaced his jacket and tie and last of all, his dog collar and went home to his wife and daughter.

As the years went by, young Frank grew and developed an adult body. He would never achieve the physical size of his father, but having listened to and having observed the behaviour between his peers and between adults; he stored all the information away in his subconscious which was destined to re-emerge in his future deviant, tyrannical attitudes.

CHAPTER TWO

Saturday 3 March

Chris Day shivered. She covered her head with the thick duvet. In spite of its insulating denseness, she had become aware of bird song. Flinging back the bedcovers and throwing off her eye-mask, with teeth chattering, nimbly, she dashed to the window and released the blind in such haste that it opened with a clatter. She glanced back, guiltily, at her still-sleeping husband, Hal. She was relieved that her noisy activity had not awakened him. She looked out on to a beautiful morning. It became crystal-clear why it was so cold. They had gone to bed and had left some windows open.

    She tip-toed out of the bedroom and made for the silent kitchen. Normally, she might have heard the sounds of their two sons, Max and Danny, but they were enjoying a sleep-over at Hal's parents' home in Higher Ridge.

    She was the lark in their partnership, usually wide awake and raring to go, but this morning she felt drained. Hal slept soundly still.

    They would not normally leave all their windows open. They were well aware of such temptation to cat burglars, but Friday night had not counted as 'all night' because it was three in the morning before they had got to their bed.

The previous evening Chris and Hal had hosted a dinner party at which former teaching colleague, Frank Hector and his wife Shirley had been their guests. Chris hated Frank and Frank returned the compliment.

She could not understand what had attracted a respectable woman, like Shirley, to Frank – a convicted sex offender who was divorced from his first wife Helen. Furthermore, she could not understand why her husband, Hal, somehow seemed to be in thrall to this odious monster.

She could still smell the stale odour of Frank's cigar. Chris addressed the absent Frank,

'Y' know, Hec, if you had any decency which I know you have not, you wouldn't light up your smelly cigars in my home. It's not like the old days when lighting your fag was automatic. Okay, so it's not in a public place, but even so, it's another example of your arrogance, you obnoxious reptile. You should've had the curtesy to ask me if I minded. I would certainly have told you to go outside if you wanted to smoke.'

She had questioned Hal's acceptance of this filthy habit by Frank in their home environment. She questioned why she had been so accepting of such impertinence from this individual whom she disliked so vehemently? She questioned why she had agreed to the dinner party in the first place?

She began to feel furious with herself for her willingness to have fallen into line with the demands of the men. However she had to admit that she had enjoyed goading Frank during the evening.

Hal had a 'live and let live' attitude. He had condoned Frank's smoking habit for several years and as he himself had been a smoker, he was prepared to overlook this grossness in Frank's behaviour and make the necessary repairs afterwards.

Hal was a decent bloke who had always seen some good in the vilest of people and Chris had admired him for that.

'...and that's why we had this damned party', she thought.

She stood by the window, deep in thought for a few moments, her expressionless face adopting a fixed stare.

'It's time I made a move. Better to let Hal sleep on. Shall I give him his breakfast in bed as a kind of apology for the meltdown at last evening's dinner party?'

She decided against this idea. If Hal would have been satisfied with bread and marmalade, she would have taken it up to him but his breakfast followed a complex routine. It was like a religious ritual and, in her opinion, was too messy an affair to have in bed. She would call him when all was ready.

Downstairs, the atmosphere was rank, reminding Chris of the stench of a city centre bar in the morning, before the cleaning staff started their work. She threw open all the doors and windows and wandered outside.

There had been another light dusting of snow as fine as icing sugar on a home-baked Victoria sponge. She would not be able to stay out long in these temperatures. She inspected the bird bath. Naturally, it was frozen over. The bird table was empty. In the last few days, some coal tits had reappeared after the winter. After the winter! It was still the winter, weather-wise, even though that day, meteorologically speaking, was the third day of spring. Great Barrow had had it easy. Much of the country was at a standstill because of the exceptionally heavy falls of snow. She would find them some crumbs, scatter some raisins for the blackbirds, replace the suet balls in the feeder and put some hot water into the bird bath. After breakfast, they would dispense their discarded pear parings and hope that the crows would feed before the gulls descended. She wandered over to Hal's pride and joy…his Koi pool…now sadly devoid of fish.

She anticipated the delights that the future would bring in the garden. As spring moved slowly and inexorably towards summer, the days would dawn progressively earlier and Chris would wake early and would be up and

about at four o'clock in the morning. Sometimes, it would seem as if the sun had never set. The following three months April, May and June were her favourite time in the garden. It was a time of new growth, of fresh green leaves on the trees and the promise of delicious scents and wild colours in the herbaceous borders. She hoped that her favourites, *Zantedeschia aethiopica* and *Verbena bonariensis* had survived the winter temperatures. She thought about what her dear, old, granny would have said, 'Well, they have two chances – live or die.' That recollection of her deceased granny brought her back to the reality that she was still outside in the chilly morning air. In order to ward off the cold, she folded her bare arms across her chest, and with hunched shoulders she quick-marched back into the warmth of her kitchen.
Replenishing the bird table and feeder had soon gone from her mind. Once inside, she tossed a few grains of rice left over from the previous night's meal into the goldfish bowl in which Remi swam sedately round and round but then with sudden movements gratefully accepted her offering. Perhaps their resident wood-pigeon would eat some of this too. No sooner had she scattered it on the patio, she heard the screech of the gull. It seemed to be saying,

'About time! You're late! I've been on this roof waiting for you to give me my breakfast. I'm due at my next feeding station'.

The gulls were down in a flash and there was a flurry of wings. How magnificent these birds were with their enormous, sleek white bodies and grey wings with black and white spotted wing tips, all perfectly preened, And what about that beak? It could tear any food to shreds. That is if, of course, the bird had not swallowed it whole first.

The dominant gull, which they had named Sydney, was not always the first to arrive, but having landed, it prevented the others from getting anywhere near, gobbling the entire offering. She had christened it Sydney, assuming it was a male bird. It *had* to be male – the way he strutted about and swaggered so that all the other smaller birds fled into the hedge. The crows did not stand a chance and the poor, plodding pigeon was way at the end of the queue. It had toddled off onto the lawn to see what food fragments were available there.

Half an hour had elapsed and she could hear movement upstairs. She decided to take a cup of tea to her sleepy husband. She felt sure that they would discuss the previous night's events over breakfast. To her surprise, Hal appeared fully dressed so there was no time or apparent need for a peace offering since it was by then ten o'clock. He said that he wanted to go to the newsagent's to pick up the Saturday paper. This was an unusual occurrence as they did not normally bother with newspapers except on Sundays when they were delivered to the door. He suggested that they should skip breakfast and have brunch a little later. This would allow them to get on with the clearing up and stacking of the dishwasher.

They had gone to bed at three o'clock and had left the kitchen in a mess. They had had such a hearty meal the evening before, with a variety of alcoholic drinks that he had been left with a dry mouth and was not at all hungry.

'Are you fit to drive?' Chris asked him.

'Hmm, never gave it a thought. Perhaps I'll walk down. It's a nice morning. The fresh air will do me good and I'll be all the more ready to eat when I get back.'

He was thoughtful for a moment. Then he added, 'No... on second thoughts, I'll take the car. I didn't drink much at all, too busy re-filling Hec's glass and, anyway, I want to go to Hec's. He left his phone on the table last night.'

No sooner had he spoken than he donned his favourite, well-worn gilet and bobble hat. He kissed his wife on the forehead and was out of the door.

Since the tea had been made and had time to mash, Chris sat down with a cup of the steaming brew and thought about what she had been doing at this time on the morning before. She had been in the process of making the soup. As she had stirred and added her ingredients, she had uttered some lines from *Macbeth,*

"Double, double toil and trouble,

Fire burn and cauldron bubble...

Something, something, something, something,

Eye of newt and toe of frog,

Something, something

Lizard's leg and owlet's wing."

She smiled to herself, thinking that she ought to look up the quotation and get the recommended ingredients if ever they should come again. This she thought highly unlikely, after the previous night's shenanigans.

Chris had gone to a lot of trouble preparing dinner. She always did. Invariably, she put in the forward planning and preparation and her methods had never let her down. She had prepared a simple meal….consisting of several courses but each one easily prepared. Carrot and coriander soup to start then giant mushrooms stuffed with rice, garlic and green pesto followed by pork meatballs in a tomato, garlic and oregano sauce, served with a Désirée potato and swede mash with lots of white pepper and butter and a sprinkling of cheese and French beans. Finally, she had served a raspberry and blueberry trifle, a platter of cheese, coffee and liqueurs and chocolate truffles. She considered that it had been a good menu. Hal had been in charge of setting the table and of pouring the drinks. She had not let her own standards slip even though she was entertaining such an evil bastard.

It was time to close the windows. The weather was deteriorating. The sky darkened and snow started to fall. Large, fairy-tale flakes fluttered thick and fast, covering the ground with a white carpet. Chris looked out of the window, anxious about Hal's whereabouts. She began to load the dishwasher. It was soon filled though several dishes lay unwashed on the worktop. It was no bother to her since she would wash the remainder by hand. Chris did not mind doing simple chores such as the washing up; it gave her useful thinking time. She filled the draining board, dried the crockery then filled the drainer again. At this point, Hal walked in, covered from head to foot with melting snow crystals, resembling an animated snowman. He shook himself like a dog might do, scattering droplets of melted snow all over the tiled floor, jumping up and down and stamping his feet in an attempt to get some feeling back into his frozen toes. Hunger pangs began to gnaw at their stomachs; neither of them had eaten that morning. Hal said,

'Let's go down to the 'Botanics' to Kat's Café and grab some soup and a sandwich. It will save you having to cook again'. She needed no further encouragement. They served wonderful food at Kat's and she was ready for some.

Then she had another idea.

'Instead of going to Kat's, why don't we go to Helen's Haven? When we were there, yesterday, we said we'd go back and we know she serves soup and sandwiches.'

The driving was a bit tricky with the soft snow on the ground, but they arrived intact and parked easily.

'I suppose the weather has frightened everybody off, said Hal, 'It'll mean we'll get faster service though'.

They were surprised to see so many people having lunch. It was obviously a popular stopping place for the traveller. Helen's business seemed to be thriving. The radio could be heard, faintly, in the background. They could hear music by one of their favourite composers, Debussy's *Poissons d'or*.

They caught Helen's eye.

'Hi Helen, we said we'd come back.'

'I never expected it to be so soon', Helen laughingly replied.

They each ordered a bowl of Smoked Haddock Chowder. Hal requested a ham and salad sandwich, while Chris chose her favourite egg mayonnaise. They shared a bowl of chips.

'These chips are just like those we had in that hotel in the Highlands…chunky, soft but crisp on the outside. Do you remember we said they were the best we had ever tasted?'

He remembered the trip well. They had participated in the annual Bridge Congress at the MacInvor Hotel and had not disgraced themselves during the various events. Infrequent players of the game, owing to a busy weekly schedule, they had initiated a monthly Saturday Bridge Club at the village hall in Great Barrow. The club had attracted a pleasing number of local residents since its inception a few years before, when they first moved into Luxor Lodge.

They had enjoyed the congress so much and the Scottish scenery was so majestic that they had decided to make it a regular event on their calendar. They recommended it to their long-standing friends, Debs and Tony, with whom they had learned to play the game as students. They had also taken the opportunity, whilst there, to call at Cromarty, the village overlooking the firth where Chris's mother had been born and had spent a few years before her father, Chris's Grandad MacDonald, had sought work south of the border. It had been a good weekend and, she agreed with him that the chips had been scrumptious.

'I'll just give your mum a call to see what it's like over there'. Chris was anxious to hear what the boys were up to. After a moment or two's chat, she switched off her phone. 'Max is snow- boarding with Jack Yates and Danny's watching *Finding Nemo* on TV. They're both fine...have had a good breakfast. There's a bit more snow but your mum thinks that the road will be OK.'

'Max is lucky to have Jack on the doorstep when he goes to Mum and Dad's,' Hal added.

Jack had been Max's main companion before they'd relocated to Great Barrow. Subsequently, Max attended the grammar school in Castleton. They met up only at holiday times or when on a visit to Grandma and Grandpa Day. Chris hoped that the two boys would escape without injury on their snow boards. They could easily have an accident coming down that hillside in Higher Ridge. She did not want Max to miss any school because he would be taking some important tests later in the year. She voiced her concern to Hal.

'Don't worry so…he'll be fine. We have to let him take a few risks… can't keep him in cotton wool any longer.'

Hal tucked into his lunch with relish. The generous serving of soup, delicious and perfect for the cold weather, was served at the correct temperature for its consumption. Helen knew that her customers could not abide a tiny portion of tepid soup served in a shallow bowl. Helen deserved to be successful because she ensured that the diners got good value and they showed their appreciation accordingly. The number of customers had started to dwindle as the time approached two o'clock. Helen was no longer run off her feet. Chris wondered how she managed to produce such amazing food for so many people without help behind the scenes. She came to join them at their table. Chris started to fish for information.

'We had Frank and Shirley for dinner last night.'

'I hope that the inevitable indigestion wasn't too severe', Helen laughed.
Chris was relieved that Helen took that news so lightly. She continued to angle for information. She asked Helen where she had been for the last few years. Helen recalled, now, the events of that February day some years previously, before she had divorced Frank Hector.

'I heard Frank yelling my name at some unearthly hour. I think it was about half past five, certainly before the whistle went for the boys to get out of bed. It was the police who'd come to arrest him. I was out of bed jumping to attention and had got to the doorway of my room when I saw him staggering up the stairs. I'd never seen him in such a state. I was stunned and paralysed by the whole performance. I couldn't speak. Goodness knows what the police thought – a wife who showed no emotion for her just-arrested husband. The police virtually carried him off to the station in Ravensborough. Then, I was in a panic because I didn't know what to do or who to contact. I never made any effort to contact the police to find out about him. I was just so pleased that he was gone from my sight. I really couldn't believe what was happening. I was out of one terrible situation but I was in another one with all these boys and two refugees. I know he took some things with him; he took his cornet because he didn't know what would happen to him, whether he'd be allowed to return to the school, for example. Somehow, I doubted it because I knew in my heart what he was like…a predatory paedophile. I was so disgusted with him and with myself for having tolerated him for so long.'

Helen paused. Her glistening eyes and quivering lip indicated to them that she was reliving the agonies of the past. After a moment silence she carried on speaking.

'Frank made all the decisions. Just as my own career was taking off, he dictated to me when it was time we started a family. Why did I go along with his command? Looking back now, I can't believe I just accepted his decision. What a scaredy-cat I was. I was so frightened of what he might do to me if I didn't jump to attention every time he spoke.

'We must have been remarkably lucky as there had not been many opportunities for me to conceive because our sexual relationship had been virtually non-existent. I had had to give up my job to look after Colin, our son, and so I became virtually a prisoner in my own home with just a baby for company. I had to rely totally on Frank for the shopping and Colin's needs.

'I had known in my heart that he was 'bent', ever since Colin was a baby. I suspected that he had interfered with Colin. I never knew the extent of it. I kept telling myself that I was imagining these terrible things about him. Did y' know it's called 'being in denial'? Colin was a baby; he couldn't talk. He never talked. He knew no different. He never complained once about his father's unnatural attention towards him. Why would he? For him, it was the norm. Frank had always been keen to bathe Colin and to do his nappy change. I used to think how lucky I was and persuaded myself that perhaps he wasn't so bad after all. I was glad that he was a 'hands-on' father. I was pleased that he took an interest rather than just letting me do all the work. Well, he certainly was hands on! I blame myself that it went on for so long but I had no proof and no one was accusing him, certainly not Colin. I worried as Colin was growing up whether he would be affected by his father's abuse of him but he seems to have been unscathed. Colin was packed off to boarding school when he was fourteen. He had been glad to leave home but was sad to leave me behind. I was gutted to see him go away to school but, at the same time, I knew that he would be safer anywhere else but at home under his father's influence.

'After Frank left, I had so much to think about... so much to do. At first, my mind was in a spin. He made no attempt to contact me. I suppose he guessed what my reaction would be. You know a lot of the story. For me, it was like a dream come true. At last, I was free of this brutal thug who had dominated my life for so long. I couldn't understand why I had allowed him to have such a hold over me for all those years. It was as if I was bound to him by invisible bonds.

'Once I had done the necessary paperwork to do with admission, he confined me to the kitchen. He never let me anywhere near the boys. All I did was to prepare and serve their meals. The only contact I ever had with any of them was when they came in penny numbers to help with the washing up. The boys never said a word against him. They were very much aware of the consequences of such foolishness. I was left with thirty boys still in bed on the February morning in the middle of nowhere. I was glad to have Andej and Anna with me. I kept saying to myself, *'Stay calm, don't overreact, take it slowly'* but all the time I was so excited, so elated, so fearful, so surprised. I had such a marvellous, tingling sensation of my impending liberty. I seemed to develop some kind of super-human strength. I didn't show what I was feeling; I continued to play the role of a subservient wife. I was good at that after all the practise I'd had for nearly twenty years. After Frank had left in the police van, I was left holding the fort until I knew what his fate would be. At that precise moment, I had thirty bowls of porridge to make and serve. I attempted to keep the routine going in the short term, because for all I knew, Frank would have persuaded them that he should be allowed to return home.

'I blew the reveille whistle and soon the boys were up and about their business, in the shower, none the wiser about the turn of events. They soon discovered that Frank was not around for the morning run. I asked Andej to sort out the boys' routine. He was so competent. He got them out for their run, through the showers and down for breakfast. He had always been kept in the background before. Frank would not loose hold of the reins to anyone else. I racked my brains for someone I could employ in

Frank's absence. You lose touch with colleagues when you're out of teaching for a few years. Anyway, I did remember some retired colleagues of mine who I had always got on well with and they were prepared to help me out. They would never have done any favour for Frank. They could never understand why I stuck with him for so long. Looking back, I don't really understand it myself. With their help, the school ran smoothly, but not as silently as when Frank was in control. The boys naturally took advantage of the change in personnel and like mice they played in the absence of the cat and who could blame them?

'I followed all the court hearings leading to Frank's jail sentence. I was left in no doubt as to what was going to happen to him. I only contacted him once, by letter, to tell him that I wanted a divorce. I had lost all interest in Frank years ago and was relieved by his downfall. I could hardly wait to turn the screw on him and on his affairs. He had kept me under his thumb for so many years when I felt incapable of retaliating. He had some strange hold on me. I was frightened of him and yet felt powerless to help myself. Suddenly, I was emancipated.

'Frank left the house at very short notice and consequently left behind all sorts of things that he would normally keep a tight control over. He forgot to take his keys. This was very significant because it meant that I could get into the safe for the very first time. He took his wallet with some cash in with him but all his other bank cards and credit cards along with a bank book in my name were in the safe along with some unbanked cash. Well... this was like opening a treasure chest or entering Aladdin's cave. I found a bank account, opened in my name, which Frank had set up to squirrel-away income from the taxman. He would explain to anyone who might ask, that it was my earnings. He never gave me access to it. It contained over four hundred and eighty grand. Can you imagine how I felt? It was as if all my boats had come in. I had to make some important decisions and number one was that I was not prepared to run the school in his absence. As soon as I learned that Frank's teaching qualification was to be revoked and that he would never return to the classroom I made an appointment to see a solicitor in Ravensborough to get some advice. To cut a long story short, his advice was that I wind up all Frank's affairs concerning the school.

'I contacted all the parents to come and fetch their sons. I reimbursed them with a term's fees which they had paid in advance. I paid off Andrej and Anna and said I would help them to find work if I could. They are both working for me now, Anna in the kitchen as before, and Andrej as my maintenance man. I paid off all outstanding loans and bills. I closed the school and put it on the market. There was little interest in it as a school because of the bad publicity. The local paper was full of Frank's arrest. Yet it was set up to function as a school. With no potential purchasers, I sold off all the furniture and furnishings and then put the place up for auction. All this was done following the solicitor's advice. A substantial amount of money was spent on Frank's legal fees. I was annoyed about this because we were still married and it meant that I was contributing to this cost. Eventually, I got my share of the proceeds and Frank was left with some cash in the bank. He was banned from associating with minors so his brass-banding would have to go. The shock of forfeiting the band on top of everything else ought to have been enough to make him want to end it all.

'His strength seemed to be magnified when he was controlling others but he's a cowardly weakling at heart. So the worm finally turned. I had escaped that snakehead of a husband. I was able to set up my business. Later, I was able to buy this place and refurbish it. Now, I am my own boss and I am well suited with my life and I just hope our paths never cross again.

'Looking back, I cannot believe what I've endured. Almost twenty years of my life...wasted! How I wish I'd never got entangled with Frank. We met when I was on holiday in America and he was working - doing all sorts of menial jobs for cash. His looks didn't attract me but there was something about his manner - his careful attention to detail. He was so tidy. I'd never met anyone like that and I thought how wonderful not to have to tidy up after a man...but how wrong I was. Frank remembered every detail I ever told him and always made sure I came to no harm. He was so attentive. Of course, I was mesmerised by his wonderful musical talent. He was like the Pied Piper and I followed him, unable to do otherwise. It was as if I was spellbound and unable to escape from his clutches and his control which worsened over the years. I felt isolated and trapped. I know it sounds incredible but he had such tremendous power over me. My parents had long since given up on me. They soon sold up and moved south. They couldn't stand him.'

Chris looked at Helen, with wide, tearful eyes and a furrowed brow, her body language displaying total sympathy for Helen's former existence.

'Goodness, Helen, that's a shocking story. We had absolutely no inkling about your horrific life with Frank... Bastard! Before the trouble, we used to see Frank now and again, about the town and we noticed how much healthier he was looking- carrying a bit more weight which suited him and we reckoned that his investment into the private school had made a good life for you all. Then the story about his arrest broke in the paper followed by his conviction. He wrote to Hal from prison. Did you know that? Hal and Frank were not exactly friends but they had some interesting debates with each other. Hal was surprised to get the first letter from Frank. Most people would have ignored it but Hal showed some compassion and they started to communicate.

'We're glad that all's turned out well for you. But now, he has another wife who may be having the same hard time that you went through. We must keep tabs on Shirley and ensure that history does not repeat itself. I must admit she did not look at all well last evening. She looked so weary and strained.'

Hal had remained silent throughout. He had been quite happy to let the women do the talking. He wondered whether he had been right to have befriended Frank when he learned about the hellish life Frank had given his first wife.

They left Helen to her food preparation and went back to the car.

'Did you hear what she said?' Hal reminded Chris. 'She said that Hec was left with some cash. He's always denied having any money. I bet he's stashed it away somewhere and is living like a parasite on Shirley.'

'The tight-fisted, control freak! That was an incredible story... I know I've always detested him, but who would have thought that he really was such a monster? And to think we entertained him so royally last night.'

Chris was silent for a few moments then she asked,

'By the way, how d'you think last night went?'

Hal was full of praise,

'Your food was immaculate as ever. Nobody in Great Barrow would have eaten better than we did. Hec drank and smoked too much, but what's new about that? As for the rest... well... what happened was bound to happen sooner or later. What's done has been done. What's said has been said. There will be consequences. But, don't worry. I totally agree with you on all matters concerning Frank Hector'.

Chris was relieved that Hal had not been too stressed about the fiasco at the table. So she changed the subject. Frank Hector had never been a favourite topic for discussion as far as she was concerned.

'By the way, why did you want the newspaper?'

'There should be a big write up about the match this weekend. One of the Premier clubs is up against our team. Some of the lads from school might be playing. It will be a great opportunity for them. I wanted to have a copy as a souvenir. I expect the TV cameras will be there at such an unusual cup tie.'

'Did you call at Hec and Shirley's?'

'No answer…all quiet… I put the phone through the letter box.'

Later in the warmth of the afternoon sun streaming through the window, Hal was dozing on the couch owing to the late hours they'd endured the previous night, the Hectors not having left until three o'clock that morning. The newspaper had slipped to the floor. Even the article he had been desperate to read had not been so engaging as to keep him awake. She studied his inactive face, peaceful in sleep. It had not changed much over the years.

It had matured, naturally. He was clean shaven at the moment. She wondered when the beard would start to reappear. It usually made a temporary appearance during the winter months. Perhaps he was giving it a miss this year as it was now March. His face had developed a few lines but his skin was still smooth for the most part. He still wore the same style of bold, black spectacle frames all those years later.

She recalled the old conundrum, 'When did Good Friday fall on a Monday?'

Answer: A racehorse called Good Friday fell in a steeplechase race in England in 1946. The race took place on Easter Monday.

She conjured up a similar question.

'When did Christmas Eve fall on the fourteenth of February?'

Intoxicated by the cosiness of their sitting room, she drifted back some twenty years.

After graduation, Chris had decided to stay on for an extra year in order to attain the Post Graduate Certificate in Education. She had drifted into it. The PGCE year enabled her to have another year of thinking time.

Her degree in Ancient Civilisations and Ancient Literature qualified her to teach those subjects. However, the schools which offered those subjects in their curriculum were almost as rare as hens' teeth. Those institutions which currently predominated as a result of the change from selective to comprehensive education in secondary schools in the 1970's, did not include Latin, Greek and other studies of the ancient world in the curriculum. She had loved Latin, considering it, together with Maths and Music, to be the most important subjects for study. She had been anxious to find her correct niche in the education system suspecting that in all likelihood, she would have to settle for the bog-standard comprehensive school. Could she have offered another subject...History, perhaps? It was the subject she loved...not the teaching of it to uninterested adolescents. If it hadn't worked out, she could have taken a job in a library, or even pursued another qualification to become a Personal Assistant in industry or the Law, or, maybe, become an Egyptologist. Now that had *really* been appealing. She had always been drawn to the mysteries of Ancient Egypt. They were uncannily fantastic. She had loved the film, *Stargate* and the eccentric archaeologist character. She never tired of watching the film. Hal had no interest in movies of that sort. Their tastes were very different in many ways.

Hal, on the other hand, had been determined to teach. He was a born teacher, his skill having been identified at all stages of the course. He was articulate, proficient in debate and seminar discussion, highly skilled in the classroom and popular with his pupils. It was forecast that he would go far in the profession.

Chris Pugh first met Hal on the train whilst travelling to grammar schools on teaching practice. It was February. They had their first date on February the fourteenth, St. Valentine's Day. By today's standards, this had been a very low key event. The University Union had staged a season of old black and white films - one a week, for six weeks; they were films that had been considered notable in their time, either for the film itself, or for the actors in it. The film in question, *Only Two can Play*, was set in Wales. It was a story about the 'eternal triangle'. Looking back, it seemed an odd choice of film for a first date. Perhaps Hal had thought that having a name like Pugh, she would enjoy it.

Hal, like the starring actor, wore black-framed spectacles. This gave rise to the pupils' nicknames for him - 'Peter Sellers', on account of his spectacles and 'Action Man' because of his boundless energy and dramatic personality in the classroom. Afterwards, they walked, hand in hand, back to her flat. She felt very strongly from this simple linking of their hands and the interlocking of their fingers that he could be someone special.

They used to spend much of their time, devoted to academic work, in the University Library, down in the Stack, where there were dinky studies off the main thoroughfare. These were intended for the use of post-graduate Theology students but Hal had frequented one for three years as an undergraduate without comment. There was no reason why Chris should not join him there.

The library closed at ten o'clock then they would stroll back to her flat, have some supper and later, Hal would take the long walk back to his own bed. And so their relationship flourished. They became qualified teachers and they were married the following summer.

Their wedding had been a fairly simple event. Possibly because of the lack of time required to organise a more lavish celebration; possibly because of a shortage of funds. They had planned their ceremony for eleven o'clock - such a ridiculously early time for a wedding ceremony, she now reflected. The groom was late, very late and she had to be driven round the block several times before the driver got the thumbs up to say the bridegroom had arrived. Hal being on the last minute was something she had grown accustomed to over the previous year so that she never considered for a moment that she was about to be jilted at the altar. They had to leave the wedding reception, soon after the wedding breakfast, in order to catch the train to the airport.

As she recollected her wedding day, she felt really quite annoyed that it had been over far too quickly and she regretted that she had not had the time prior to the ceremony to anticipate and relish the main event and its subsequent celebration with family and friends some of whom had travelled long distances to witness their marriage. She certainly regretted having had to leave the party so early. She would have liked to have had the opportunity to savour to the full this special occasion.

Her colleague's daughter, Chloe, had organised her wedding most sensibly; a two o'clock ceremony; a sit down wedding breakfast for close friends and family; an evening party and dance for other friends; an overnight stay at the hotel and all together for a full English breakfast the following morning before everybody set off for home and the happy couple set off for their honeymoon. Chloe had missed out on nothing.

Hal was appointed to the staff at Burnside Grammar School in Broadclough as an assistant English teacher. Chris had continued to search for her dream job. She ultimately joined the staff at St. Ambrose Girls' School, an inferior, independent institution which had taken a lease on Pinchbeck Hall, situated in the rural outskirts of Pinchfold Castle. Here she was able to teach her own subject. However, in her opinion, this fee-paying establishment represented the worst kind of educational experience for both pupils and teachers so she escaped into the state system as soon as she was able, offering her services as a teacher of History. She had always remembered her experiences at St Ambrose's and wondered how those young, trapped girls had fared in later life.

Chris reflected on her years with Hal. Throughout their marriage, they had pursued different interests, but still had much in common. He had been a keen sportsman in his youth, playing football, swimming and cross country running and had continued to participate in them. Before marriage, Chris had toyed with fencing and dance, but these activities had fallen off and she had pursued more typical domestic hobbies such as baking and the reading club. These fitted more conveniently with family life. They had enjoyed playing tennis before the boys were born, but now their main activity was walking in their glorious countryside. There were so many different paths to tread to the foot of Beacon Scarp, the hill which dominated the landscape. They both loved the garden; Hal found satisfaction in constructing paths, ponds and pergolas whilst Chris preferred pruning and propagation. They relished the combat of the daily battles with Sudoku and Crosswords. They enjoyed a game of Bridge. Their sons' education was a major concern. They spent a lot of time together, frequently in companionable silence, but it was nothing like the stifling relationship such as the one Helen had described to them earlier that day.

  As she studied Hal, he stirred as if he was aware that he was under scrutiny. He opened his eyes and yawned, stretched and asked what o'clock it was. It was approaching a quarter to five. He jumped up and grabbed the remote. He found the programme he wanted, *Sports Scene.* He wanted to see the football results. He was out of luck. Most matches had been cancelled because of the wintry weather.

  'Let's have a drink', he said.

  Chris countered, 'Beer or wine? Don't suppose there's much left. Hec drank most of our stock last night.'

'No…I meant a cuppa…it'll be better for our gut.'

'OK, I'll make some tea. Anyway, we ought to go and fetch the kids. Your mum will be ready to see the back of them. Let us not kill the goose *blah, blah, blah*.'

In order to get to his parents' home in Higher Ridge, they had to drive past Frank and Shirley's house. They noticed that a police car and an ambulance were parked on the street. Hal said,

'That's odd. I wonder if the problem is at Hec's or at the neighbours'. Shall we stop and see?'

'No, let's not. We'll soon get to know if there's a problem. You know what they say… 'Bad news travels fast.'

Chris hoped for her sake that the Hectors weren't suffering from the food she'd given them the night before. She had fantasised about Hec choking on the meatballs and the vile ingredients she might use for soup should he ever dine with them again but in reality she would be mortified if her food was found to be at fault. She would not have shown so much concern if they had dined out at a restaurant but it was *her* food and her booze they had consumed. But, why were the police there?

Obviously, Hal was not inclined to pursue this line of thought. His mind was fixed on the task of getting to his parents' home to collect their two sons, Max and Danny.

He put his foot down on the accelerator pedal and they sped away from the scene.

They left Scarp Edge in the valley and started to climb up the Turnpike Road towards the crossroads known locally as 'Top o' th', so called as it was the watershed from which descended four roads. A cluster of local shops clung to the immediate area

On one corner, was situated a delicatessen which catered for the most epicurean of tastes. The proprietor knew his customers' tastes and the sizes of their pockets. This was an affluent spot and his prices reflected that. But the quality of his commodities never varied; It was always first class. The shop also served morning coffee with which the most excellent cakes and scones could be consumed. Four tables were set up by the front window - a pleasant place to while away half an hour or so and watch the world go by. During the summer months, there was an overflow of tables onto the broad pavement outside. At lunchtime, speciality sandwiches were available. Carlo obtained his bread and confectionery from the neighbouring premises, Bower's, an artisan bakery, from which, all day long, excepting for Saturday evening, emanated the most tantalising of aromas. Roy Bower also baked superb Cornish Pasties which the Days had enjoyed on many occasions as a take-away. At this time on a Saturday evening, these shops were all in darkness.

Fred Milam ran the newsagent-cum-general store-cum-Post Office situated across the road on the opposite corner, adjacent to which was Dave Byard the Butcher and Jim Norton the Greengrocer who specialised in the provision of local produce.

On the third corner, stood an old-fashioned iron monger's shop, Arthur's, where it was still possible to buy nails by the pound. Arthur was a very obliging fellow and could get his customers virtually any product they asked for. His motto was 'Once asked for: forever supplied'. He stocked both black and green rubber Wellington boots, wheelbarrows, weather vanes and a wealth of varied products. His shop was like the overcrowded Cave of the Forty Thieves, but he knew where to find every item of his stock. Arthur was not only the proprietor and main sales person, he also operated as a local handyman when time permitted and he had a list of customers anxious for his expertise. He was the guru who freely gave advice and would not sell a product unless it was the correct one for the task. Chris would go into his shop whenever she could, simply to inhale all the delicious scents on offer. Next door to Arthur's was located the seed merchant's. This was another emporium in which Chris revelled. She loved the hessian sacks bulging with all sorts of animal feed, seeds, grains and pellets, every sort of food for livestock- from domestic fowl to pet rabbits, straw and hay, bedding for pets and packets of flower and vegetable seeds with their multi-coloured illustrations. Inhaling these scents was a relaxation therapy for her. Hal had the opinion that she was quite mad.

The last corner housed the Turnpike Inn, renamed 'The Turnpike Gastro' by the new owner who served Real Ale and high-quality food, a step above the conventional pub grub, all day long. Travellers along the Old Turnpike were so delighted to happen on such an eclectic assortment of traders that Top o' th' was a well-used shopping experience for locals and tourists alike. At these cross roads, they took a left turn immediately starting a steep descent into Dene Bottom, a hamlet of a dozen or so ancient weavers' cottages. At this point in their journey, the road conditions became treacherous. No gritting had been carried out so far. The road rose just as steeply out of the hamlet and caused them some anxiety as the wheels started to skid, on the slippery surface. However, they arrived safely at the residence of the senior Days.

Grandma Day welcomed them in with a mug of steaming beef tea. In the spacious family room, the log-burning stove burned hot and bright. At the substantial table, both boys and Grandpa Day were engrossed in a many-pieced jigsaw. The TV was switched off. There was no iPad in sight. They were engaged in some old-fashioned family fun. The idea of decamping from this cosy environment appalled their two young sons and after much discussion Hal and Chris agreed to let them stay another night. Max was pleased because he would now have more time to consort with his old friend Jack Yates. They would carry on snow-boarding the next day, weather permitting. Danny was content to sit in the company of his Grandpa and work with him in order to complete the jigsaw depicting a map of the world. Grandpa Day's opinion was that all pastimes wherever possible should be of educational value. Hal and Chris, relaxing in the warm comfortable surroundings of their elders, were reluctant to leave. Hal suggested that a late departure would give the council workers more time to do their work. Grandma Day, always content to have the company of her son and daughter-in-law, encouraged them to stay for as long as they wanted. They watched the late news at ten o'clock and decided to leave before the start of one of Hal's favourite programmes, *Match of the Day*. He was not too bothered about missing it as most matches had been cancelled due to the snowy weather. He could always watch it the next morning if he were awake. They had set it to record anyway; nothing was lost.

It was agreed that they would return the next day to collect the boys. Chris was concerned that Max was up to date with his homework. She did not want any last minute hurried assignments to be left to the following day especially as they had decided to have some family time before the end of the half term. They said their goodbyes and were relieved to discover that the road surface had been treated and so they had a safe and uneventful journey back to Great Barrow.

CHAPTER THREE

Sunday 4 March

Chris opened her eyes. The sun was streaming in.

'Damn this sun.' she said out loud.

She had forgotten to put on her eye mask the night before. She would have preferred to have slept in as she still felt weary after the extremely late night, two days previously, following the never-to-be-forgotten dinner party. She glanced at the clock on the telephone. It was half past seven. She was wide awake – amazing, considering the two late nights they had just experienced. This early bird hopped out of bed and moved quietly out of the bedroom so as not to disturb Hal who was still dead to the world. He was no lark.

In the kitchen, it was wonderfully warm due to their brand new-to-them, cranberry-red Aga. In some ways, she had regretted the loss of the underfloor heating which they had enjoyed in their former home in the nearby village of Higher Ridge, near to Hal's parents. They had found the underfloor heating difficult to control, sometimes having to throw open all the doors, on the coldest of days, in order to breathe in cool air. It had taken a long time for them to adjust to it. Not in this house though. There was a multitude of cracks and gaps through which draughts could drift. It was a rediscovered pleasure. They had needed to make compromises, swapping the brand new, all singing, all dancing, *box,* with breath-taking views of their beloved Beacon Scarp, that *Leviathan,* rising out of the mists in the valley like some great, grey whale, for their new cherished home in Great Barrow.

Chris opened the blinds. The sky was a brilliant blue. The sun was glaringly bright. It was a wonderful start to an early March morning. Then she noticed that it was white over. There had been a fall of snow during the night. She wondered what it was like elsewhere. The weather forecaster had promised a very cold snap with copious snowfall anticipated in various parts of the country. She switched on the news and listened for the weather forecast. She gasped and repeated what the faceless voice on the radio had revealed,

'Blimey, some parts of the country are deep in snow and Rome has had its first snow in six years.'

She looked out at the garden, with its shallow layer of snow which sparkled and glinted under the radiance of the sun. How peaceful it was. Not a sound. Normally, there would have been the babble of children's voices but they were enjoying an extra night and day at Higher Ridge. Grandma Day was in charge.

She popped a peeled grape to the aged Remi, the goldfish which had been acquired by Max some years before. As the fish swam in circles, Chris wondered how happy she, or was it he, was. At least, Remi had life, not like some of its unfortunate cousins - Hal's precious Koi, who had been mercilessly murdered by a hungry heron the previous summer.

She slipped a coat over her pyjamas and found her wellington boots in which the bright red wellie socks, a gift from Father Christmas, were waiting. She was glad that she had remembered to wrap up warmly compared with the day before when she had ventured outside with her arms uncovered. She walked towards the bird feeder. Already, the birds had been to look for their daily rations. She recognised the large, forked footprints of the crows and the webbed patterns of the gulls. She crunched her way across the lawn, studying the state of the flower beds. Snowdrops were very much in evidence. Tiny, golden crocuses were gleaming, their petals contrasting with the pure whiteness of the newly fallen snow. Daffodils, too, were showing their leaves and some were already in bud. Come the better weather, she would be amongst them with her secateurs cutting down all the dead foliage - a job she thoroughly enjoyed.

She raised her eyes to the rear aspect of the house. It appeared to be quite ordinary compared to the front. She retraced her steps and opened the side gate which allowed her access to the side and front of the house. She gazed up at this graceful residence which she now called home, and she had an incredible feeling of gratitude for being the custodian of such a grand abode. An elegant edifice constructed in the late nineteenth century by skilled craftsmen, it was Georgian in design, heavily influenced by the architecture of Ancient Greece. She particularly admired the pair of massive pillars which supported the portico. They had decided to rename the house. Even though there was a huge Grecian influence, she had decided that the house name would be changed from The Lodge to Luxor Lodge, in deference to her admiration of the Ancient Egyptian civilisation. Those pillars were a reminder of the wonderful temples at Luxor and Karnak. Hal had had no objection.

Hal, she blessed him, had performed a considerable feat in obtaining this former mill owner's mansion from the Fortunes. Hal had seen the details in the estate agents' window in Great Barrow. The price had been reduced.

'We'll have this', he had thought to himself.

He had taken Chris to look at the details and photograph of the property in the estate agent's window.

'We'll never be able to afford this, even though the price has dropped.'

'Pessimist! It hasn't sold. Why? We'll go and view it. I'll talk to the agent and find out what the story is.'

Lily had married Peter Fortune, a fishmonger by trade, but Lily was an enormous snob, and felt that his fishmonger's business was not sufficiently elevated for her perceived status in the society in which she moved - namely the local church and her charity fund-raising affairs. She had persuaded Peter, against his better judgement, to invest his funds into a factory which had become available. It produced wrought ironware whose metallic craftsmanship was totally alien to his capabilities. Eventually, the business diminished to such an extent that they could no longer afford to keep the house. But Lily was not prepared to surrender it without a struggle. Apparently, there had been numerous interested parties who had given up their interest because they were not prepared to tolerate Lily's prevarications and procrastinations. Hal, normally a peaceable and easy-going fellow, had inherited his father's stubbornness and had no intention of letting this jewel of a property slip away. He had made an offer which, remarkably, she had accepted but then her delaying tactics began - demanding an unreasonably extended date for completion. Lesser mortals had conceded defeat but Hal had been determined to beat her. The battle raged on. Eventually, faced with the threat of being ditched by her agent, she succumbed.

How Chris loved this village of Great Barrow. It was like a nugget of gold in the midst of a grey, barren landscape, a vibrant organism in a deluge of decaying dereliction. It had evolved from a simple mill village into one of desirable location. Extensive sandblasting and other evidence of renovation and refurbishment to Victorian properties were a common sight. Run-of-the-mill shops had been transformed into purveyors of quality goods. Chris did regret the loss of the seed merchant's business whose aromas she had always savoured. It had evolved into an establishment selling clothing and tackle to the hunting, shooting and fishing fraternity. The scents emanating from sacks of all sorts of grain were now a thing of the past in most villages; they were now only fond memories. The village had all the shops and amenities they could ever desire. They needed never to leave it. She was suddenly overcome by a feeling of great joy, as if her heart would burst. She had a wonderful family, a palatial home in one of the best locations on Earth. She wished that she could live there for ever.

She thought about Shirley and felt very sad. Chris had everything and poor Shirley was stuck with that opinionated windbag, Frank, living in a little terraced house in downtown Scarp Edge. She decided that in future, she would be a better friend to Shirley. She would patronise her Beauty Parlour and in that way she would be supporting Shirley's business.

Chris suddenly had an urge to protect her. She felt that Shirley needed looking after. She seemed so pale and depressed compared with her appearance on her wedding day. Chris's mind went back to that day when Frank had made promises to Shirley,

'...to have and to hold.....to love and to cherish till death do us part'.

God had not been involved.

Frank and Shirley made their marriage vows at the Ravensborough Registry Office. Hal had been asked to act as witness and Chris had naturally accompanied him. It was a day that Chris would remember all her life. It must have been a very expensive affair. She couldn't believe that Frank had had much money, so she surmised that Shirley had footed the bill.

In those days, four years earlier, Chris and Hal were living in a new house, built on the site of a former farmhouse. It was an ultra-modern, but characterless property in the village of Higher Ridge, which lay on the hillside rising from the valley, in which was located the town of Scarp Edge, affording it a panoramic view of the dominating hill - Beacon Scarp.

It was a cosy place in which to live and it was safe for the children to play, situated as it was at the foot of a long, fairly steep driveway, from the top of which were superb views across to Beacon Scarp. Whatever the weather, Beacon Scarp stood proud. Even when the valley was shrouded by a thick blanket of mist, obscuring the grey, ugly mass that was Scarp Edge, Beacon Scarp's summit and Big End emerged from the white, pillow-like softness, along with the grade II listed former mill chimneys of Scarp Edge, giving the scene an ethereal, magical, fairy tale like quality.

The drive-way, as well as being fairly steep, had two dog-leg bends. First time visitors were usually terrified as they crossed the cattle grid separating the driveway from the road, for it felt as if they were driving off the top of a cliff.

She could remember watching the sleek, metallic silver wedding car glide tentatively down towards their door. She was glad all danger of frost had passed as their drive could be very tricky to tackle in the slightest ground frost.

'Look at this! A Silver Ghost', Chris had shouted to Hal.

It was not a recent model; it showed its age, but so what? They had never before been in such an opulent vehicle with a liveried chauffeur, not even on their own wedding day. They had rather enjoyed their drive, luxuriating in the pale leather upholstery which still had that aroma of real leather despite the age of the vehicle, to the little terraced house in Sylvan Way, Scarp Edge to collect the bride and groom. Shirley emerged from the house looking like a glowing, golden goddess. She wore a full-length, flowing coat and dress in shimmering gold lace and she carried a small bouquet of gold roses. What an exquisite outfit it was. Chris stared at her in awe and wonderment. Shirley had had such an air of elegance.

What a pity that it would probably have been worn only once. The four of them then drove in the wedding car to Ravensborough Registry Office. The ceremony had been brief, with no other guests, and before they knew it, the next party was being ushered in. Shirley's elegant outfit had been admired by only a minority of onlookers. The limousine emerged, as if by magic, from a side street and carried them, slowly, around the town meandering through the narrow streets until they reached their destination. They had watched Frank as he sat next to the chauffeur, waving to the populace as if he were royalty. How he must have enjoyed being the centre of attention. Their destination was the Palm Grove, an up-market bistro which had been closed to the public on that day because Frank had booked the entire restaurant for their wedding breakfast. The feast consisted of several miniscule courses - bare mouthfuls, but tasty. This had been Chris and Hal's first experience of nouvelle cuisine, and they had never repeated it, preferring one of the many local, alternative, excellent restaurants, such as Franco's. However, it was the Hectors' 'do' and they were paying. The Days joked that the Palm Grove ought to have been named 'The King's New Clothes' because all the food critics raved about it but the uninitiated left the restaurant almost as hungry as when they had entered.

    The Silver Ghost loomed silently from around a corner as if by remote control and in a few minutes they were back at Sylvan Way. Thus the celebration of the Hectors' marriage ended. The clock struck the hour - six o'clock, Hal was eager not to delay. He had performed his duties, now what he wanted was a square meal. Frank and Shirley were left to start their married life on their own. Chris and Hal knew nothing about the relationship between Frank and Shirley, assuming that it had been similar to their own – close, caring and loving.

In fact, nothing was further from the truth…Shirley had married Frank for a variety of reasons: pity: gratitude for bringing her son to his senses: an admiration for his intellect and musicianship. She had never been attracted to him in the physical sense. His 'wedding tackle' would not be required by her that night or any other night. They had had sufficient occasions during their pre-marital state to get to know each other's preferences. Theirs was a marriage of convenience; they had had no illusions about each other. She wanted to look after Frank because he had had such a bad time whilst Frank wanted a drudge with some accessible cash. She could not foretell on her wedding day what the future held in store for her.

Having been chauffeured back home, Hal suggested immediately that they ring their local chippie, Porgy's Plaice, in order to book a fish supper. 'What'll it be, Chris?'

'Since it's Hec and Shirley's wedding day, I fancy cod and chips now and banana custard for afters.'

Chris wondered whether Shirley had ever worn her wedding dress in the four years since their wedding and whether she might consider selling it to her. They were about the same size. With that idea firmly planted in her brain, she put her reminiscences from the past into a safe compartment in her memory and returned to the matters of the present day.

She glanced again at the giant, metal skeleton wall clock, which dominated the wall. *Tick-tock, tick-tock,* it stuttered…loudly… slowly… ominously, interrupting the silence of the kitchen. Hal was and had always been on the last minute so she had bought the unusual timepiece for his fortieth birthday as an encouragement to be less tardy. This peccadillo had been a constant grumble all their time together. She should have known what was in store for her when on one of their early dates, a theatre visit to The Alhambra at Bradford to see Pete Postlethwaite in *Macbeth*, they had had to run for the train.

It was approaching nine o'clock. She put the kettle on the hob to boil in order to make some tea. She would take him a drink while he watched the Sunday morning politics show. She started to prepare their breakfast. They were very much opposites in most things. Hal was quite predictable with respect to his breakfast: Always the same prosaic fare: A peeled pear, prunes and porridge. She liked a bit of variety …sometimes porridge … sometimes peanut butter with banana. She thought about the taste of the sweet slippery slices of banana mingling with the crunchy saltiness of the peanut butter spread and rejected it. That morning, she fancied smoked salmon with an egg. She put the coffee on the hob to brew - Columbian, medium roast. Soon it was crackling, bubbling and smelling divine. God, how she wished it tasted as good as it smelt. It reminded her of the times when as a child she had gone with her granny to a particular high class grocer's shop where a coffee grinder still took pride of place on the counter. Coffee beans were purchased and ground while you waited. In the old days, her granny had informed her, coffee was purchased in a paper bag and not in a glass jar.

She put bread rolls into the oven to warm. The combined smell of freshly brewed coffee and baking bread almost made her dizzy. Daydreaming came to an abrupt end as she heard a yell from the bedroom; Hal was shouting at the TV.

'Why don't you ask the right questions? Why do you always interrupt? Let him answer the question. I want to listen to him, not you.'

The letter box clattered. The newspapers had arrived. They always took a couple of quality newspapers and the local Sunday rag, the *Mercury*. These publications would keep them occupied for a week. They could get the daily news on TV and their iPads. Hal picked up the *Sunday Times* and turned immediately to the crossword. He needed to get a head-start on Chris. She picked up the *Mercury* and started to glance idly at the headlines. She was not one for reading every word unless the caption grabbed her. This one did.

'Hey, guess what?' Hal looked up and peered at her through his new spectacles in an absent-minded sort of way, not really wanting to be disturbed.

'That slime-ball *friend* of yours is dead'.

She was referring to Frank Hector, their former teaching colleague who, two days before, they had been entertaining to dinner with his wife. Chris felt a tingle run up and down the innermost core of her body - a kind of thrill which she found hard to understand

'Who?' Hal scratched his head.

Chris quoted from the *Mercury*,

'Frank Hector, former Principal of the erstwhile Abercrombie Restorative Academy and former music teacher at the James Ratcliffe High School, has been found dead in his sauna by his wife on Saturday.'

'Hec?'

'Well,' she said somewhat sarcastically,' the sauna clue does rather give it away. How many slime-balls d' you have for friends anyway? How many people do we know who have a sauna? ... that odious toad, Frank Hector, of course.'

Hal continued to stare at her. He put his newspaper onto the table, forgetting his crossword. He removed his glasses and held them in one hand while he absent-mindedly placed the end of the pencil between his front incisors and considered what he had just heard. Then he looked across at his wife, his eyebrows raised and his sad eyes expressing his thoughts, *'Well, he's finally got his comeuppance.'*

She continued to stare in disbelief at the newspaper.

'I can't believe it. They were only here on Friday night. D'you remember, we were still at the dinner table at half past two and I said that if they stayed much longer, I'd have to serve them breakfast?'

She began to gabble furiously as she considered all possible scenarios for his untimely death,

'D'you think it was my food or did he kill himself? Has something tipped him over the edge? You don't think it was anything I said, do you? What a way to go… a bit like Marat in his bath, but Marat was murdered, wasn't he? You don't suppose Frank was murdered? Shirley seems too nice a person to be capable of that. Do you think we ought to get in touch considering all that argy-bargy on Friday night?'

'OK .Will you phone or shall I or should we call round with some flowers?'

'Well, he was *your* friend, so you decide.'

She wanted nothing to do with Frank Hector any more. She had had her fill of him. She wanted to wash her hands of him.

Hal needed to consider what he was going to say to Shirley under these bizarre circumstances and so he delayed making contact with her in order to give himself more time in which to compose his condolences.

They spent a lazy Sunday morning, with only themselves to be concerned about. They put the dead Frank Hector out of their minds. Hal was happy with the Sunday newspapers. He always sat in the bright front window where he could doze off in his favourite armchair. Chris was happy pottering in the kitchen. She spent some time looking through the hundreds of recipes which she had collected over the preceding twenty years of marriage. She would carry out this task every so often and discard duplicated recipes and those which she knew she would never attempt. Even so, the folder contained a vast number of papers of all sizes and still she continued to add to them. The job completed, Chris put on the kettle to boil. She made a beef tea for Hal and a cup of fruit tea for herself; she opted for lemon and ginger.

Hal decided that it was time that he spoke to Shirley. He had read the news about Frank in the newspaper and so felt duty bound to make contact. He dialled their number and waited...there was no answer.

Chris asked Hal to leave his newspaper in order to help her change the bedding. The vile foulness of Frank's cigars and the stale odour cooking of Friday's dinner party were, to her nose, still permeating the house. She needed to throw open all the windows so as to admit some clean air and to put some fresh, cool, crisp cotton sheets on their bed.

Hal was quite content to follow his wife up to the bedroom. She went to the linen cupboard to fetch the clean linen and while she was sorting them in the bedroom, he came up behind her and put his arms around her waist and spontaneously kissed the back of her neck. She let go of the sheets and turned towards him and they enjoyed a spontaneous, lingering embrace. They fell back, laughing, onto the unmade bed. They each removed the other's clothes, and lay back each fondling and exploring the other. They stroked and licked each other's bodies. They began to caress each other in turn taking their time in order to enjoy every second of this unplanned, exquisite intimacy. Their bodies were hot and wet as were the sheets under them. They relapsed into the fantasies of their younger selves.

Peter Pointer and Toby Tall, stiff legged, marched determinedly over the familiar path across the low, smooth plain towards their favourite Mount Venus. They climbed the mountain, slowly. Descending into the valleys, they went in search of the opening of the tunnel which would lead them to the secret cavern. They had to scramble through the thick undergrowth which hid the entrance. The two inseparable buddies penetrated the deep dark tunnel and slid on their bellies along its slippery floor with a constant dripping from its walls onto their heads. They reached the entrance to the secret cavern. It was impenetrable. They moved back and then forward again, repeating this action many times, eventually retreating. They made their way from the tunnel's entrance to the raised spot which they called the pleasure dome. There they enjoyed jostling each other with frantic urgency until finally they fell off the dome exhausted, accompanied by the sounds of intense, unbearable, indescribable waves of pleasure from within the dome.

    Chris and Hal lay back, exhausted, for a moment or two. Then, raising herself on to her knees, Chris gazed at his engorged, personal instrument, his *askaulos*. It had been their preferred, though imperfect, attempt to devise an alternative private expression, unique to themselves. They had borrowed the name of a musical instrument which was exotic, original and private, unlike scrotum and penis which were far too clinical. It lay motionless, quietly waiting, against his warm, glowing, glistening body. She slipped her hands into his groin and clasped with both hands the bag of rough, skin which immediately tightened and puckered under her touch. His phallus sprang up, and began to throb under her delicate fingering. She licked and bit him gently. She prolonged her attention to him in order to make the final climax come slowly and ferociously. They lay in each other's arms and giggled gleefully at their private, intimate practices.

They very rarely had the house to themselves without the anxiety of the boys bursting in on them so it was a heaven-sent opportunity to relax in each other's arms and feel the frisson of the sexual exploration of each other that they had enjoyed in their early days together.

'Maybe we'll get that bath now', thought Chris, thinking back to Friday afternoon when she was relaxing in her bath before the dinner party. 'Come on, Hal it's a long time since we got in the bath together.'

They stepped cautiously into the warm, welcoming, water, facing each other and leant against the ends of the bath. The warmth and the silkiness of the water felt quite exotic and erotic as it penetrated all the crevices of their bodies. Hal took Chris's feet and massaged them with the lavender scented bath oil. He turned round so that he sat between her opened legs, his back towards her, so that she was able to rub against him with her smooth, soapy, slippery breasts and the insides of her legs. She used the loofah to scrub his back until it reddened with her exertion .He turned again and while her legs were apart and available to him he took the opportunity to enter her with his massively erect phallus. He slid slowly and rhythmically into her moving to and fro, to and fro, again and again, the warm soapy water lubricating his movements. He began to move more urgently until finally, they both shouted out in a violent climax to their passion He collapsed against her, shuddering in ecstasy. They were reluctant to stop. Afterwards Chris wondered why they had not indulged in such an erotic activity more often and determined that she would make more time available for its more regular occurrence in future.

Later, they returned to the bedroom to resume the original task of bed-making. Chris looked forward to bedtime and anticipated getting into bed and stretching her legs into the cool depths of that tightly made bed.

Hal's thoughts returned to Hec's demise and Shirley's failure to answer the phone.

'What time shall we collect the boys? Let's ring your mum and suggest that we go to Franco's for supper.'

'Look, love... I'll have to ring Shirley again. We must show our concern. If there's still no answer, we'll call on our way through Scarp Edge. It's on our way to Mum's.'

She nodded.

Hal rang Shirley's number...again no response. They stopped at Sylvan Way on the way to Higher Ridge...again no response to their rapping on Shirley's front door.

'We can't do any more. No doubt the police will be at our front door in the morning asking for information. We might as well enjoy this evening at Franco's.

'Franco's Portuguese Restaurant was situated in the upmarket village of Higher Ridge, where the senior

Days resided. It was usually filled to capacity with diners chattering excitedly, their plates clattering noisily in the well-lit, cheerfully decorated restaurant. Franco served the most delicious food imaginable and his portions were more than adequate. Merely reading his menu with its vivid descriptions of the fare made the saliva flow. He was a great asset to the village and his clientele came from miles around. Hal rang Franco's before setting off and were lucky to be able to book a table for six o'clock which was deemed a suitable time for all concerned.

Hal and his father ordered a starter of whitebait. A dish filled to the brim with the crispy, fried tiny fish hardly left any room for a further course. Chris and her mother–in-law chose sticky Portuguese *palio* wings, followed by *Caldeirada,* a wonderful fish stew. Hal and his father, after a surfeit of whitebait, ordered a small steak with a green salad. The boys had *Linguica*, a smoke-cured, pork sausage with paprika and garlic. They never refused sausages. After the meal, the senior Days had a short drive home whilst for their son and his family it was a twenty-minute drive home to Great Barrow. Chris was already relishing the thought of an early night, watching the Sunday evening movie on TV, in her crisp, clean, cotton sheets and snuggling close to Hal.

'What did you do with Grandpa and Grandma?'

'After we'd finished the jigsaw, Grandpa got out all of his old photographs and we saw lots of Dad when he was little. Tomorrow, can we look at your old photographs?

'Alright, love', replied their mother thinking that it was always interesting to remember the way they were. As they settled down in their freshly made bed whose sheets were fragrantly scented with lavender, the MGM opening credits of the old black and white movie appeared on the screen.

'What's the movie tonight…I forgot to look in the paper with all that business about Hec.'

'We'll soon find out. It's just starting.'

They looked at each other in amazement as the opening credits of the 1944 movie *Gaslight* filled the screen with its accompanying, disturbingly discordant, frantic, melodramatic, climactic score.

'Is that the weirdest coincidence or what?' Chris gasped.

The film depicted the kind of marriage that both Helen and Shirley had endured with Frank Hector.

CHAPTER FOUR

Monday 5 March

A frantic sensation in her bladder woke Chris; she needed the bathroom urgently. She glanced at the clock on the bedside table next to the still-sleeping Hal. It was four minutes past seven. She sensed that the temperature had risen. She raised the blind slightly and peeped out of the window. The temperature was such that all the snow had disappeared. The weather had changed. The garden had lost its glistening, white coat and everything even the snowdrops looked grubby. The air was still and chilly. The sky was grey. The sun would not shine today. Even the birds were nowhere to be seen. The stillness had a doom-laden intensity as if a storm were brewing.

Hal awoke. She must have disturbed him. He, too, dashed off to the loo. They had consumed a lot of water the day before in order to cleanse their systems from the toxic overindulgence of the Friday evening's dinner party. They needed to be fit for work on the following day.

It was the last day of the spring half term holiday. It had really been a long weekend as the four-day break had included the weekend. Later in the day, she would experience that 'end of the holiday' feeling. She wondered whether she would get these feelings all her life. She would soon get over it as the new day dawned and work beckoned.

She had experienced such feelings many times over the years. As a schoolgirl, on a Sunday evening, the programme on the radio –*Sing Something Simple* used to be broadcast around tea-time. It was a reminder that the weekend's homework had yet to be completed. Remarkably, it was still being broadcast during her PGCE year. It signalled the fact that she and Hal had only a few more hours together before they said their 'goodnights'. She had this 'end of the weekend' feeling more keenly whilst on teaching practice when they tended to see less of each other.

'We've had quite an eventful half term break. Who would have expected Hec to die the day after he had been a visitor at our home? When will the police come?' she thought.

She experienced a discomfort in her throat. Her glands informed her that a sore throat was imminent and was possibly the start of a more serious malady. She was not prepared to take sick leave, as so many of her colleagues were prone to do. Hal was of the same opinion. They both believed that school managers had to lead by setting a good example to their staff. She would prepare a honey and lemon for each of them, in order to pre-empt such an eventuality and she would make a pot of tea. Hal, no doubt, would have the same symptoms as she. She made a salt-water gargle for herself. A belt and braces approach worked best, she felt.

There was a tapping on the French door. She responded and opened it. In walked their handsome black and white pet - Bastet. The cat had spent the night outdoors. He ignored her totally and strode, in a determined fashion, straight to his dish of biscuits. He wanted breakfast and a long, undisturbed sleep on his blanket. Later, he would come to her for some attention, but in his own time and on his own terms.

Carefully, Chris made her way up the stairs back to the bedroom, carrying her tray of hot drinks. She snuggled up to Hal under the duvet and stole some of his bodily warmth. She lay across his chest and encouraged his hand to stroke her back. This pleasant, cosy state would not last much longer and such intimacies were less frequent during the working week which began the following day. They could hear sounds from the boys' rooms. Max and Danny were not ones for lingering under their bedclothes. Considering their age difference, Max was on good terms with and had a lot of patience in relation to, his younger brother. Chris and Hal felt blessed and relieved that their children were good-natured, and were not problematic to them.

Considering Max's school experience to-date, they had escaped such a fate. How difficult it was for parents with awkward offspring. She had met many distraught parents in her previous job at the James Ratcliffe, and also at her current job over at Pinchfold Castle High in north Lancashire. She had great sympathy for them and endeavoured to help ease their burden.

They stayed in bed just long enough to swallow their steaming cold cure and drink their tea and then they were up, and down to breakfast. The children were already downstairs. Max, quite a broad, fourteen year old, was not very tall but he still had a lot of growing to do; he was an intelligent, cheerful individual with enthusiasm for most enterprises. His early education had been rather messy, on reflection. As teachers, it might have been expected that his parents would have navigated a safer passage for him through these turbulent early years of his schooling. Like most parents, they had considered that their actions had been the correct ones at the time.

At two years of age, he had been accepted at an excellent day nursery where he had stayed until the age of four years. Chris and Hal would deliver him on their way to and collect him on their way from the school where they both had teaching posts. The Head of the nursery school was of the opinion, that even though Max was so young, he was ready to commence his formal education in primary school. She had suggested that they contact the local primary school to discuss the matter with the Headteacher.

They followed her advice and had taken Max to meet Mrs Cass, a very pleasant, Christian lady, who lived in the house adjacent to the school. Mrs Cass talked to Max and assessed his potential. She proposed that if the Days were agreeable, then she would accept Max into the Reception class in August, at the commencement of the next academic year. So, Max embarked on his school career at St. Andrew's C of E Primary School in Scarp Edge. He was totally contented; his class teacher, Mrs Ogleby, was a gem of a teacher. He could not have had a better one in his first year at school. His subsequent experience with Mrs Blake was less perfect. Her practice was to listen to the children read out loud to her at her desk. Events came to a head when it was discovered that Mrs Blake was in the habit of listening to a group of children at the same time, all reading from different books. Chris and Hal took up the problem, as they viewed it, with the Headteacher, Mrs Cass, who realised that Max was too bright to be held back and she recommended that a more high-powered establishment be sought.

Max moved to another school. He was enrolled into the junior department at the King George V Independent School in Broadclough. At seven years of age, he was fortunate to find himself in a group of children with similar abilities to himself and so for three years it was plain sailing for Max. The crunch came at the age of ten years when it was time to move into the senior part of the school. In order to qualify for a free place at the KGV Main School, certain conditions had to be met, one of which was the passing of the entrance examination. This had not been an anxiety for Max. He had sailed through. The obstacle had lain with his parents' income. They earned too much for qualification for a free place; they would have incurred school fees.

After a lot of soul-searching, it was agreed that Max would not continue in that institution but would move to a non-fee paying high school with an excellent reputation in Higher Ridge. This had the added benefit of being within walking distance of his home and that of his paternal grandparents. So Max moved again. However, it soon became obvious that an error of judgement had been made. Max was no longer the happy, contented child he once was. He suffered in the classroom where the intelligence level was somewhat lower than that to which he had been accustomed; he suffered in the playground because he was the new boy who did not belong to a friendship group; the dreaded word *bullied* was voiced for the first time. Max was the archetypal square peg. The fateful event which was to be the cause of yet another change of school was a day's exclusion from the school. An ineffectual teacher, having been late to his lesson, found the pupils in uproar in the corridor, their school bags and their contents strewn about and two or three pupils involved in a brawl. Max was pounced upon to give account of where the blame lay. This he had refused to do. The consequential punishment of exclusion had been the final straw.

In his thirteenth year, his parents were successful in gaining a place for him at the Grammar School in

Castleton, in the adjacent county, which meant a bus journey of about forty five minutes morning and afternoon. But, at last, he had the ideal environment in which to thrive… and thrive he did.

Danny was eight years old, a lot slimmer than Max had ever been. He favoured his father in many physical attributes and had an aptitude for gymnastics. He was not as academically gifted as his brother, preferring running to reading. Of course, it was early days. He had, totally naturally, performed forward rolls from the age of two years. He would probably never have been a contender for the fee-paying KGV anyway. Danny could walk to Higher Ridge County Primary School but then had moved to the local school in Great Barrow. Hal's parents had always been very much part of his pre- and post-school child-care on school days since both Chris and Hal had had to travel several miles to their respective schools, and so had to leave home well before the time that Danny needed to set off. They were fortunate to have parents who were prepared to give so much time and personal inconvenience to their family's needs. Their children, similarly, benefited from the close, loving contact they had always had with another generation whose experience of life had been so different from their own.

It was useful that on that occasion, all the family had shared the same half-term holiday. Grandma Day had held the fort and had overseen Max's homework, which meant that they could spend the whole of the last day of the holiday as a family. They had decided to go to their local leisure centre where Hal and the boys could swim and Chris could indulge herself in the sauna and Jacuzzi. Hal had taught both boys to swim at a very early age. They had taken to it like ducklings to water. They had been veritable water babies. They were, all three of them, strong swimmers. The boys were not yet interested in the relentless haul up and down the pool as was their father. Hal could swim for a mile, effortlessly, and did so every week, sometimes more often. During visits to the pool in school holidays, other children would shout and splash and jump or make otherwise deliberate moves to intercept his relentless progress, length after length, but he was undeterred and was determined to swim all the more strongly.

    Chris was not a lover of the water, unlike Capricorn, her sea-goat sign of the Zodiac. However, she could and did swim, but she lacked the confidence needed to become proficient in the water. She would never contemplate swimming in the sea. She preferred to have her feet on the ground. Having the qualities of determination and ambition of her Zodiacal sign, she taught herself the crawl stroke simply by observing and copying a swimmer with a good style. However, her maximum number of lengths was twenty, after which she grew bored and was ready for a change of activity. Frequently, she would leave her menfolk in the water while she went to the gym next door. There, she would be perfectly happy on the walking machine until it was time for them all to disappear into the café and have a hot chocolate and a custard pie.

In a very short time, the sports bags were packed with swimwear, goggles, earplugs, towel and coins for the lockers. In this household, tidiness was the order of the day so that anything required could be located immediately. *'A place for everything and everything in its place,'* she could hear her mother's voice echoing as she collected everything together.

Hal had gone into the garage to get the car out onto the driveway. He seemed to be taking longer than she had expected. She walked through the utility room to the internal door to the garage and noticed that he was on the driveway talking to a police officer who had just arrived with a colleague in a police car. She put her hand to her forehead. She had completely forgotten that the police would be likely to call on them. Hal appeared to be bringing them into the house. Her thoughts immediately were on the state of the kitchen. In her haste to sort out their swimming gear, she had forgotten to clear the breakfast table.

The police officers, in their stuffy, officious way of talking, announced that they had come to make some enquiries about the Days' friend, Dr Frank Hector who was now deceased and lying on a cold slab in the hospital. What information could they provide on the matter?

'There goes our family day and our trip to the baths'. Chris thought.

She went upstairs to break the news to the boys. They would have to find some other entertainment now. It did not take long for the Xbox to be set up and the two brothers were happily engaged in their latest game, a gift from Father Christmas.

After the police had departed, Chris and Hal did not have the energy to return to their original plan. They made some coffee and sat at the kitchen table to go over the events of the previous hour. It appeared that Frank Hector had been found dead in his sauna, by his wife, late on the Saturday morning, appearing to have suffered a massive heart attack. The police were treating his death as unexplained. Chris and Hal had been asked the usual questions about their final encounter with Frank Hector and were asked to contact the police again should they remember any other, hitherto forgotten, details.

A lot of muck from the past was about to be raked up, they both agreed.

Danny, having finished his game, came into the kitchen where his mother and father were still deep in conversation. He interrupted them.

'Can we look at the old photographs like you promised?'

Chris was amused by his use of the word *old*. In his young life, he had only ever known mobile phones and iPads. He had grown up seeing his parents use their iPhones for talking, texting and taking pictures which were stored automatically. He had viewed images only on the small screen of the iPhone or iPad; watching a slide show would have been unknown territory. Traditional photography was something of a mystery. The tangible, printed photograph was becoming part of history to the majority who had availed themselves of the advances in technology in order to store their images on memory sticks or in folders on the hard drive of their computers. This cold, clinical practice which was by far the most economical way of storage in the current, technological society enabled the elimination of images by the mere touch of a button. Users, lacking the technical knowhow concerning image preservation, lost their pictures forever when advancing computer technology caused their hardware to become obsolete. Chris could envisage a future when the bottom drawer of the family's treasure chest no longer contained well-thumbed photo albums but instead boxes of inaccessible memories on obsolete sticks. There was something special about the physical nature of a photograph. It could be kept in a wallet or in a pocket, under a pillow or in a frame on a shelf. Chris could remember her practice of taking to the photo shop, the undeveloped reels of film from her camera and her excitement and anticipation when the printed photographs were due for collection. The printed photographs caused her either delight or dismay. It was impossible for Chris, as well as her parents and grandparents before her, to destroy a photograph. She suspected that in homes across the country, old photographs of forgotten, long since dead family members and unknown people and places people were stored in biscuit tins or shoe boxes, without names or dates, gathering dust in attics, waiting to be jettisoned by future generations.

She presented some albums to Danny,

'There you are... four albums to look through.....all old photographs. All our recent ones are on a memory stick'.

Danny enquired about some photos of his mother as a child.

'Who's this with you?'

He pointed to a photograph of herself with Debs on holiday at Berrow in Somerset. Chris's mother - Granny Pugh, had taken her and her best friend Debs to a caravan for a week while Grandad Pugh had gone for a week's fishing with Bob, their next-door neighbour. Chris could remember her mother's annoyance at the lack of vital equipment in the caravan, her friend, Debs crying herself to sleep every night because she missed the tyrannical, time-keeper mother of hers, and the great expanse of sand but no sea.

'Don't you recognise Aunty Debs? That's us when we were ten years old at Berrow. 'She's got funny glasses on. What's this one of? All I can see is you and piles of stones.'

He was looking at a photograph taken on a school trip to Chedworth Roman Villa, one of the finest specimens in the country from the Roman occupation. The journey took four hours to reach Chedworth, and four hours to return home. That was the occasion when her interest in the ancient world began. The trip had been organised by her two favourite teachers, nicknamed Jessie S and Flossie S. Jessie taught Latin and Flossie brought to life Ancient History. Jessie was well-known for nodding off in the class whilst her pupils were working from their text books. Evidence of her snoozing, when marking homework, was evidenced by faint red markings on the page as if a drunken spider had weaved its way over the page after first treading in some red ink. Jessie owned, to accommodate her huge, corpulent frame, an extremely, ancient, roomy car which she had intended to use until it finally rusted away under her. They had frequently car-shared, presenting a highly amusing sight to onlookers, because of their substantial girths, crammed like two well-fed groundhogs into Flossie's Fiat 500.

Chris rose from her chair and went over to the window. The weather was on the turn again. The stillness of the morning had morphed into a wind which was becoming increasingly gusty. As it picked up speed, the windows and gutters of the old house started to vibrate producing a familiar, eerie whistling sound together with a loud thumping crash every now and then. As she watched through the glass, evidence of the boisterous gusts could be observed by the movement of the branches of the gigantic Douglas Fir tree which was rooted about a hundred feet distant. The incessantly, bouncing branches simulated a throng of long witch-like, bony fingers beckoning the unwary. It was a truly magnificent specimen. She hoped that if ever it became uprooted in the future, under such windy conditions, it would fall in the opposite direction from where she stood otherwise they would be for it. As she watched, great chunks of foliage became detached like the limbs of some hapless surfer being wrenched from its torso by a great white shark.

    The telephone rang adding another raucous, cacophonous sound to those already being experienced from the rattling windows. It was Grandma Day on the line. Grandpa had been taken ill. The paramedics were attending to him as she spoke. She was calm and spoke in a steady voice as she gave them details. The paramedics seemed to think it was a heart attack, she reported. She intended to follow the ambulance to the hospital at Broadclough where she would stay overnight in the special facilities afforded to the next of kin. She had yet to pack his favourite, paisley design M & S pyjamas and other essential requisites for them both. The family agreed to meet up at the intensive care unit as soon as they were able. There had been no time for lunch. Chris made sure that the boys had enough to keep them occupied during the impending, potentially extended interval at the hospital. They decided that they would get a snack in the hospital canteen since it was open all day.

Eight years had passed since Chris had eaten hospital food… in the maternity unit. She had found the food most palatable unlike some of the new mothers It had always amused her that the women who had moaned the loudest about their meals were often those from the lowest level of society where incomes were sparse. These women had the pale, pinched and wretched appearance of those who had never eaten a square meal in their lives.

Chis took with her a writing pad so that she could note down any facts, important in relation to Frank Hector's death. They had already decided to call at the police station in Ravensborough after their visit to the hospital. She suspected that Hal would agree to her taking the notes as he would be too concerned about the health of his father to have his mind on any other matter. By the time that they had reached the hospital, Grandpa Day had had his initial assessment and the decision had been made to admit him to the Intensive Care unit for at least twenty four hours.

They waited in a small area opposite the door into the Intensive Care ward. Only two visitors were allowed in at any one time so Chris was left with the boys in the waiting area whilst Hal accompanied his mother at his father's bedside.

They all had had good experiences at this hospital, although the occasions had been minimal: two stays at the maternity unit for Chris: some outpatient appointments for Hal: a broken arm for Max and a case of suspected concussion for Danny. There existed a calm, bright, light, airy, clean, hygienic atmosphere which had instilled confidence in the recipients of NHS treatment.

The boys were engaged watching downloads on their tablets and Chris similarly was busily scribbling notes on her pad. Meanwhile, Hal was in another place, far away with his thoughts about his father.

Grandpa Day had always been a stubborn man as was his father before him. Hal had inherited the same characteristic. Grandpa Day had always been a keen member at the church in the village and his wife and son similarly had to follow where he had led. They did not altogether share his beliefs. Grandma had meekly acquiesced for a quiet life. It had been a requirement for Hal, in his childhood and early youth, to attend church on Sunday mornings and evenings with extra attendances at

Sunday school, Bible study and prayer meetings. Grandpa Day had been a *big fish* in his little church - handing out hymn books, caretaking and acting as an occasional, emergency preacher; he was an indispensable member of that community. Grandma, too, did her bit to support him by preparing refreshments after the Sunday services. Hal had grown disillusioned with the whole charade, as he had believed it to be. He had discarded religion whilst at university; he described himself as an atheist. This had not prevented members of his extended family from proselytising him at every opportunity. He believed, as did a notable, German philosopher and sociologist from history, that religion was a man-made invention used by oppressors to make the gullible populace feel more accepting of their lot in life. His experience of church attenders over the years had intensified his belief that many of these were not truly Christian people. They would treat a person with the insincere, effusive bonhomie engendered by their presence in the *House of God*. Subsequently, they might ignore that person in the street and even stab that same person in the back, metaphorically if not literally. In many cases, they had used their position of influence to abuse the young and the innocent. In his own profession, he had encountered superiors in the hierarchy who sported the sign of the fish showing favouritism to similar badge wearers. It was like the emblem of an elite club whose members gave mutual support to each other. It had frequently dictated the rate of progression in the profession. Hal was highly sceptical of anyone professing himself to be a Christian. His habit was to quietly observe whether Christian action spoke louder than Christian words.

The charge nurse emerged from the ward and beckoned to Chris. She could go into the ward with the children for a moment or two to see Grandpa Day who had awakened. He was lucky in that his heart attack had been slight. Since he was a fit man, the damage to his heart had been minimal, but it was stressed to them that this was a warning and under no circumstances was he to do any strenuous work in the future. In all probability, he would be allowed home after a couple of days.

'That means no more shovelling snow,' his wife reminded him, using a hectoring tone of voice so that all he could do was to nod meekly and obediently in agreement.

Hal and his family said their goodbyes and left Grandma Day to spend the rest of that day and night at the hospital. Meanwhile, they headed north to Ravensborough Police station where the officer on duty was expecting them.

Chris gave an account of the events of the previous Friday night. She explained that they, the hosts, had witnessed the deceased drink much whisky and liqueur, consume several pain killers and appear to doze off between courses, at the same time being enthusiastic about the 'adult party game' that he was in the process of developing. She referred to his sarcastic, provocative, cantankerous manner during his lucid moments. Hal mentioned Frank's previous history at Her Majesty's Prison at Pinchfold Castle in case that was relevant to their investigation.

On their way back to Great Barrow, they called at Sylvan Way where they hoped to catch Shirley in. This time they were in luck. They relayed their events of the day to her.

Shirley looked well considering her shocking, recent bereavement. She described the circumstances in which she had found Frank on Saturday morning. It had been quite late when she woke up, because she had slept in and had assumed he had done the same. When Frank did not appear, she had gone to his room to discover that his bed had not been slept in. It was then that she looked in the sauna and found him, dead under a towel with whisky and pills beside him. She described that in her state of shock she had sat, stunned, for a few minutes while her brain got back into gear. It was then that she called 999. After the elapse of two days she had got used to the fact that Frank was dead and was able to consider the consequences. She said that she fully anticipated the necessity of a post mortem because of the nature of Frank's death but she was not dismayed at the prospect as she felt sure that the findings would show that Frank had consumed so much whisky and Zymkase that the verdict would be accidental death. She promised that she would keep them informed of the timetable of events. There was something about Shirley's unusual authority and confidence that Chris and Hal got the feeling that she was anxious to end their conversation so they took the hint and took their leave, leaving Shirley to grieve on her own while they headed home in order to get ready for school on the following day.

On the journey home Chris, her brain buzzing, bombarded Hal with non-stop questions,

'You rang Shirley twice with no response. Where was she? We called at her house on the way to your mum's on Saturday evening. Where was she? Why didn't she call us to let us know about Hec? We should have asked her those questions. Why didn't we?

Hal merely shrugged his shoulders. He could offer no logical explanation.

On that last evening of the spring half–term in bed, sipping a hot chocolate, they reviewed, together, the events of the preceding Friday which had possibly contributed to the shocking, surprising demise of Frank Hector.

CHAPTER FIVE

1

Friday 2 March

The day of the dinner party had at last arrived, Friday 2 March. This was an event in her social calendar which Chris had not welcomed. Good natured Hal had invited Frank Hector, and his wife, Shirley to their home. Hal had an odd liking for Frank's intellect and his debating skills. The fact that, in Chris's opinion, he was an utterly contemptible member of the human race was not an issue with Hal. They had entertained Frank and current wife, Shirley, and Frank and divorced wife, Helen, on a few occasions in the past, but after each event, Chris had promised herself that it would be the last time that she would entertain an individual whom she abhorred. Now, here she was again, about to provide an evening's entertainment for this booze-guzzling glutton with a conviction for child sex abuse.

That morning, Chris and Hal delivered their two sons, Max and Danny to Grandpa and Grandma Day's for the weekend. She did not want their children to be anywhere in the vicinity of the odious Frank.

On leaving Great Barrow, they had passed through the neighbouring village of Great Ridge. They noticed that a new tea shop had opened for business. The name over the top was Helen's Haven and it was just across the road from the Tourist Information Office and in the optimum position for an ample passing trade.

'Let's give it a try on the way back if there's time,' Chris had said.

On they drove through Scarp Edge to the crossroads where they turned on to the old turnpike road which took them to Top o' th' and then on to Higher Ridge. At Top o' th', Chris requested that Hal stop outside Mr Norton's as she needed a few items of greengrocery and at the newsagent's to buy some *Maltesers.* In no time, they arrived at the Senior Days'. The boys were going to stay overnight while their mum and dad got on with their entertaining. The boys loved having a sleep-over at their grandparents'.

The snow was quite thick on the ground and Hal was glad that he had decided to change his car for the four-wheel drive version before the onset of winter. This particular model had very substantial tyres with a deep tread which was just ideal for the sort of weather they were experiencing that weekend. Grandpa Day was exerting himself with a snow shovel, clearing a path to the door and sprinkling rock salt on to the cleared track. Grandma Day was busy in the kitchen, baking the sort of buns and biscuits that her grandchildren delighted in as treats. Their particular current favourite was a chocolate, Malteser tray bake.

'Chris, did you remember the Maltesers?' asked her mother-in-law.

'No problem, Ma' said Chris, shaking the box, like a maraca, above her head.

Grandma Day addressed Danny,

'Now, young man, you can learn how to make this cake since it's your favourite. I'll find you a pinny to wear.'

Danny did not seem too pleased at the prospect of wearing a pinafore. He rolled his eyes and sighed loudly but obediently put it on when his grandmother handed it to him. He would not admit it but he was glad to be involved in the making of his favourite cake and it would be good to tell his teacher about it. He decided to take her some, the next day, on his return to school.

Chris and Hal did not accept their parents' invitation to stay for elevenses as it was obvious that Grandpa and Grandma were busy with their labours. Grandma Day already had her hands full with Danny and the melted chocolate. Chris and Hal took the opportunity to have a closer look at Helen's Haven on the way home.

Having parked the car, they looked across at the new teashop. The external doors and window frames had been repainted in a cheerful, delicate yellow, like primroses in spring. The random gritstone, stonework had been sandblasted and repointed to reveal its delicate muted, fawny-grey colour. It presented a most welcoming image. The pavement was sufficiently wide to accommodate bistro tables and chairs in more favourable weather. They went inside and sat down at one of the tables in the window where they could watch the world go by. Each table had a yellow and white check tablecloth with a small vase of intense blue grape hyacinths. The curtains were in a similar material. The original oak floorboards had been sanded and polished until they gleamed and the wallpaper bore poppies, primroses and bluebells. Chris and Hal felt very much at home here in the comfortable, warmth of this environment, especially on this cold, snowy morning and they were becoming increasingly intoxicated and drowsy with the scents of freshly-baked bread and newly-ground coffee.

    Hal picked up the menu, hand-written in ink on a fine quality card. He had been impressed. This was more than a teashop. It offered morning coffee and a selection of other enticing beverages, toasted teacakes, home-made flapjack, shortbread and other tempting confectionery. They opted for a hot chocolate, without the cream or marshmallows, and a slice of carrot cake. On further reading, they discovered that Helen also served light lunches of soup and sandwiches and afternoon tea with toasted crumpets, a variety of sandwiches and home-made scones with jam and cream. It was Helen, herself, who came to take their order. They had looked at her open mouthed. It was Helen Hector, Frank's former wife who had divorced him while he had been locked up in Pinchfold Castle Prison.

'Helen Hector! ... Fancy seeing you... it's so good to see you again'. Chris's voice had been genuinely enthusiastic in her greeting. 'We've not set eyes on you for ages. We thought you must have moved away.'

At the greeting, Helen positively flinched. Her face reddened and she blurted out,

'I'm not called that any more. I've gone back to my maiden name. I can't bear the name *Hector*. I go by the name *Sutcliffe*. I realise that it's a far worse name than Hector because it's the name of the Ripper, but at least I grew up with it and it was mine for twenty years before I married Frank.'

Helen explained that after Frank's imprisonment, she had started divorce proceedings on the grounds of his unreasonable conduct. She had indeed moved. She had gone to Dorchester to where her parents had retired but she had found life rather dull. She had also tired of their constant reminders of the unsuitability of Frank Hector as her husband. Her parents were in good health and had no need of her services. Her son, Colin, and his wife were living in Scarp Edge with their new baby and this had been the magnet for her return to the area.

She explained that her experience in the teaching of Home Economics and the subsequent catering and administration at Abercrombie Hall had provided her with the invaluable expertise which she had been able to draw upon in the setting up of her catering business. She had started, in a small way, by providing dinner parties for clients in their own homes and then she had found the vacant shop premises to renovate and convert into a café. Thus, her business developed into a two-pronged venture.

Helen told them that Frank had never intended that she would have any money but the cash he had stowed away in an account in order to avoid tax had come in very handy when purchasing the shop. He could do nothing about the situation since the account holding several thousands of pounds had been put in her name. He had never allowed her access to it but the name and signature in the book was hers. Frank was helpless and could not touch it. She chuckled gleefully as she remembered finding that she had access to all those funds which Frank had never intended her to have.

They could have sat there all day listening to the stories of Frank's obnoxious behaviour but Chris and Hal, having long finished their snack, noticed the time. They said their goodbyes to Helen with a promise that they would return.

In the car, Chris said,

'D'you think we should have mentioned our dinner party tonight with the dreadful Hec?'

'No…we can tell her about that when we see her next time. I'm sure we'll call again because her food is so good and it's on our doorstep.

CHAPTER FIVE

11

Friday 2 March

'We've got three hours before they arrive.' Chris thought, *'That's ample time for me to enjoy a long, luxurious soak'*.

Their deep Victorian, iron bath was so capacious that to fill it to the level she desired was extremely extravagant. But there would not be enough hot water for them both to bathe. She started to work out the logistics of the bathing procedures for each of them. She decided that Hal would have to take a shower. If he showered first, with minimal water, then she could take the rest of the hot water from the tank. She and Hal took few baths, not because of the waste of water, but the act of bathing seemed to take an age. A shower was so much easier and faster; and they were both busy people. On this occasion, however, Chris decided that a bath it would be so that she could relax. She could make use of some of those oils and lotions that she had received as gifts which were cluttering up her bathroom cabinets. It was impossible to use those scented bath oils and bubbles in the shower.

She needed some time to relax in order to prepare herself for the ordeal of the forthcoming dinner party. She hated Frank more than ever since listening to Helen's account of his beastly behaviour.

They could have got in the bath together. It was big enough for two but the better idea was to take a bath together after the dinner party, not before. She weighed up the pros and cons. She assumed that Hal would not like all the perfumed products she planned to use in the bath. However, she would ask him. Chris suspected that he would refuse the bath oils and consequently would opt for the shower. The discussion would prevent him from being aggrieved, not that he ever would be. He really was the most considerate husband she could have wished for; she was less considerate. She felt somewhat guilty about the devious plan she had for getting a bath. But she need not have worried.

'I fancy a bath, what about you?'

He removed his reading glasses and looked in her direction. He thought for a moment.

'You go ahead. I'll get a shower once the water's had time to warm up again. Anyway, I'm in the middle of doing this crossword. I'm on the same wavelength as today's compiler so I'll crack on; maybe I'll have a snooze.'

He replaced his spectacles. He was sitting in the window of the sitting room. This spot caught the afternoon sun and the temperature in there could get up to twenty seven degrees. He would nod off without a doubt.

'I'll get my shower about half past five and take my time'.

'What are you wearing tonight?' she asked.

'Something cool, something cotton. It's going to get hot tonight in more ways than one', he forecast. 'I'll wear that striped cotton check shirt with the summer-weight, cream trousers. I'll keep cool that way. What about you?'

'I've got out that blue *galabaya* with all the Egyptian motifs; I wore it to that party on the Nile boat. I've only worn it the once.' An idea popped into her mind. *'Perhaps Shirley will do a swap with me - my galabaya for her wedding dress.'* She carried on talking, 'It's cotton and pretty loose fitting. I'll stay cool. I'll wear my gold cartouche necklace too and that blue beaded cap. I might as well go the whole hog. It'll provide Frank with something to rib me about, but if he does, I'll be ready for him.'

She was transported back to that holiday in Egypt, on a Nile cruise boat.

'D' you remember, Hal, that day when the crew on the boat tried to get people to buy stuff for the galabaya party from the kiosk on board? Debs and Tony were taken in and paid far more than they needed to have done. I got my outfit from the *souq* for half the price and you refused to fork out at all. Tony originally sided with you but he allowed Debs to persuade him to change his mind and he became unreasonably irritable about the whole business. They were annoyed and called you a tightwad. So Mohammed suggested that you should go in your cream suit and a white shirt, and that he would use my scarf to make a turban for you. You looked great, really handsome, especially with your sun tan. D' you remember where I got that scarf? It was at that stall on the left as we approached Hatshepsut's temple. I bought it to keep the sun off me, but I never used it. You wore it as a turban and it's never been worn since.'

Hal remembered the occasion and laughed out loud.

'Yes I remember it well….Tony was really cheesed off because he'd spent over the odds. He looked such an oaf in those flowing, white and blue striped robes of the Sheik. He called me a spoilsport for not joining in. Well, I did join in, and felt good in my suit and turban and it hadn't cost me a penny. That was one in the eye for 'Tightwad' Tony, controlling busybody that he was.'

Tony Thomas was a man who liked to call the shots, at home, at work and on holiday.

Chris giggled at the memory,

'I think he still had his trousers on when he wore that robe. That's why he looked so bulky.'

Chris disappeared upstairs to collect together all her bottles of bath oil, bubble bath and scented candles and made her way to the bathroom while Hal disappeared into the front sitting room window to make the most of the early March sunshine. He would be perfectly content to sit there for an hour or so with his crossword, reference books and his iPad to use as a last resort.

Chris swung open the door of the ornate, Victorian, green and white tiled bathroom and stepped onto the tiled floor. The intricate, geometrical pattern of bottle-green and white tiles met her eye. She could not look at it for long without feeling dizzy. She was so glad that they had not modernised this room. They had been sorely tempted by the offers made by Castleton Museum to purchase these historic pieces of Victorian sanitary ware, but they had resisted the temptation. She admired the deep green canopy shower bath. Not only did it have a shower rose but also body jets around the canopy. She loved the white, oval washbasin, with its Grecian pillar-like pedestal and the lavatory with that fantastic flushing system. They both considered that the modern design might be neat and sleek but they were not a patch on the old systems. Modern lavatories had been designed to save water, but how could water be saved if they had to be flushed more than once? The world had gone mad in her view. Functionality had been compromised in the name of progress.

Chris selected her towels, and started to run the bath, adding this potion and that oil and the relaxing crystals all with the perfume of lavender. She lit a couple of scented candles. She started to cough as the candle vapours caught her throat. She did not respond well to the vapours from the candles so did not over-use them.

'Some people must spend a fortune on candles to use in the bathroom. They look so pretty and romantic, flickering as they do and yet they really upset my nose', she thought. She was glad that she normally took a shower.

Somebody had told her that it was more efficacious to layer perfumes so in her self-pampering mode that is what she would attempt to do. She wondered if Shirley was doing likewise. After all, she had all the knowhow. Chris decided it would be a useful conversation to have with her.

Into the bath she stepped, carefully and deliberately. She was not used to this procedure and she did not want to slip. The water was deep and she could stretch full length and get her body totally submerged. The water was wonderfully warm and made her feel drowsy. She was soon immersed in her favourite topic of the moment- that exotic Egyptian holiday taken twelve years before.

Hal had breezed in, some twelve years before. It was a late Saturday afternoon in November. She had been enjoying a cuppa whilst watching an old movie on TV.

'I've got a surprise for you. Three guesses.'

She had absolutely no idea. She could not even hazard a guess. A meal out would be no big deal. Hal would never get so excited over that suggestion.

'Go on then. Spill the beans'

'I've only booked a holiday in Egypt to celebrate us being thirty: next April: the Easter holiday: two weeks: fly from Gatwick: a week cruising the Nile: a week in Luxor: Debs and Tony are on board.'

It had been the last thing she could have imagined. She could not believe her ears. She had wanted to go to Egypt ever since being fascinated by Egyptology during her undergraduate course. Her mother and gran had kept putting her off the idea. Her gran had been forever saying,

'Mark my words; there'll be trouble in the Middle East before long.'

And she had not been wrong; there had been that terrible massacre of tourists at Hatshepsut's temple in 1997. After that atrocity, in what she had considered to have been an idyllic location, she had given up on the idea of ever holidaying there.

She had leapt out of her seat and had given her husband a polar bear hug.

'Hal, I can't believe it! Egypt: the Nile: Luxor: Debs and Tony too...they're always good for a laugh. We can get some Bridge...... What about Max?'

Hal explained that he had discussed the subject of Max with his mother. She and his father would take Max away with them to Whitby. Max would love the sea and the sand and in any case, Egypt was no place for a toddler. It would be too hot for him even in April.

As she luxuriated in her bath, Chris savoured that particular river cruise. Every aspect of their holiday filled her with a sense of well-being.

The conditions in Luxor Airport had provided Chris with an interesting, never-to-be-forgotten experience. The airport was crowded and suffocating with the heat of the day. Jostling for attention at the bureau de change were haphazard masses of robed, turbaned members of the indigenous population and weary tourists on whose bodies lingered the stench of stale sweat which entered their nostrils at every turn of the head. It was a necessary procedure which they would not have endured for any longer than they had been obliged to. Their relief was great when at last they had been able to escape into the stifling but slightly less pungent atmosphere of the airport environs.

Their cruise boat, *Naqada 11*, had seen better days and lots of tourists before them as had many others, she observed, all in the same shabby, yet romantic, state of disrepair. These Nile boats were often parked up to five abreast because there were so many of them operating in the tourist trade on the river. To board *Naqada 11*, they had to traverse three other boats. It was a new experience for them but for the crews, it was an everyday part of the job. On their arrival on deck, they had been presented with a steaming hot flannel with which to wipe the sweat and dust from their faces. What an unexpected treat it had been.

Just downstream from their berth, containing eighteen cabins and five suites and fitted with the period furnishings, with its own berth was the SS *Sudan*. This alluring pleasure-paddle-steamer, dating from 1885, had originally belonged to King Fouad and, subsequently, it had featured in the movie *Death on the Nile*. Chris wondered what the cost would have been for them to have cruised in the SS *Sudan* and she was determined to research it just in case they ever returned. She would travel in the premier suite as Agatha Christie had done. She would take a copy of the novel, *Death on the Nile,* and would totally immerse herself in the dramatic events of that story as it unfolded on their voyage in that glamorous, fascinating paddle-steamer from that bygone, romantic age. She had anticipated with delight the prospect of bringing Max and Danny on any future trip.

While *Naqada 11* chugged peacefully through the waters of the Nile, her passengers had all the time in the world to relax on the sun deck to take a dip in the pool and to enjoy long, cool drinks all day long if that had been their desire. This had been marred only by the scent of the effluent fumes and the flecks of soot from the stack but this had been a small price to pay for such an idyllic environment. The ambient temperatures at that time of year were already high even at six o'clock in the morning and as the day wore on, so the temperatures rose. In order to visit The Valley of the Kings, the travellers had to disembark at that early hour in order to join the armed convoys of coaches setting off for the West Bank of the Nile where the pharaohs' burial sites…the world-famous tombs which over the years had been ransacked by locals and researchers alike, were to be found.

Chris's favourite Egyptian, Hatshepsut, was thought to have been entombed in this valley along with all the other pharaohs, some of whose tombs yet remained undiscovered. She had been fascinated by this queen who married her half-brother and bore him a daughter. On his death, she had acted as regent to his infant son by a concubine. From this point, her regime of power took off with a vengeance. In less than seven years, she had assumed the title of pharaoh with all the powers of that role. She relinquished her femininity by ordering that she be portrayed as a male pharaoh; images depict her wearing a beard and displaying a muscular physique. She had been an extremely successful ruler, bringing prosperity to the region, but on her death, her successor had attempted to obliterate her from history. Chris had been overwhelmed by the enormity of the mortuary temple which Hatshepsut had constructed and her thoughts went back nine years to 1997 to the massacre of tourists that had taken place in the very spot where she stood and she tried to imagine the horror of that day.

After such excursions in the searing heat, it had been a relief to arrive back on board, to be welcomed by the stewards with steaming face flannels and glasses of mint tea…and it was still only nine o'clock. Whilst *Naqada 11* was moored, there had been ample opportunities to disembark and absorb the local atmosphere. Their preference had been to take the opportunity to relax on the sun deck, take long drinks of iced water, and play some Bridge. Otherwise, they believed that they would have found themselves exhausted by their holiday rather than refreshed. Debs had frequently complained about the heat and the others had been perfectly content to stay with her in the coolest spot they could find.

They had enjoyed the evening entertainments on offer from the Swirling Dervish to the silly party games. Hal, always ready to make a fool of himself to amuse others, had been very successful in the childish game in which a potato pendulum suspended from his waist was used to direct another potato along to the finish line by the to and fro thrusting of his lower body. Chris laughed at her mental image of his bodily movements thrusting forwards and remembered the cheering of the audience as this grown man excelled in a prize winning performance.

Another of Hal's successes had been in the cocktail competition in which every contestant had free access to the bar and to all the spirits and liqueurs with which to concoct a prizewinning cocktail. Hal, not being a serious drinker, had used selected fruit juices with a modicum of alcohol and in due course he had been pronounced the winner. He had been presented with a papyrus certificate, which now hung on the wall in their sitting room in Luxor Lodge, in that corner devoted to Egyptian memorabilia. It had been his first and last experience with a cocktail shaker.

They had enjoyed sailing in a *felucca* which like the cruise boat had been multiple-parked, meaning that the tourists had to clamber over the other obstructing vessels in order to board their designated felucca. Pre-pubescent boys in tiny, coracle-like crafts navigated their passage to the sides of the felucca in order to sing to the passengers and so to beg for *baksheesh*. They would be rewarded with showers of Egyptian one pound notes, virtually valueless and so unbelievably tattered and dirty that the sanitising hand gel was in constant use.

Such activity demonstrated the vast differences in the culture of their home country compared with the Nile where scant regard was paid to the health and safety of the little boys who risked their lives to earn a few pennies.

As their cruise boat joined the queue of many others to enter the lock at Edfu, a long wait ensued. Local traders would come in their small rowing boats laden with galabayas, linens and other locally-embroidered cottons to tempt the captive audience of waiting travellers. Great entertainment was enjoyed by watching the young men hurl their wares up to the sun deck, maybe three cabins height from their position in their boats, for the perusal of the passengers who would then either decide to buy or not to buy. Cash or the unbought item would then be tossed back to the vendors, sometimes landing in the boat and sometimes in the water. This episode had provided entertainment which had been one of the highlights of the cruise and Chris reckoned that such a method of trading could happen only on the Nile.

Chris remembered the shock on entering her cabin on one occasion to find a fully-clothed, female figure lying on her bed. Mohammed, their cabin steward, practised towel sculpting for the entertainment of his clients. He had ransacked her wardrobe to find a dress, a hat and a pair of her sunglasses for his creation. A lesser mortal might well have suffered a heart attack caused by the shock at such an unexpected sight.

All too soon, their cruise on the Nile came to an end and they spent the remainder of their time in Egypt in Luxor, just a five-minute walk from the local Temple of Thebes.

The temples at Luxor and Karnak contained some incredible images. The one which had made them all smile and which obviously had been a source of interest to generations before them had been an engraving at Luxor of the fertility god, Min, depicted with an outrageous, erect, blackened phallus. The colouration, as they were informed by the guide, had been caused as a result of the touching and rubbing of it for 'good luck' by generations of greasy-fingered tourists. Some of them may have been the Ancient Greeks who it was alleged by the guide, came to Egypt to holiday and left evidence of their visits in the form of archaic Greek graffiti on the walls of the Ancient Egyptian temples. The story about Min described him as a weakling who was not strong enough to fight and so was rejected as a warrior. He was left behind when his peers went off to war. On the return of the warriors, it was found that Min had impregnated all of the women. As a result, he was publicly dismembered. Subsequently, ironically, he was deified as a fertility god. His image depicts him with only one arm and one leg but with an enormous phallus.

At this point in her recollection of Min's mighty phallus, the vision of Frank Hector had entered her thoughts, not because he might have been similarly equipped but because it had been alleged during his trial that he was particularly fond of touching and rubbing the phallus of other males. She wondered if the phallus of Min had been so mauled by Frank's grubby fingers on the occasion of his visit to Luxor. Maybe she would ask him that evening should the opportunity arise. A naughty smile momentarily appeared on her face at the prospect of his potential embarrassment to such an impertinent question.

Chris's recollections of the celebratory holiday to mark the start of their thirties reminded her of Hal's forthcoming birthday in a couple of weeks' time on 17 March. He was going to be forty three years of age. She smiled as she thought of Grandpa Day going to register Hal's birth. If Grandpa Day had had a sense of humour like that of her own father, Hal would not have been named *Henry John* but, *Patrick*.

Memories of their Egyptian holiday with their close friends would stay with her for ever. It had been quite a holiday for Debs and Tony to remember for a different reason for it was during this holiday that Debs suspected that she was pregnant with their first son, James.

Chris and Debs had been friends since early schooldays. Chris might have thought that their friendship would last a lifetime because it seemed as if they had known each other for ever. . As children, they had spent most of their free time together, either at Debs' or at Chris's. She would have described them as bosom pals, but of late, she had had some reservations and had finally come to the realisation that she did not know her friend very much at all.

Debs had been adopted as a baby and during her childhood she had been kept on a tight rein by her mother. There was no father now; he had died at an early age, and so Debs's mother became a widow with a small child to rear. She had been something of a tyrant, giving her daughter strict instructions about her appearance, clothes and her comings and goings. On reflection, perhaps she had just been a protective parent - concerned that her child was safe. Perhaps, too, the mother had been lonely and needed Debs for company. So, maybe, she had been a dictator with the best of intentions. But the two growing girls found that their activities had been curtailed by such severity and it had been a source of girlish resentment. Many a time Debs had left, to the last minute, her departure from Chris's home to be seen running for dear life to get for her lunch at the stipulated time. This performance would be repeated throughout their young lives.

They had attended different universities where they had met their respective spouses. All had gone into the teaching profession. Hal's and Tony's careers had followed a similar path and they were then both in Deputy Head Posts. Debs and Tony had two sons, James, younger than Max by two years and the other, Philip, slightly older than Danny but near enough in age to have the same interests. They used to meet up at each other's houses for a weekend about every six weeks or so as they lived several miles apart. Hal always took his tool box because inevitably there was some urgent DIY to be done and Tony did not know one end of a screwdriver from the other. The only tool he possessed was a hammer.

The girls' careers had not been similar. Debs had ceased working when James was born and so was a stay-at-home mum. Chris, on the other hand, had taken maternity leave for both Max and Danny and so had never really relinquished her hold on that greasy pole that she was attempting to climb to the glass ceiling. She would be lucky to progress any further. Her current boss had told her that she 'had done very well for a woman'. Meanwhile, both Hal and Tony had aspirations to Headship.

Over the years, Chris had become aware that her friendship with Debs had soured somewhat. She had not been able to fully understand the reason, but suspected that it might have had something to do with her husband, Tony. Over the years, Chris and Hal had become aware that their friends had become almost miserly.

Invariably, Tony insisted that the whole family should use the same bath water in order to save money. Their cupboards were full of empty *Tupperware* containers; there was no bulging pantry as could be found at the Days'. Chris and Hal had nicknamed him 'Tightwad' Tony since the he and Debs lacked a reciprocal generosity of which, considering the lavish attention they had received from the Days, was hurtful to Chris. Hal had even taught Debs to drive when her own husband would not give either time or funds for the task.

Superficially, their reunions had gone well but there had been harsh, derisive, sarcastic, misanthropic comments made from time to time which Chris would always ignore for old times' sake and to keep the peace. It had been particularly noticeable on the Thomas's first visit to Great Barrow. Chris might have been expecting congratulatory comments about their beautiful new home, but instead all she heard from Debs was,

'What do you want with such a big house?'

From that moment, Chris realised that her friend had always been a *taker* and not a *giver* and she had taken a husband who was similarly inclined.

Chris began to think about their friends and friendship in general. She came to the conclusion that she and Hal had no true friends apart from each other. Hal was her best friend, in whom she had absolute trust and to whom she could speak frankly and who shared her highs and lows in life. And he reciprocated. They needed no other friends as they had each other. Some friendships had been forged via their children but frequently they had not survived, usually through some niggling behaviour on the part of one or another of them. The closest friends they had had outside of themselves were Hal's old school friend, Michael and his wife Sally, both sadly deceased. There were people whom they regarded as social acquaintances but friendship with them was only skin deep. Colleagues from the workplace necessarily had a courteous relationship with each other in order that friction did not mar the day's achievements. Then there was Frank Hector.

Chris shivered as his name came to mind. Could Frank be described as Hal's friend? He was certainly no friend of hers. They were pushing the boat out for him that evening. What was their reason? Indubitably, it was not in the name of friendship on her part. She positively hated the man, and yet there she was, making massive efforts to feed, water and entertain the creature.

The chilliness of her bathwater caused her to return to reality. All was quiet in the house. Without further ado, she hoisted herself out of the bath, remembering that time was of the essence and that she still had to dress, to deal with her hair and to apply her makeup. She hoped that history would not repeat itself and that the Hectors would not arrive early and catch her unawares. She slipped on a bath robe and went in search of Hal whom she suspected would be fast asleep in the sitting room. She heard him singing. Sounds emerged from their newly installed wet room where he was obviously showering and oblivious to his wife's whereabouts.

CHAPTER FIVE

111

Friday 2 March

Frank Hector had been in his bedroom all afternoon, lying on top of his bed trying to get some relief from the nagging ache and shooting pains in the leg that he had injured some years before. He wondered why he had consented to go to the wretched Days. Theirs was not a true friendship. He barely tolerated Chris and the feeling was mutual; in fact, they could not bear each other. He considered Hal to be a good bloke and a useful one. Frank hoped Hal would give some valuable advice concerning his new project. Hal was prepared to sit down and have an intense debate with him not like those other half-baked, so-called academic wannabes at the James Ratcliffe. He then remembered the reason for their forthcoming visit. They were going to the Days in order to discuss his project. He could milk Hal dry whilst getting a good supper and a skin full of whisky into the bargain. He reckoned, though, that although Hal was a capital fellow, he must be lacking in something to put up with that imperious wife of his. He recalled the time at the James Ratcliffe when Chris, the external candidate, had beaten him in interview.

The job was Frank's for the taking. He and another young hopeful, Andrew Sykes, a biology teacher, a nice lad, but still wet behind the ears in Frank's opinion, with bags of confidence despite a twitching eye disfigurement in his disfavour, were the two internal candidates for the Pastoral Head of Year post, a post which carried increased status and salary. Andrew was enthusiastic, energetic, and popular with the hierarchy and the brats, whom he was always taking out to hunt for pond-life and bugs which lurked under stones but Frank was older with more experience. Both Frank and young Andrew knew the kids inside out and their families too. What possible chance could an outsider have? Frank considered himself to be the acme of control in the classroom and he was a talented musician to boot and conductor of the respected Great Scarp Brass Band. Yes, that job was meant for him. He had grown tired of his current post in the music department. He considered his boss, the head of department, to be an idiot. Frank had had his fill of clumsy urchins ruining his beloved music and treating his instruments with disdain. He was renowned in the school for his iron grip on discipline. That's what these brats needed. Which Headteacher wants a member of staff who cannot keep control in the classroom? Yes, he had felt extremely confident that the job was his for the taking. He rather fancied himself in a caring role. Taking on a pastoral function, he would tackle the job like his old mentor - the Reverend Edward Pickering would have done. It would be a wonderful, exciting adventure for him and his charges. They would learn about each other together.

But, there was an outsider up for the job - Mrs. Day. Nobody knew her but they knew of her. Her husband Henry Day was Faculty Head of the Arts subjects at the James Ratcliffe. Another young woman was to be interviewed that day. Mrs. Felicity Drew was a music teacher who specialised in singing; she would be an addition to the music department. She would be an underling for Frank, if he should fail to be appointed Head of Year.

Frank was unsuccessful; Chris Day was appointed. The two of them had been at daggers drawn ever since. However, Mrs Drew was appointed to the music department. The only positive outcome for him was that now he had another young female soul to mould, manipulate and train in his ways and from the look of her, he judged that this would be an easy task.

Frank fell into a disturbed sleep. His head was fuzzy with all the painkillers he had consumed. Random, nightmarish glimpses from the past flashed disparately in and out of his drugged mind, including transient images of his mother on her hands and knees, donkey-stoning the front door step. This activity had been the only opportunity she had had to join in the gossip with her neighbours. She was the listener and they the gossipers. Much of their gossip would be behind her back- about her little emaciated body which showed signs of some ill-treatment. They would look and frown but dare not speak out because all the households lining their sombre street lived in constant dread of discomposing their fearful neighbour, Big Frank Hector and they reckoned that his retaliation would have no bounds. Frank could remember the giggle-gaggle which snaked between the houses linking their pitiful terrace to the main route to the pit and the vast frame of his father striding along in his size eleven hobnail boots, coughing and spitting as he marched forward.

Frank visualised those two *silly puddens* as he had called his two wives - Helen from the past and Shirley in the present. Why on earth, he wondered had he married them. Plainly it was not for love because he did not even like women. Had they made him happy? Had he ever been happy? What was happiness anyway? No, he had merely satisfied himself by exerting control over them. His early, unfortunate experiences with the village girls in his early pre- and post–pubescent days had caused his absolute antipathy to the female sex. Women were there to be used by him, for menial tasks - to prepare his food and keep his house clean. He wanted no relationship with them physically. He wanted to rule them, to make them do his bidding, and to impose on them the consequences in the event of their failure. That is what excited him about women - his power over them and their absolute obedience. Both wives, he considered to be 'lazy cows'- self-willed and therefore not naturally obedient. He was always mindful of the marriage vows which demanded obedience from the female partner.

He remembered how he eroded Helen's self-confidence in order to achieve her total obedience. She had been a shy, slightly-built, nervous little thing when they first met in Philadelphia in the USA and she had seemed to be in awe of him. He had been drawn by that quality in her because he realised that she would not give him too much trouble. As soon as they were married and away from the influence of her parents, he had found the best way to get control was by causing her pain or merely by threatening her. It had been easy to manipulate her. She soon learned that the slightest deviation from his expectation would be a fierce glare or a slap. Sometimes, he would administer a 'Chinese burn' on the wrist; at other times, she would receive a good shaking.

Ultimately, he had been contemptuous of her weak nature. She had been unconditionally dependent on him. As long as she behaved herself, he treated her tolerably well. She knew that conversation about their home-life was forbidden outside their four walls but in fact there was little opportunity because one by one her friends had deserted her.

In spite of his despicable treatment of Helen, their marriage had lasted nineteen years and had produced their only child, Colin. He had sent Colin away to boarding school as soon as the decision had been made to set up his academy.

At his academy, he had forced Helen to take on the role of secretary so that he was able to monitor her movements at all times. He remembered how his father had only had to look at his mother to get her entire subservience and he had put it into practice in his own marriage. But Helen had escaped on that day in February when the police had come for him.

His second wife, Shirley, had been a good support to him in difficult times. She had been grateful for his 'knocking into shape' her son, Linus. She had had a lot to thank him for. He was aware of her sympathetic response to his plight. She had written to him and visited him in Pinchfold Castle Prison. She had been his sole visitor. He had got to know her well. She seemed to be mesmerised by him; she had ample means and was malleable. He anticipated that she would be so easy to control and he was positive that he could further mould and manipulate her into the kind of drudge he required.

He remembered the day he married Shirley. It had been a pure formality. After all, they had been living together more or less since he was released from prison. He had declared to her that he had little money. He said that all the profits from his school had long since been spent on his legal fees and his divorce from Helen. Shirley had some savings and she had her own mobile beauty business so he thought that he might just as well be the beneficiary of any funds which might come his way.

He had deliberated upon how he could demonstrate to all those holier-than-thou critics of his, just how superior and unrepentant he was about his recent past experience. It occurred to him that a stylish wedding might be the answer. Shirley would be pleased even if she were paying for it. He would get Henry Day to be a witness. Of all his acquaintances, Henry Day was the least offensive. He had enjoyed the verbal tussles they had had in the past. It was that vixen of a wife who utterly appalled him. Frank could hardly omit Chris Day from the event in which her husband would be a major participant so he gritted his teeth and issued an invitation. He would ignore her as much as he could. He forgot the pain in his leg as he recollected with pleasure how on that day, money had been no object. How great his delight and satisfaction had been at the surprised and admiring glances that had come his way from bystanders. He had showed all of them that he was not cowed by his status as an ex-convict.

He had made sure that the Days always remembered that wedding. What a remarkably smug pair they were in his opinion. Chris had an attitude which was outside Frank's control and he could not come to terms with it .The mere thought of her lording over him had made him squirm. She had beaten him in interview and in the eyes of the hierarchy at the James Ratcliffe, she had superior status over him- an intolerable situation which enraged him. Even in his fitful sleep, his cheek began to twitch with the tic he had developed at times of stress and discomfort. He believed that she used to act in a condescending manner towards him as if he were some inferior creature which she might find under a stone.

At this memory of opulent extravagance, he subconsciously stretched and preened himself. He had hired the most expensive vehicle in the hire firm's brochure. He had booked the entire iconic five-starred restaurant solely for their party of four for the wedding breakfast. He had smiled at his plan to make sure that the Days would talk about his wedding day for years to come.

Subconsciously, his cheek began to twitch as a distasteful memory of the day surfaced. On their return to Sylvan Way, those ungrateful mongrels could not wait to take their leave. He had expected them to stay for a while, to compliment his organisation of the event, to rave about the splendiferousness of the celebration, while he would bask in that glory. But that did not happen. They took their leave immediately, making use of *his* wedding car to ferry them back to Higher Ridge. He and his new, current, wife, Shirley, only had each other for company. He did not appreciate her company; she fussed over him too much; she tried to mother-hen him; he had nothing in common with her. She had made it very obvious to him that she admired him. He had married her because *she* had wanted to marry him. He desired a comfortable life-style and to have access to her money; it was his sole reason for the marriage. He had no interest in her sexually; he did not like women. He preferred the company of his constant companion, St John, known formerly as 'Eddie'.

Her money had bought them that little terraced house on Sylvan Way in downtown Scarp Edge and she had furnished it to *her* taste. She had bought him his Bechstein Grand piano as a wedding present. He had accepted all her expenditure as his right. He accused Shirley of being cold and frigid. He told her that he would get a better response from the fishmonger's slab. It was not true, of course. It was he who was the cold fish. They had shared a bed for a very short while. But very soon they took to sleeping in separate rooms. He had speculated that she would be a push-over with regard to his ascendancy but he had been in error. He had had to work on her to get under her skin with his snide comments about her weight, a topic which upset her. He had deprecated her cooking and baking abilities which he alleged were not up to the standard of his former wife, who was well versed in the art of preparing attractive and delicious dishes from fresh produce whereas Shirley relied on frozen and ready-meals so that cooking did not interfere with her work schedule which she regarded as sacrosanct. It was the only reliable source of their income.

He had tried to discipline her by sharp slaps whenever she displeased him but he soon learned that she did not respond well to pain. He constantly nagged her about her sluttish behaviour which he contended had remained unaltered. She had reacted better to the spoken word. He had the skill of articulacy, and the making of sarcastic comments was well within his repertoire. He grumbled perpetually about her untidiness in the kitchen and bathroom. He expected the towels to be neatly folded before being replaced on the rail and her lack of diligence in this simple matter had infuriated him so much that he deliberately would spill tomato ketchup over the scorching gas hob and stand over her while she scrubbed it with a toothbrush to remove the stain. He would spill flour and sugar on the floor which she had just swept so that she would have to repeat the task. If the spice and herb jars were not lined up, alphabetically, with their labels facing forward she would be rewarded with a bellowing in her ear. He would take his glass of red wine into the front room and deliberately upset the glass so that her newly purchased carpets were continually being stained. He would return to a cupboard not inspected for a day or two and it would satisfy his obsessive compulsive nature to carry out his inspections until he found one not to his liking and so his 'curriculum' would be revisited until his requirements were met every time. He would run his finger along the picture frames and hold his supposedly grimy finger under her nose,

'Look, yer idle cow. D'yer expect me to live engulfed by such filth?'

She had been a slow learner like some of the dimwits he had taught over the years. But he conquered her eventually.

She knew better than to contradict him or he would threaten to smash those antique dolls she valued so highly.

On account of his behaviour, she had moved herself out of the conjugal bed, an action he had not discouraged, into the spare bedroom which originally had a lock and key. All these old houses had internal, lockable doors, but he had removed the key and had forbidden the locking of the door. In this way, he could and did invade her privacy at will. When she had been at work, he would enter her bedroom and investigate her wardrobe. He would inspect every nook and cranny to know all about her and her possessions.

So Frank reflected that he had not been happy whatever happiness was, for several years. He had been content in those far-off days with the Pastor. But, in truth, was it happiness or the innocence of youth not knowing what happiness was? It was just a word. He knew that as a small boy he was not happy with his situation at home. His long-suffering, oppressed mother had endured his father's loathsome conduct. Why had she allowed herself to suffer? Had she loved his father? What was love anyway? Had he loved Helen and had she loved him? What was love anyway? Both were always at work; she was concerned perpetually with child care; he had had Band commitments every evening. They each had their own lives with little affection for each other. He was only happy when he was 'Banding', either playing his cornet or conducting the band.

Frank never knew or cared how much he was hated by both Helen and Shirley, because of his obsession with controlling their every move. Both wives, in his opinion, had had their slipshod ways of attending to mundane tasks. He was not slapdash. He demanded order in everything – everything regimented: everything tidy. He would not countenance any slipshod behaviour in his sphere of influence. He exerted his authority over his women, his child and his pupils. For him true contentment lay in his complete domination over his women, his child and his pupils.

He had trained and rehearsed on his tiny son, Colin. He never minded changing Colin's nappy or bathing him. Helen had been so pleased that he had taken an interest in the childcare as she knew, from her acquaintance, that other fathers left all the infant care to the mother. Frank delighted in the nakedness of his small son and became aware that even at this tender age his infant son could achieve an erection simply from the handling required during a nappy change and a rub down with a towel after a bath. So started this weird relationship with his son and Colin being such a tiny being, was wholly under the control of his warped father. Colin knew no other behaviour. He accepted his father's attention as normal behaviour.

All went well until Helen, somehow, became aware of this malpractice. Frank never knew how she found out. Her attitude altered somewhat. He sensed he could no longer rely on her absolute submission. No matter how he tried to make her comply, she seemed to have found some inner strength to combat his control and yet she remained as his wife. She tolerated her situation for the sake of the child. Eventually, when he decided to send the boy away to school, she supported the decision. Ultimately, apparently still in awe of him, she became his secretary cum housekeeper at Abercrombie Restorative Academy. Eventually, she broke free and secured a divorce when finally Frank was put behind bars.

Why had she stuck with him for so long? She recognised him to be a creepy paedophile. Was he a paedophile? Frank could never see the harm in his actions. Why didn't she make her escape earlier? The fact was that poor, shy Helen could not face life on her own. Life with the *beast,* Frank, must have seemed marginally better to her - better than being alone. But was he a beast? The truth was that he believed he was not. He merely believed that obedience should be absolute. He had not hurt his son; indeed, he loved his son; Colin was never a naughty boy like some children he witnessed - children with their mothers in supermarkets, being noisy, troublesome urchins. Frank's child was ultra-quiet, exceedingly well-behaved and never was he noisy. He was a 'speak when spoken to' type of child who obeyed his father absolutely.

Frank could not abide noise; it was cacophonous to his ears. He revelled in the sounds of melodious music from an instrument expertly played, not the discordance he experienced from those arrogant adolescents at the

James Ratcliffe playing their recorders. He picked up his cornet and rubbed it on his sleeve. It had not been played since his release from Pinchfold Castle Prison. It was best left in the past; he replaced it on the shelf in his wardrobe.

He remembered Leo from his teenage Sally Army days at the Citadel in Ravensborough. Leo had taught him how to play the cornet. Leo was man in his middle-age when first they had met. By this time, Frank had left home. He had grown taller, but still stick-insect thin, but older and able to think for himself a bit more. He had had his fill of his father. He had resigned his mother and sister to their fates. They would have to look after each other. His mother would not have much time left on this Earth. Big Frank would browbeat her into an early grave.

Frank had persisted at school because it was the most obvious, crucial action to take. He was no dunce; he had a brain and he used it. He was articulate, a skill he learned from his earlier involvement with the Pastor. Halfway through his teenage years, he outgrew both the Pastor and his Mission. Instead, he sought solace with the Salvation Army in Ravensborough where he had met Leo. Frank was sixteen; Leo, at forty six, was a man of mature years. In his fitful sleep, Frank twisted his mouth into a smile. Frank would himself be forty six in a year or two.

Leo had been a proficient tutor and Frank had been a fast learner. He had an aptitude for the instrument; he could make it sing; he became a skilled performer. Leo and he shared other interests down in Ravensborough Forest in a deserted, derelict shack, obscured from view by the cover of conifers. Leo assumed the role of 'the Pastor'. As the major tutor to the youths in the band, he justified a need to inspect their genitals, believing that there was a connection between the size of their bodily *instruments* and the quality of the music which they played on their brass instruments in the band. Brass instruments were hard to the touch. Leo required that his protégés' phalluses had the same quality. Frank was no fool. He had known the game that Leo was up to, but had he minded? No, he had not. He revelled in the attention from Leo who was the kind, gentle man who had taught him to play the cornet. Leo simply had a predilection for young lads. Where was the harm in that?

Lucidity returned for a moment as he looked at his watch.

'Bollocks! Is it that time already?'

It had turned six o'clock. He supposed that Shirley was somewhere in the house, maybe in her bedroom, getting ready for this jaunt. Poor, silly Shirley, a good woman at heart, but deadly dull; there had been no spark about her. She had no conversation, interesting or otherwise. She was no match for him. She had deserved her treatment at his hands. True, she had been a friend in the early days of their relationship, when he had been banged up. She wrote to him and visited him when no-one else did. Helen had finally discarded him. No matter, he had thought; there would always be another salivating bitch in the queue. Then along came Shirley. Shirley had money. That had made her an attractive proposition. She looked after herself too. She was an attractive woman.

'Well, she's in the beauty business isn't she? But she's a slut in the kitchen, a slut in the bathroom…messy bitch! I can't abide mess.' Frank murmured in his disturbed sleep.

His mind drifted back to Ravensborough Citadel. By his own admission, he had made use of the Sally Army to suit his needs. They had truly lived up to their title. He had been found temporary accommodation in the town and, most importantly, he had been taught to play the cornet. Before too long had passed, he became a regular member of the band. But Frank was not a believer. He expressed an interest in escaping from the area, and, in due course, with the help of Captain Challoner, he obtained a passport and set off for Philadelphia, Pennsylvania, USA where the Captain had personal links with members of the Salvation Army. Frank had lodgings with one of the Captain's acquaintances, and had behaved faultlessly in order to ingratiate himself with his foster carers. His mentor's wife accepted him into her family and treated him as a son. She advised him on his appearance and attire and he appeared to appreciate her attention. It had all been a charade; it was a means to an end.

He obtained a succession of lowly paid jobs, always being paid in cash. This was important to him because the authorities were unaware of his illegal residence when his visa expired. He enjoyed working in the supermarket, stacking the shelves. He took particular pride in ensuring that all items were stacked neatly and carefully. He used to become irritated when shoppers took an item from the back of the shelf because it disturbed the order. To supplement his earnings, he took a job as a waiter at Joe's Diner where he would wipe tables, refill condiment containers and restock napkin repositories He used to keep his tables spotless and received praise from both his boss - Joe and customers alike. He stayed in Philadelphia for three years.

Eventually, he met Helen Sutcliffe, who was on an extended holiday in the affluent suburb of Byberry, with family members who had emigrated there some years before. She, like he, had a visa for temporary residence. But his visa had become out of date. Helen was a quiet, shy girl who he believed suited his personality. They met regularly and he decided that they would become engaged to be married. She had not disagreed. Frank decreed that it was time to return to Lancashire.

Frank lodged at her parents' home. The Sutcliffes lived in a rural hamlet, north of Ravensborough, in a large house with enough room to accommodate him in a separate annexe. Her father worked for a large profitable company and had a good income for many years. They were an affluent family. The social group to which they belonged was totally alien to Frank. They liked to host

Bridge parties and were stalwarts of their local Bridge and Golf Clubs. Frank had not the slightest interest in card games of any kind; golf similarly bored him. He could see no point in batting an inert ball around an uneven golf course. The Sutcliffes had no interest in the genre of music which Frank enjoyed. Helen's mother had not been impressed by him. She considered him to be of scruffy appearance, rather ugly and generally unprepossessing. Furthermore, she had been very much aware of the constant twitch in his cheek which she found highly disconcerting. Mrs Sutcliffe wished that their daughter might have brought home a more attractive boyfriend, but, believing that attraction between the sexes should not be by looks alone, they went along, reluctantly, with her choice of man. She had been bewildered and perpetually kept guessing about what had attracted Helen to him.

In those days, Helen had firm plans for her future. She had always, from being a young girl, intended to train as a teacher and since her main interest and skills lay in domestic pursuits, she decided to apply to train in Home Economics. Frank was intrigued by her passion to pass on her knowledge and skills to the younger generations. He was determined to do likewise. He became excited at the prospect of being in charge of groups of children who he could mould and manipulate to his way of thinking. Both Frank and Helen trained at the Metropolitan University in the west of the county, she in Home Economics and he in Music.

In the January of their first year as undergraduates, Frank decided that they would marry. He had disliked her parents from the first meeting and they had made it plain that they disapproved of him. He needed Helen to focus on himself instead of being under the influence of her parents. Frank had to demolish this relationship, so that her parents would become the outsiders and he would assume supremacy. As a result of the ill-feeling in the household, a registry office ceremony was suggested by Mr. Sutcliffe who had no intention of funding a lavish reception for friends from the Golf Club and his other social groups in order for them to observe and make comments on this scrawny, scruffy individual who was about to become his son-in-law.

The grey, rainy day dawned in early January, when the marriage between Helen Sutcliffe and Frank Hector took place. The building which housed the registry office was drab. The designated room for the ceremony displayed a sombre atmosphere with cheerless paintwork in serviceable shades of brown and cream. A solitary vase of pink carnations lifted the gloom and the mood to a slight degree. Little did Frank know that he would be back in this same room in a little more than twenty years, with a different bride holding on to his arm. After the ceremony, at which only the Sutcliffe parents attended, the newly-married couple returned to their annexe in the main house. There was no honeymoon as lectures started the following week.

After three years of study and practice, they qualified as teachers. They were in their twenty fourth year. Now they had to find work. Frank planned their futures, decreeing that they would both apply for posts in schools country-wide. They would consider anywhere in the land. The first of them to secure an appointment would thereby determine where they would live. He was impatient to move forward then and glad to leave that stifling annexe which had become their first home together. In this environment he had been like a fish out of water.

Helen was appointed to the staff at Great Scarp High School. Frank soon achieved a post at Scarp Edge High School which was located about six miles distant. He would soon be back in his old stamping ground. It appeared to prove the widely held belief that the folk from this valley might leave for a while but that they always returned. Not long after, the Sutcliffes moved far away to retire in Dorchester.

'Good riddance', had thought Frank, *'now, there'll be no more interference from them'*.

He woke up with a start. His head ached with the indescribable, disjointed visions which had roamed relentlessly through his slumbering brain. He glanced at his watch and immediately remembered that a distasteful evening lay ahead. He regretted the eagerness with which he had accepted Hal's invitation to dinner. He could well have done without associating with the witch, Chris Day. He sighed. The clock was ticking. He had better get a move on. He tried to be positive. After all, he would be testing his game in the very situation for which it was devised. The dreaded visit could prove to be productive. He had better make the most of it. Some good may come from the evening, he hoped. His bed-cover was crumpled as a result of the incessant squirming during his reveries. He hobbled off the bed and painfully returned it to its former flawless state. He limped over to the wardrobe to select his attire for the evening, opting for an olive-green, polyester shirt with a button-down collar, a colourful tie with a pattern evocative of the end-papers in antique bank ledgers. He chose to wear his favourite brown, corduroy trousers. Bright yellow socks completed his ensemble. He grinned momentarily as he donned the socks; he had always loved extreme colours for socks and ties. Having replaced the empty coat-hanger into his well-organized wardrobe, Frank inspected his bedroom. How orderly it was; nothing was out of place.

Frank checked his medicine cabinet. His large stock of pain killers seemed to be diminishing so he resolved to maintain a regular prescription which would afford him the necessary relief. He decided to have a peek into Shirley's room where all was quiet. She must be downstairs. Opening the door of her wardrobe a flimsy silk blouse fell to the floor. She had not arranged it carefully enough on its hanger. This small indiscretion of hers totally unnerved him and in this frenzied state, he tore every garment off its hanger and onto the floor. With his facial tic, at its most uncontrollable, he raced to the head of the stairs and bellowed so loudly that she could hear him, wherever she was.

CHAPTER FIVE

IV

Friday 2 March

In the Day household, it was fast approaching half past six. Frank and Shirley would be arriving at any minute. If Frank acted true to form, they would be early just to try to catch her unprepared. She had no intention of that occurring. It had happened once before and she had learned from that experience not to let history repeat itself.

Chris well remembered that occasion when Frank and Helen had come to dinner. It had been a lesson for her. She had heard the door-bell ring. She was dressed but still had her hair to comb out. Rollers, in profusion, were still enmeshed in her hair. She panicked. Hal had not been able to come to her rescue….he was still in the shower and would be oblivious to the early arrival of their visitors. She could not do her hair; that would take too long. She could not leave them standing on the doorstep; she was too polite. Of, course, that is precisely the action she should have taken. She wasn't ready simply because they were too early… a good fifteen minutes. Stuff them! She should have made them wait. If she had known Frank better, she would not have rushed to admit them. In those days, there was not a great distance between their two homes. Therefore, he must have been deliberately trying to wrong-foot her. Helen, his first wife, was suitably embarrassed but Frank thought that the episode was very funny; he was visibly amused - sniggering and fidgeting in his inimitable manner - a huge grin spreading from ear to ear, obviously highly delighted to have caught her in rollers.

'Are we early?' he had enquired with that wolfish smirk.

Chris had passed off the event with apparent sang-froid but inside she had been seething. Frank had made jocular reference to her unpreparedness from time to time. It had been best to ignore him, but, she had stored the memory in the recesses of her brain. The mere recollection of it now enraged her.

All was ready in the kitchen - soup was simmering on the hob; mushrooms were ready to go into the oven at twenty to eight. The main course of meatballs in tomato sauce was already bubbling away in the oven. The pre-prepared mash with its topping of grated cheese in an oven-proof dish was ready to pop into the oven in order to warm it through at half past seven. There remained just the beans to be cooked. Her Chef's Candle, scented with basil, patchouli and geranium, was ready for lighting at the appropriate time. Dinner had been planned for eight o'clock. The trifles had been previously prepared in individual sundae dishes because she hated the messy business of spooning trifle from one big bowl. Cheeses had been unwrapped and placed in position on the cheeseboard, accompanied by shelled walnuts, green grapes and a selection of knives. Coffee cups and saucers, cream and brown sugar crystals and chocolate truffles were in place on the sideboard. She had decided to use her beautiful Wedgwood *Meadow Sweet* china which she had purchased at auction. She really loved the design and had enough pieces for that night's meal.

Hal had been in charge of setting the table. He used the lace tablecloth and her place-mats depicting birds of prey both of which had been given to her by her granny. Hal made sure that their silver-plated cutlery was in good order and he arranged them to display the rat's tail design on the reverse of the spoons and forks. A small vase of early jonquils and some table lights completed the setting. She needed some matches to hand. Hal had forgotten the napkins. She went to her sideboard and brought out her best white linen napkins. He had remembered to put out the whole grain mustard, the sea salt and black pepper mill. She did not use much salt in her cooking. She considered that individuals ought to add seasoning to their own taste. She could anticipate that Frank would add salt before even tasting her food. She inspected their provision of drinks. Bottles of Sauvignon Blanc, Chardonnay and sparking water were already cooling; a couple of bottles of Australian Shiraz, her favourite red wine had been opened and were on the sideboard. Port for the cheese course, cherry brandy, Cointreau and Advocaat were also at hand. Craft beers had been put to cool. She also had some fresh apple and ginger juice just in case it was needed. She would be offering either gin and tonic or a good blended whisky as a reception drink. She knew that Frank preferred single malt whisky.

'Tough,' she thought.

She recalled the dinner parties hosted by their friends, Frans and Bridget Bakker. Frans was a Dutch National who had moved to the UK as a child. His wife, Brid, was Irish. They had met at university just as had Chris and Hal. They had got to know the Bakkers through Max, their son. Max and Paul Bakker had formed an immediate friendship at KGV and so had both sets of parents. It was a common occurrence for adult friendships to be made in this manner, but they were often transient, lasting little longer than the presence on the scene of their offspring.

Frans' gin and tonics were *the works,* the best she had ever tasted. He had told her his secret,

'Keep everything ice-cold; keep your gin in the freezer; keep your tonic and lemon in the coldest part of the fridge; use crushed ice, not ice cubes; and serve in tall, fine, highball-tumblers which you've also cooled in the fridge.'

The resulting nectar was invariably heavenly. She followed Frans' advice and hoped that her skill in the preparation of the G and T, ice and slice equalled his.

She deliberated upon the extent of energy and expense which she was expending on the forthcoming dinner party for a creature whom she detested. She needed to produce the best entertainment she could both for her own pride and for the maintenance of her solidarity with her revered husband. How had she allowed herself to be manipulated into this position? She remembered the occasion well.

She and Hal had been doing their weekly supermarket shop when they spotted a frantically, waving hand along an aisle. The hand had belonged to Frank Hector. After a few pleasantries had been exchanged, Frank took no time in requesting Hal's help with some scheme or other which was fomenting in his mentally disordered psyche. Hal, being an English specialist, had been ready to oblige. He then did something totally out of character; he issued an invitation to Frank.

'Why don't you come for dinner one evening? Perhaps we can get our heads together, then.'

Chris could not believe her ears. Hal knew how much she detested Frank Hector and it appeared that she was going to have to entertain him and his wife. Normally, Hal would have discussed such an evening with her first.

Needless to say, Frank had jumped at this opportunity to nosey around their new house. Naturally, Chris had not intervened. She regarded such behaviour beneath her. She would never have disagreed with Hal in public. Such discussions were for the privacy of their home and she intended to make her feelings known to Hal as soon as she had him on his own. She rubbed the dry, scaly patch on her finger. If she was turning into a lizard, she would be in good company, on the forthcoming designated evening with that snake in the grass.

CHAPTER FIVE

V

Friday 2 March

In the Hector household the antique grandfather clock chimed the half-hour. Shirley checked the time on her watch, half past five. Frank was still in his room. Meanwhile, Shirley sat in the sitting room waiting for Frank. She was nervous as she looked around, checking that all was in order and nothing out of place. On this particular evening, she did not want him to find fault with her. She needed to remain calm. She wore a navy suit with a cream trim. It was a suit that she had rarely worn and she could feel it fitted rather too snugly. *'Time I shifted a bit of weight,'* she told herself. She opened the sideboard door to take out her favourite perfume – Miss Dior: *Blooming Bouquet*. She removed the cap then she hesitated. She decided that she would not wear any perfume on this occasion.

Shirley was in her early forties but looked older. Her hair was still blonde, but whether that was her natural colour was hard to determine. She was, after all, a beautician and knew the secret of successful hair colouring. She had deep lines around her eyes and darkened skin under them. She had the appearance of a critically unwell woman. She tried her hardest to hide from the world the misery of her recent life. She had grown to detest Frank, her second husband who was an ex-convict, a man whom she had formerly admired and whom she had felt had been misjudged, but, during that four year period of marriage, he had changed from a friend into a sadistic swine. Shirley and Frank had not shared a room for most of their four years of marriage. She would have locked the door of her bedroom but he had not allowed it.

Shirley could well believe the story of Doctor Jekyll and Mr Hyde. Frank's 'Henry Jekyll' had long since disappeared and she was faced on a daily basis with 'Mr. Edward Hyde.'

Shirley had always been in awe of Frank, ever since she enrolled her son, Linus, at Abercrombie Restorative Academy, Frank's independent boys' school.

At first, before they had married, he had been an attentive suitor; he used to bring her flowers, chocolates and unexpected gifts. He had been amusing and had made her laugh. He had displayed impressive intelligence and in company had proved himself to be an informed conversationalist. He was a proficient musician who, before his prison sentence, used to play the cornet beautifully. In no time, he had moved into her small flat and before long he had proposed marriage to her. She had accepted, trusting that a happy future was to be had. She loved his talent. She was not interested in having a sexual relationship with him and she knew that he felt the same way. Soon after the wedding ceremony and the lavish, though tiny wedding breakfast which had lulled her into a false sense of security, Shirley realised what his cunning motives had been. She had been like a mackerel ready to jump on to the silvery hook as it was lowered into the shimmering sea. It was too late. As in her former marriage, she had made her bed and on it she was obliged to lie.

During her first disastrous marriage, she had received scant attention from her husband, Alf, whom she had eventually divorced because they had had nothing in common except the boy. She was married at twenty four and pregnant. At her age, she should have known better. She had met Alf at a dance. Tall, fair haired and good looking, he was also an accomplished dancer. He had led her to believe that his father was a professional academic. He had given her his father's business card on which was printed Professor Jimmy Entwhistle with the address, 'Holly Grove'. He had never taken her to his home until after they were married by which time it was too late. She had been naïve. An innocent who had been sweet talked into bed by Alf Entwhistle, she should have been more inquisitive. She should have asked more questions about the family. Shirley recalled her thoughts at that time,

'What sort of academic calls himself 'Jimmy' on his business card? He's no academic, a confidence trickster, more like.'

She took not the slightest interest in his family after that. And it was reciprocated. None of them had ever shown the slightest interest in her or Linus.

She believed that their son, Linus, was going to develop into a wastrel like his dad. He had been the archetypal 'teacher's nightmare'. She had been at her wit's end, forever having been called into his school since he was aged five, on account of his poor attention to work, insulting to the teacher, shouting out in class and threatening behaviour towards his peers. The list of his misdemeanours had seemed endless. She had grown weary of treading the well-trodden path to the Headteacher's door especially since Alf never would accompany her. He had found his son's contempt for authority somewhat gratifying. Alf had been more interested in dog racing and playing darts at The Dun Cow. The boy was seven years old at the time. Eventually, she decided that enough was enough and she walked out.

She could not remember their ever having danced again after Linus's birth.

She had seen an article in the local newspaper. There was to be a new school in Scarp Edge Fold, in the isolated rural hinterland of the town of Scarp Edge.

Scarp Edge, had been a thriving town in times long since gone. There were still some magnificent buildings in the town, constructed in the Victorian era with money from the cotton industry. The Town Hall's primary facade was faced with the beautiful local stone; marble pillars, built in the classic Corinthian style, marked the main entrance. Other buildings were a mixture of brick with ornate stone sills and architraves. But Scarp Edge had become a dreary place to live, as a result of the decline of the cotton mills, the movement of the population out to find work elsewhere, the consequential lack of money and the influx of less desirable citizens.

Rows of dilapidated, unkempt terraced houses covered the close environs of the town centre. Occasionally, a well-maintained property could be spotted like a primrose in a dismal, neglected garden. The sort of people who inhabited such dwellings were those with proper values and had probably been residents of long standing who had had the misfortune of watching, with despair, the decline of their neighbourhood and the inevitable devaluation of their properties.

The newspaper article had stated that this new establishment, *Abercrombie Restorative Academy,* had been the brainchild of Dr Frank Hector, a former teacher of music at the James Ratcliffe High School. Frank Hector had seen the need to provide an education for boys, aged nine to fourteen - the archetypal square pegs who had not fitted into the standard education system. The school aimed to provide good discipline, music appreciation, and a sound basic education in the three Rs. The aims, especially the one about good discipline, caught her attention. It was like music to her ears. It sounded just the sort of institution that her problem son, Linus, required and would benefit from. She decided to make enquiries. This would be a fee-paying, private school. This had made her anxious, but she thought it would do no harm to find out more. So, she had made an appointment to discuss Linus's needs with the Principal, Dr Frank Hector. The mere sound of his name filled her with hope for the future.

After her separation from Alf, Shirley had to set about earning enough money to support herself and Linus. She had received nothing from Alf after the divorce. She was already a qualified beautician, specialising in the treatment of hair and nails. She contacted her former employer, Sian Protheroe. Shirley, having been a conscientious employee before her untimely pregnancy and unfortunate marriage and in possession of beautiful hands and nails and an immaculate personal style was immediately reinstated by the owner of the Salon. There had been no hesitation. Sian Protheroe reckoned that Shirley would be a fine ambassador for the Salon. She required Shirley to provide a home-based service to clients who were usually highly-paid working women, with little time to sit in salons, and the wealthy elderly who still took great pride in their appearance but found travelling for treatment at the Salon difficult.

Shirley had clients in some of the most prestigious homes. For the most part, they were located in the affluent, desirable villages of Long Barrow, Great Barrow and Great Ridge all of which were in the green belt, a short, but significant drive from the dilapidated town in the valley, Scarp Edge. She had witnessed elegant houses with their opulent décor, furniture and their grand limousines. This was the kind of lifestyle that she had wanted for herself. She had worked diligently and had elevated herself to a position of self-respect. She also enjoyed a substantial income. Her generous employer, who rewarded her therapists well, was rapidly approaching retirement and she had not objected when Shirley decided set up her own business. Shirley had already acquired a long list of satisfied clients and the future of her mobile beauty business looked promising. She had managed, by a careful, economic lifestyle, to acquire a healthy bank balance. The school fees appeared to be within her capability.

The day had arrived for her visit to the school – Abercrombie Restorative Academy. The institution was located in Scarp Edge Fold, a substantial drive out of Scarp Edge, in the wilds to the west of the town. She had stopped at the huge iron gates which guarded the entrance to the grounds. On the twelve feet high stone walls flanking the gates was a large sign with the words *Abercrombie Hall*. She drove up the winding driveway to a large country house which had obviously seen better days. On the door was a brass plate on which was etched,

ABERCROMBIE RESTORATIVE ACADEMY

PRINCIPAL: DR. FRANK HECTOR

She had been ushered into his office by the secretary, who she later had discovered to be Mrs. Helen Hector, the Principal's wife. On the door of his office was another brass plate which bore his title. Shirley immediately was struck by Frank Hector's unkempt, physical appearance. He stood about five feet eight inches in height, thin, gaunt and looking underfed with a poor complexion. He was rather a poor specimen for a prospective Principal of an independent school she had thought. She had considered that for a man of his status, his hair was too long and it clung greasily to his scalp. That had been obvious to her trained beautician-eyes. His suit hung baggily on his bony, angular frame. His overall, scruffy appearance probably would have inhibited some potential clients, but in her desperation, she was inclined to give him a chance. She found excuses for his unprepossessing appearance. Perhaps his personal wellbeing had taken a back seat during the setting up of his new venture.

She had scanned his office, noticing its immaculacy. It seemed to be in such stark contrast to the man himself. Books were neatly lined up in order of height on the shelf. A container of newly sharpened pencils, all of the same length stood in a cylinder on his desk. His professional qualifications, mounted and framed, hung on a wall. They had included a B.A. (Music) from North Ravensborough City University and PhD in Child Psychology from the Thornton Institute of Philadelphia, USA. A collection of black and white photographs of various fungi were mounted on the wall behind his desk. The extreme tidiness struck her as slightly bizarre and somewhat creepy. There seemed to be not a thing out of place. Shirley was not to be deterred by her observations. She convinced herself that this man would be the answer to her prayers and that Linus's improved life chances in the new school would be her salvation.

In many ways, Frank Hector's teaching methods had been commendable. His methodology had been task-orientated; the boys had to complete their assignment before moving on to the one following, otherwise the penalties imposed upon them would have been severe. He had been a strict disciplinarian. This was what these boys had needed. This had been the reason why this establishment had been the obvious choice for them. No other school would have taken them. The parents of these boys had been at the end of their tethers. They had been glad that there was someone in charge who would control their recalcitrant heirs and leave them, the parents, free to pursue other demands on their lives. The school had provided a musical education; Frank Hector was convinced that if he could have instilled even a smidgeon of music into their souls, they would always find peace and satisfaction in their own solitude.

Abercrombie Restorative Academy was a boarding school.

Shirley heard a roar emerge from upstairs, causing her to stir rapidly from her private thoughts. It was the sound of Frank's angry tones emanating from her bedroom. He reverted to local dialect more and more.

'Where are yer, Woman? You gret lump o'lard. Get up here reet now. This wunt do! 'Ow many times have yer got to be telled? When will yer get it into yer thick skull? Yer know 'ow I want things done and it aint like this.'

She scurried up the stairs and into her bedroom. He walked slowly and deliberately towards her. 'Ye'd better give me an explanation of this. Yer slut.'

Shirley looked in the direction of his bony, pointing finger. All of her orderly, immaculate wardrobe had been scattered. Frank, in his frenzy, had swept everything to the floor.

'Now, get that all picked up and put back proper or yer'll feel this'.

He shook a fist in her direction.

'Mi old injury is giving me gyp as well. I'll have to tek some painkillers to get me through this pigging evening.'

Shirley could have done without this tiresome task, but she obeyed without complaint. She felt rather light headed and drunk on the thoughts running through her brain at breakneck speed of Frank's impending comeuppance at her hand later that very evening. She actually smiled at him, but he was too concerned with his pain to notice.

He was aware that strong opiate painkillers would not mix well with the alcohol that he intended to consume at the dinner party at the expense of the Days. But he had thought, *'What the hell?'* He had to rid himself of this chronic ache in his leg.

'Yer'll have to do the driving. Serve yer right for being such a sluttish, cowin' bitch.'

His usual educated vocabulary lacked sufficiently appropriate words to express the vehement loathing he felt towards her at that moment and his chronic facial spasms were gathering alarming momentum.

Shirley said nothing. But she thought all the more. She gave the outward appearance of being the subservient wife. It suited her purpose that evening. She completed her task of tidying her wardrobe whilst he went off, hobbling, in search of his pills. She found her car keys, turned down the central heating, and went to start up the car. She could keep her thoughts to herself under the pretext of driving safely. He stumbled out. It was obvious he was in pain.

'Do you want me to help you, luv?' she asked, her voice quiet and showing concern for his discomfort.

'Nah…. Yerv made us late enough already. Put yer foot down and let's get to this swanky new house of the Days. God knows why they want such a big place'.

It was a twenty minutes journey to Great Barrow. They uttered not a word to each other. Frank had his mind on the pain in his leg. He had, however, remembered to bring paper and pens for use later that evening. Shirley had plenty on her mind too. She had thought back to that day in early February, when an envelope containing an invitation had come through the letter box. Before slitting it open with her paper knife, Shirley had studied the handwriting on the envelope and recognised it as that belonging to Chris Day. They had not been to the Days' home for several months and then their visit had been to the Days' former address in Higher Ridge. The Days had certainly moved a few times - first Scarp Edge, then Higher Ridge, now they had moved further out to Great Barrow into a posh new house. Shirley would have liked to live in Great Barrow. It was a tasteful village with various architectural styles, a mixture of ancient and modern dwellings. She had known in her heart that this would never happen. It had been an invitation to dinner at eight o'clock on the evening of Friday, 2nd.March. Drinks would be served at half past six and dinner would follow at eight o'clock. An RSVP was requested.

Shirley had eagerly anticipated the outing. She had been hatching a plot for some time, going over and over it again in her mind, refining it to the 'n'th degree so that it was perfect and fool proof. This was going to be the ideal opportunity to put her plan into action. She had read somewhere, 'Revenge is a dish best served cold' but her revenge would be anything but cold. She shivered in tingling, orgasmic anticipation that her scheming was finally approaching its climax.

CHAPTER FIVE

VI

At Luxor Lodge, Chris stood, hands on hips, in the kitchen, staring at the enormous clock face which dominated the wall.

'*Wretched guests!*'

She swore to herself under her breath. She was not in the habit of swearing; she might utter a mild oath occasionally, but nothing to offend anyone. But now, in the privacy of her thoughts, she let rip...

'*BUGGER! BUGGER! BUGGER FRANK HECTOR!*'

The clock read twenty minutes to seven. They had been due at half past six. From her previous experience of entertaining the Hectors, she had expected them to be early; Frank could squeeze in an extra drink that way. This was a specific dinner party for two invited guests, not one of those occasions when guests, having noted the starting time, had turned up an hour later expecting to find the party in full swing, their reason being 'Who wants to be first at a party?' This was a dinner party for four. She had made the preparations and the least they could do was to arrive on time - not early: not late, but on time.

'Put yer foot down, will yer. Hopeless driver that yer are! Should 'a' driven 'ere meself, after all. Can't trust yer t' do owt reet.' Frank was livid. His use of local dialect accentuated his venom.

Shirley ignored his comments. She was in control of the car. She felt for the first time in several years that she was totally in control of everything. She was driving, not fast, but, not slowly either; she was driving carefully. Virgin snow lay on the ground. And as they approached Great Barrow, the depth of snow made driving more dangerous. The roads in this rural area had not been cleared by the council, and the gritting wagon had not been that far out of town. They had not been invited to the Days' new house before so that in the darkness and under the weak, inadequate glow of the intermittent street lamps, they struggled to find it. All the houses were well-separated and were not always numbered. They had to search for a house name in the dimly-illuminated road. Fortunately, the snow on the ground helped somewhat in reflecting the headlights onto the garden boundary walls. They spotted the house sign and the driveway entrance.

'Luxor Lodge'...'pretentious plebs!' scoffed Frank.

He had overlooked totally the fact that he was about to gorge himself at the Days' table and relieve them of a large quantity of alcohol. Shirley navigated their way up the sweeping driveway to the portico which housed the front door. In the wintry conditions and the darkness of the early March evening, they were aware of the imposing façade of the building. The wide, white-rendered, rectangular edifice had four deep, virtually ground-to-roof, windows, a central entrance and double opening doors, flanked by two large columns, thus producing a portico. This was surmounted by a triangular pediment. Frank believed the building to be Georgian. He wondered what it had cost them and vowed to utilise the internet back home to find its true value. He reckoned that it could be worth nine hundred grand or even a million. He reflected on his own modest dwelling in Scarp Edge. Some might be described as a slum property because of the decline of its surroundings, but at the time of its construction, it would have housed a respectable family, probably originally owned by a skilled textile worker. It was a compact, stone–built, terraced house with three bedrooms, the smallest of which had been converted into a sauna. With gloating cynicism, he wagered that the Days had no such luxury in their 'Luxor Lodge'.

Frank alighted from the front passenger seat with a groan and a pained look on his face. The snow crackled beneath his shoes and he took care not to slip on the untreated surface.

'Yer'd think they'd have cleared t' bloody drive,' he spat at the cold air. *'These damned pills are tekin' th' time to work…probably out-of-date…should 'a' swallered the new prescription',* he thought.

He did not cast a glance in his wife's direction, leaving her to make her own exit from the driver's seat and to lock the car. He limped at a gingerly pace to the huge, heavy, timber, black-painted door and pressed the bell. It was ten minutes to seven.

Hal opened the door to them. His face beamed.

'Welcome Hec and Shirley. Come into the warmth. Let me take your coats'.

There was nothing else to take. The Hectors had brought no gift of wine, flowers or chocolates. The aromatic aromas from the kitchen regaled their senses as they entered the hallway. Momentarily, Frank emerged from his black mood,

'By Jove, Aitch, this dinner smells good!'

The face of this insufferable reptile had visibly altered chameleon-like from a swarthy purple to a rosy pink. Frank appeared to have cheered up somewhat. How could he not, when greeted with such enthusiastic affability by his old, debating adversary?

Whilst their outer garments were being put on coat hangers in the cloaks cupboard, Shirley took her chance to have a surreptitious glance around. Frank's appraisal was more obvious and outspoken.

'This place will have cost them an arm and a leg. I bet they've no brass left to update it', Frank smirked amused by his mental speculation.

'Georgian is it?'

'No', Hal corrected his assumption. 'It's actually Victorian.'

'Will have cost you a bob or two, I bet'

'We reckoned that it would be a good investment,' Hal responded without going into details of its actual cost which had actually stripped their savings bare.

Shirley felt comfortable in this house. Although the ceilings were high and the rooms large, the house was warm and welcoming. The proportions, certainly, in the hallway were pleasing. The Days had their own personal style of furnishing which was not to her taste, but then it was not her home. She thought about her own modest dwelling in Scarp Edge. It was cosy with fine furnishing and some valuable antiques. It was not large but then she had to cut her cloth accordingly. She loved her little house. She had paid for the fabric and all the furnishings. It was just a pity that Frank's name was also on the deeds.

'Come into our sitting room, and let's fix up everybody with a drink',

Hal invited them into a large, square room. The ceiling had an ornate cornice, and a magnificent plaster rose from which hung an impressive, sparkling chandelier. There was an abundance of wall-lights. Frank wondered whether the chandelier was made of crystal or glass. He was no expert. There was a pale green, fitted carpet, on top of which sat a sizable Chinese rug, in shades of pink and green. Their Duresta three-piece suite, although several years old, but still in too good a condition to be replaced, did not look out of place. Frank noticed gleefully, with that critical, eagle eye of his, evidence of pulled threads on the rear corner of the sofa. Their cat had left his indelible mark.

In one corner of the sitting room, a shelved alcove displayed Chris's souvenirs from Egypt… a cast bronze bust of Nefertiti… one of King Tut… a figurine of Bastet… some fine blown-glass perfume bottles… a crystal pyramid containing a laser etching of Bastet and some framed, papyrus paintings.

'God! What excremental tat!' Frank was almost beside himself with scorn for her treasures, but he kept his own counsel and expressed a feigned interest.

'Interesting idea, Aitch. Yours or yer wife's?'

Chris entered the sitting room. Frank stood and, ostentatiously, held out his arms to greet Chris with a hug, kiss and pat on the back. She was not enamoured of this sort of chummy greeting and, internally, recoiled without making her distaste obvious.

Against one wall stood a Yamaha electric piano, purchased by Hal for Chris's fortieth birthday. Frank became almost hysterical. He fidgeted and squirmed as his face twitched.

'What's this then?' asked Frank, his whole being resembling a small grotesque goblin.

'At least it doesn't need tuning every five minutes; neither does it eat anything,' retorted Chris, her blood already beginning to boil and her face beginning to redden and they had only just arrived. 'I don't even have to play it. It came with twenty pieces in-built, so all I have to do is to switch it on.'

Frank pulled himself up to his full height and puffed out his puny chest,

'Yer can't beat a Bechstein. It's the best'.

His magnificent Bechstein grand piano, a wedding gift from Shirley, occupied most of their front room.

Chris ignored him. It would be the best way to survive the evening. She said,

'What'll you have, Shirley… gin?'

Hal left the room just as Chris said the word *gin*.

Shirley hesitated momentarily; Chris's gin and tonics were legendary.

'Yes, please, I would love a gin.'

Shirley was determined not to have more than a couple of alcoholic drinks. She would enjoy Chris's gin and tonic and would also take a small glass of wine at the table with the main course. But, she wanted to keep her head clear. And in any case, she would have to be careful that she did not exceed the limit, in case she was breathalysed on the way back home.

'What about you, Hec, Do you fancy a gin?'

Hal reappeared bearing a bottle of Scotch and two glasses.

'Gin is for women and pansies. No thanks, Aitch, I'll have a whisky.'

'Help yourself then'.

Frank took the bottle and looked at the whisky on offer. He was not impressed. However, he poured himself a generous slug, looked for the most comfortable seat and sat down. He lit a cigar. He drained his glass in one gulp and reached for the bottle, hoping that the strong alcohol would deaden the agony in his leg.

'Frank, dear, why don't you get some more of your Zymkase capsules down you if your leg's so bad?'

Shirley began to act as a worried wife, showing concern about Frank's chronic pain in his leg caused by the old motor cycle injury. Her actual intent was to instil into the Days' subconscious minds, Frank's dependence on

Zymkase, and to enable them to confirm to the police, when they inevitably would call on them, that Frank had been taking these strong opiates to ease his pain on the Friday evening at the dinner party.

Both Chris and Hal were intrigued by Frank's vocabulary. Why had he used the word 'pansy' so disparagingly when it was obvious to everyone that homosexuality was his preference?

'Oh dear, Hec, have you got a bad leg? What can we get you for it…some paracetamol perhaps?'

Of course, she was being sarcastic. Chris had overheard what Shirley had said about his painkillers.

'Perhaps another whisky will help to ease the pain? Let me help you to another.'

Shirley smiled. She could sense some kind of kindred spirit in Chris.

'Yes, go on Frank, I'm sure it will help you to take your mind off your pain.'

Frank did not argue. He enjoyed his drink and could hold it well. He forgot that the whisky was a blend and not the single malt that he preferred.

CHAPTER FIVE

VII

'Look Hal, I'll go and see to the first course. Shirley can help me whilst you and Hec talk about his project.'

The women left the men to their discussion about Frank's project. His aim was to produce a new adult game for people to play at a dinner party, around the table or indeed at any time. It would be flexible in that way and would lessen the boredom of the usual kind of chat that often prevailed at these kinds of event.

Always assuming that he could produce a game that was of sufficient quality and interest, he said that he needed somebody with Aitch's expertise to ensure that the English was grammatically correct. Frank, himself well able to write grammatically correctly, did not actually need Hal's services, but he wanted a second opinion and he knew that he could trust Hal's judgement. He believed that Hal would be unbiased. To Hal, this seemed to be an easy task. If it helped Frank to regain some self-esteem, he would be pleased to give whatever help he could. They discussed the proposed game and other projects that

Frank might try. Hal suggested that Frank might attempt a writing project about his time in prison.

In the kitchen, Shirley and Chris were discussing home, family, clothes, and food….in fact the sort of things that women often talk about. Neither Shirley nor Chris mentioned Frank Hector. Shirley was anxious to convey to the Days that she and Frank had a happy, comfortable relationship. She was not going to admit to any of the foul, sadistic acts to which she had been subjected over the previous few years since their marriage and yet she felt that Chris was sympathetic to her plight without knowing what had been going on.

Chris could not tell this woman standing in her kitchen about the absolute disgust and hatred that she felt for her husband. To Chris, Frank Hector was a walking abomination and yet she felt that Shirley had some empathy with her intense aversion to him. He was the so-called 'elephant in the room'; their best option was to steer clear of discussing their respective spouses. Shirley complimented Chris on her evening gown. Chris could not believe that Shirley would not recognise that her galabaya was, actually, a very cheap garment that she had purchased for a few pounds from the souk in Luxor. The garment, very ornate with lots of embroidery was machine-made from cotton, not a mixture of natural and man-made fibres. In that regard, it was a quality item. Chris had believed that all such items of clothing sold in Egypt would be made from Egyptian cotton, but she had seen some in the souk which appeared to be a mixture of cotton and man-made fibres. In her opinion, this was yet another example of deteriorating quality in the so-called progressive world economy.

She did not contemplate for a moment that Shirley might have been patronising her; she felt that Shirley was too decent a person for that. Chris debated with herself as to whether she should broach the subject of the gold lace wedding dress, but ultimately she thought it better to leave that issue for another time. It was early days in their relationship and in any case they had the soup to attend to. They left it on a low heat and returned to the sitting room where Hal and Frank were in discussion.

'The soup will be ready shortly', announced Chris.

'Hec would like to explain his project.' Hal said pre-empting any pronouncement from Frank. Hal thought that Chris would see red if Frank started pontificating so he was trying to ease the way forward.

'OK', Frank stood and wiped his brow. His cheek began to twitch. He opened his mouth wide in an attempt to arrest it. He spoke,

'The idea is that provocative questions are posed to stimulate debate. The game is based on a favourite philosophical question of mine. I'm calling it 'Truth or Belief.'

Chris mouthed the words as Frank uttered them. She was almost beside herself with disbelief. This was the very question the venomous Frank always threw at her at every social opportunity. What was she to do? She decided that the best plan was not to get annoyed because that is what Frank was out to achieve. She would play him at his own game.

'What *is* the difference between truth and belief?'

Frank raised his eyebrows at her impertinence in tossing the question back to him. Chris was obviously being provocative; he and Hal had debated the topic many times in her presence. He carried on as if she had not uttered a word.

Frank had come fully prepared. He was going to exploit Hal and the others for all he was worth. He had brought papers and pens, pilfered from places of past employment. He issued to each in turn a sharpened pencil and a few identical pieces of plain paper and instructed them,

'Now...everybody, tek a piece of paper and write down a question. Then fold the paper in half then in half again. I'll shuffle 'em up and select one at a time and see how we go on. Include the word *truth* or *belief* or any word which implies that idea,' he instructed. 'Avoid useless, mundane questions. Be thought-provoking'.

He wondered what sort of inane questions these ninnies would come up with. The room was quiet...

everybody deep in thought... chewing pencils... writing questions... folding papers.

'Right, here goes. Here's the first question. 'What's in a name?' Tell the truth... how much do you like your name?'

All the questions were to be anonymous. No-one knew who wrote which question with the exception of Frank who would recognise each individual's handwriting.

'You specifically forbade mundane questions. If this isn't one then I'm a Dutchman,' said Chris.

'Hardly a probing question', thought Shirley.
Hal was the first to answer. He had been christened Henry John Day, Henry, after his maternal grandfather and John after his father. He was called *Aitch* by Frank and *Hal* by his friends. *Day* was an odd sort of name; but it was quite uncommon; *Henry Day* sounded OK.

'On the whole my name is perfect,' said Hal.

'Is that it? Aren't you going to say anything else?

'I've answered the question, haven't I? Rather a mundane question if I may say so, Hec.'

Shirley announced that she hated all of her names except for her maiden name of *Mackintosh*. She disliked her Christian name. She wished her mother had been more adventurous in naming her only daughter.

'I don't care for *Hector* and I wish my mother had called me *Helen* or *Miranda*', she concluded.

'Yer faggot! I don't care for Shirley or Helen or Miranda. Just yer wait, mi wench. I'll mek yer pay for that comment about my name.' Frank's eyes were staring, blankly, into the middle distance. He was conjuring up the next act of cruelty to be practised on his wife.

Chris thought for a long time before she gave her answer to the question. She had always been embarrassed about her name. She rarely used it so why hadn't she changed it? She supposed that she had not changed it because it had been given to her by her parents, whom she loved dearly and would not have wished to hurt. In any case, she was secretly pleased to have an unusual name even if she had kept it secret.

Her father, always the Joker, had gone, somewhat inebriated, to register her birth which had occurred on the twenty fourth of December,

'What are you going to name her?' the Registrar had asked.

'Well, she was born on Christmas Eve. So be it. She will be called *Christmas Eve*. The Registrar had endeavoured to hide his amusement and had looked quizzically at the father, but Mr Pugh had returned the look with a straight face.

'Did you say *Christine* or *Christmas*?' the Registrar had asked, now with a broad grin stretching from ear to ear.

'First name – *Christmas*: second name - *Eve*: surname - *Pugh*,' repeated Mr. Pugh with an irritated sigh.

So in the regulation violet ink, in his beautiful handwriting, the Registrar had written her name on the birth certificate.

She considered that her surname, *Pugh* was ugly. She could still hear in her head, her school chums chanting the firemen's names from the popular children's programme, *Trumpton,* starting with her own.

She had rarely announced that her first name was *Christmas.* She used it only when absolutely necessary such as on her passport or driving licence or when asked for her birth certificate. Even at her wedding, she had asked the vicar to call her Chris during the ceremony. If she was ever asked if Chris was short for Christine, she would always fib and say,

'No, I am just called Chris'.

When she had first met Hal she was amazed to learn that his surname was *Day*. She decided there and then that it was fated that they should marry so that she would be named *Christmas Day.*

'I do like my name because on paper, it is ambiguous as to whether I am male or female.'

She hated her Christian name - *Christmas*. It was a joke. *Eve* was OK because it was a short name and easy for her as a child to spell. However, she was not prepared to disclose her full names to the present company. She certainly preferred her married surname ...Day to her maiden name... Pugh...ugh!

'A little bird told me that you 'ave a very funny name', Frank probed as he characteristically fidgeted and grinned, his snakelike eyes glittering with malice, intent on embarrassing her.

'*Which dork was that?*' she pondered.

Chris could not think who might tittle-tattle about her name at the James Ratcliffe. But she spoke calmly, denying the accusation, saying that he had obviously been misinformed. She was determined that her registered birth name would remain undisclosed. She would not give Frank the satisfaction of being in a position to make jocular comments at her expense. Not even on her application for jobs had she admitted it. Why had her father called her Christmas Eve? She had known any number of girls called Holly, Carol, Noelle or even Mary who had birthdays at Christmas. She could only think that her father's wicked sense of humour together with his drunken state on the occasion of the registration of her birth had caused him to saddle her with that name.

However, to his credit, he had not overburdened her with all the names of his favourite football team as one infamous father had done in 1966.

Frank announced that he liked his strong name...*Frank Hector*... He lied.

In fact, he hated his name. It was a constant reminder of Big Frank who had treated him, his sister and his poor mother so mercilessly. He wished he had changed his name when he was first legally entitled to...at the time when he left home.

'Yes, Hec, your name suits you ....Hector by name: hector by nature', was Chris's cynical response.

'*Surely the soup's ready.*' Chis thought, as she marched out of the room.

'OK folks… we're ready to eat.'

They stood, Frank with a grimace on his face, Hal with a beaming smile at the prospect of the meal to come and Shirley behaving like a concerned wife would when her soulmate was in pain. The Hectors waited for Hal to lead the way into their grand dining room.

This room, like the main sitting room, occupied the front of the house. The two rooms were separated by the main entrance and hallway. A log-burning stove was burning brightly, crackling away musically and throwing out lots of heat. Hal closed the door of the stove. He thought that there would be enough heat created in the room that evening without further contribution from the stove. The dark, heavy, bespoke, rectangular, oak dining table had four place settings which Hal had carefully placed earlier in the day. The Tudor-styled, green and gold upholstered carvers stood at either end of the table. Chris directed Frank to the chair furthest from the door.

'You can have the carver Hec, just to show that there are no hard feelings.'

She normally placed a male guest in the opposing carver to Hal, and even though she resented Frank, she was not prepared to change her habit. Hal took the other carver, and she and Shirley took the stand chairs on each of the long sides. She stared at the table with approval; Hal had done a very good job. She stared at Frank in amazement; he was adjusting the table settings and the positions of the condiments, much to her annoyance.

'What on earth is the matter with this guy?'

She was beginning to think that too many opiates had affected his brain. Choosing not to make a fuss, Chris asked Hal to find some suitable, calming music.

'The John Denver... he's easy listening...let's relax for a while,' she suggested.

'Is that the best yer can offer?'

Chris took her iPad and tapped the screen a few times. The familiar strains of *Jailhouse Rock* could be heard.

'Is this more to your liking, Hec?'

Chris hid a smile in her handkerchief.

'Ha bloody ha', said Frank, blood draining from his cheeks, as he looked at her with narrowed, daggered eyes.

Shocked into silence at this unexpected reaction of Chris's to Frank's question, Shirley and Hal simply stared at the table.

Hal shuffled uneasily in his seat, whilst Shirley started to cough in an attempt to stop herself from laughing out loud.

So they took their soup, not speaking, as *'Take Me Home, Country Roads'*, *'Annie's Song'*, *'Leaving on a Jet Plane'* and others songs from their favourite country singer calmed Chris's and Hal's frazzled nerves.

Soup dishes were cleared away with compliments galore directed at the cook. Carrot and coriander soup was always well received. Frank remained silent.

A somewhat discomposed Frank barked, anxious to get on with his parlour game.

'Now…of which of the seven deadly sins are you most guilty?'

He could recognise Chris's handwriting from all those infuriating memos she had been so fond of sending to him in their James Ratcliffe days.

'We'd better be reminded what they are', growled Frank.

Between them they arrived at: Envy: Gluttony: Sloth: Wrath: Pride: Lust: Avarice.

'What's Avarice?'

'Extreme greed'

'Doesn't Gluttony have the same meaning as extreme greed?'

'Yes', confirmed Hal.

'So, what's the difference between Avarice and Gluttony?'

'Someone…look it up please'.

'Let's agree for the sake of argument that Gluttony is more like a personal over-indulgence and greed is the taking of something so that you prevent someone else from having it.'

Chris spoke first.

'I am envious of Shirley's beautiful hands and nails and her immaculate dress sense.'

At this statement, Shirley gave a broad smile which lit up her, usually, care-worn face.

Chris continued, 'I am proud of what I have achieved in my job and materially as a family.'

There were nods of approval from Hal and Shirley and a dirty look from Frank.

'I also suffer from Wrath or anger. Are they the same thing?, When I see injustices in the world, such as criminals getting better treatment than their victims and the inability of politicians to make what I consider to be obvious decisions.'

Shirley announced,

'I am not guilty of Sloth because I work hard for my income. I am not envious of other people's possessions because I love my little house and everything about it', and under her breath, she added, '*I am envious of other people's happy marriages*' but she would never acknowledge that for fear of the consequences.

She, certainly, felt a great deal of wrath towards her husband, but that confession would have to remain a secret between herself and her conscience.

'I certainly do not suffer from Lust'.

'You can say that again you frigid, old, moo.' said Frank under his breath, somewhat disingenuously.

Hal admitted to being guilty of Sloth at the weekend but apart from that he was free from sin.

'Smug bastard!' Frank opined to himself.

'What about you, Hec? What are you guilty of?'

Chris taunted Frank who was considering his answer. Before he could utter a single word, Chris had attacked him. 'What about *Pride*? You're an arrogant Devil aren't you? And *Lust*. Don't you lust over anybody?'

'It depends on what you mean by *Lust*.'

'Didn't you lust after the little boys in your school? Didn't they put you behind bars for that?'

All Frank could do was to give her another black look; the 'if looks could kill' black look.

Another brief period of embarrassing silence followed that brief volley of shots below Frank's belt. Chris apparently, totally unaffected stood and walked towards the kitchen. She had hidden the effects of her outburst well whilst in the presence of the others. Now in the privacy of the kitchen she started to breathe heavily and her hands were shaking; her heart was beating nineteen to the dozen and the veins in her temple were throbbing. Perhaps she had overstepped the mark, she thought. Everyone seemed to be soft-pedalling around his time in jail. Why would he try to invent a game like this one if he did not expect comments about him being a jailbird to surface? She wondered whether a reference of this kind might help his rehabilitation. She would have another 'go' at him when the opportunity arose.

Shirley followed Chris into the kitchen.

'Crikey, Chris! That was going some! I didn't realise what you really thought of Frank and now I'm getting the picture.'

Chris searched for the most appropriate words to apologise to Shirley for her savage outburst. After all, she was married to Frank and must have feelings for him.

'I'm terribly sorry if I've offended you, Shirley. I have a lot of time for you but I'm afraid I have no time for that husband of yours. I've known him for several years now both as a colleague and socially and my opinion of him has deteriorated day by day. The very sight of him annoys and distresses me so. It's a wonder I don't burst a blood vessel.'

Shirley nodded. She had a warm feeling about Chris and could only agree with her comments about Frank but she must not let down her guard.

'Don't worry, luv, it's all good feedback for this game of his. Don't give it another thought'.

Feeling somewhat calmer after Shirley's comments, Chris busied herself getting out the next course. She had prepared some giant mushrooms stuffed with a garlicky mixture. As Shirley watched and did what she could to help, she quizzed Chris on what Frank had been like in the days before she had known him.

Chris thought back to the first time she had met Frank Hector. It had been at the interview for post of Head of Pastoral care at the James Ratcliffe High School. She had been the sole external candidate in competition with Frank Hector and Andy Sykes who were already teachers at the school. It had been impossible for any of them to predict the outcome - each one of them believing them self to be the prime candidate.

'Why would the Headteacher have two internals and one external candidate? Why not just appoint an internal? Why not hold the battle between two internals? Why bother with an external at all? These were all questions which she had asked herself.

From the appearance of her two adversaries, Chris had known that she had stood a good chance. She had been smartly dressed, though a bit plumper than she would have liked. She had always been on a diet; she had always been what was called a yo-yo dieter. She had tried them all with mixed success.

She was basically a ginger nut… a carrot top. She assumed that this blessing had been bestowed on her from her Scottish ancestry. Her mother's family hailed from Cromarty; they were members of the Macdonald Clan. As a child, she had had a mop of unruly, orange curls and ringlets which, over the years, had been tamed somewhat and her hair had developed into an attractive shade of auburn. She had lost the masses of curls. She was lucky not to have any grey hairs; red heads do not go grey, their locks just fade into the colour of pale golden corn. Her lashes and eyebrows were light so she had to darken them. She had a few, soft-hued freckles on her nose and cheeks. She had to keep out of the sun so she never tanned, unlike Hal who bronzed at the mere utterance of that word - *sun.*

If the decision had been made from appearances, she would have beaten them both. Chris had known that her reference was excellent. The Headteacher at Ridge Top High School had rated her highly and had encouraged her to seek promotion. He had been an exemplary and particularly supportive Headteacher in devising the curriculum so that she was able to teach Ancient History across the board. She had been sorry in lots of ways to leave his school.

When the messenger had come to fetch her back into the Head's office, the two men must have guessed that the game was over for them. Andy had been quite philosophical and had congratulated her warmly. After all, he was a few years younger than she and still had plenty of time to achieve some promotion. Frank had not been so pleased. He was older and obviously had felt slighted by this rejection. Basically, he was a thoroughgoing misogynist. She had estimated that some interesting times lay ahead. Their antagonistic relationship had started from that point. Chris had assumed a philosophical stance. She had taken an instant dislike to the man and she would have been surprised if her instincts had been proven incorrect.

She soon learned what an extreme disciplinarian he was. Not a sound would emerge from the music room apart from his voice, the piano or some musical recording. In other neighbouring classrooms, pandemonium reigned. On occasions, she would venture into the music room on some business to do with a pupil to find them all seated in rows in absolute silence, all looking down at their books with not a glance in her direction. She would ask him for the child in question to be released from the class. He would respond ungraciously and comment on the disturbance to his lesson and the work that would be missed by the absence of the child. He would bark out the name of the pupil who would scuttle to the front and out of the door with her.

Frank was in the habit of taking time off school through personal sickness. He had never looked healthy so she had felt some sympathy for him in the early days. However, he had taken sick-leave rather too frequently; she wondered whether he was something of a lead-swinger. At such times, a relief teacher would have been delegated to take his class. Sometimes it was a colleague...at other times a supply teacher would be employed. Whoever it was, the chaos and hullabaloo would be extreme. All concerned, except for his pupils, prayed for the return of Frank Hector, if only to get some peace and quiet on the music corridor. She could not blame these urchins for making the most of his absence and making hay.

If Frank were ever the relief teacher, it was possible to sense the groans of the waiting pupils as they watched his approach, hoping that he would walk by. An ominous silence would descend like the cessation of bird song during an eclipse of the sun.

There were a multitude of tales to be told about Frank in the classroom and on the corridor. His reputation had been well reported amongst the feeder primary school cohorts who anticipated with some trepidation their inevitable future contact with him. On her patrol of the corridors between lessons, pupils would wait outside the room in an orderly fashion until the arrival of the teacher. This was the theory if not the practice. One of her jobs had been to patrol the corridors to quieten the waiting pupils or to allow them into the classrooms in order to try to maintain some sort of order. Outside Frank's room, he would stand with his next group. There would be no sound. He would line up the pupils in a straight line and slowly inspect each one of them for discrepancies in their uniform. Nothing escaped his eagle eye. All the boys would be made to tuck in their shirts and girls their blouses. He instructed them to use some item of their uniform to rub the mud off their shoes. Their ties had to be adjusted correctly. All buttons had to be fastened. No one was allowed to enter the room until everyone had succumbed to his demands. Only then, would he admit them into his music room. Although several minutes of teaching time was lost at the start of every lesson on these disciplinary matters, as soon as his pupils sat at their desks they worked at their highest level so as to avoid his wrath further.

Chris recounted to Shirley some of the ways in which Frank *the Wank* as some wag had nicknamed him, exerted control over his classes. One of his favourites had been the gym shoe on his desk at the front of the classroom. Whenever a new class arrived, Frank would introduce the class to the gym shoe. He would instruct the class to say in unison, 'Good morning Mr Wallop' or 'Good afternoon Mr Wallop'. He would show them a list of misdemeanours for which Mr Wallop would be reintroduced to their rear ends. He made sure that they all knew the consequences of their actions so that nobody could complain about the treatment received at his hands. In fact, this was an idle threat. Corporal punishment had been outlawed years before.

Another favourite was the roll of sticky tape. He possessed a marionette which had a moveable mouthpiece. He would introduce the class to Willie

Wagtongue. The children thought this was hilarious. Frank would make Willie talk incessantly and then he would threaten Willie with the sticky tape.

'If you talk any more, Willie, I'll stick this across your mouth to shut you up'.

As Willie kept on talking, Frank applied the tape to his mouth and Willie ceased to chatter. Once again, Frank's hands were tied by current disciplinary practice. But his pupils were reluctant to take any chances.

Most classrooms were installed with white boards but Frank insisted on keeping his traditional blackboard and chalk. The Headteacher, anxious to save unnecessary expense had not been inclined to disagree. Over the years, certain teachers had developed an expertise in aiming, at pupils' heads and ears, old fashioned chalk and board rubbers. Frank, having achieved a high standard in this regard, refused to relinquish these weapons. If he were deployed as a relief teacher, he would bring the class into his own domain, containing the blackboard, Mr. Wallop, and Willie Wagtongue. Failing that, he would carry his instruments of torture in a canvas bag to be displayed on the desk in the foreign classroom. He always kept on his desk a large bunch of keys for his numerous cupboards and store rooms. A quick whack on the head with his bunch left the perpetrator stinging for long enough not to want a repeat performance.

Chris stopped for a moment and said,

'Shirley, you must be getting fed up of listening to all this?'

'No, luv… carry on… it's fascinating. Frank never talked much about school.'

Chris obligingly carried on with her story about Frank's disciplinary methods. Frank used to oblige a pair of naughty pupils to stand somewhere out of view of the corridor with outstretched arms and compete with each other to ascertain who could bear the heaviest load. He would load their arms equally with all manner of objects. He would describe it as a 'gladiatorial contest'. The boys never complained. They rather relished it at the time but they rarely repeated the offence. His favourite ordeal was to make the offending pupil kneel for the duration of the lesson on a prickly mat which was placed in front of the blackboard, his nose touching the blackboard.

Chris was of the opinion that Frank Hector was not a sadist in the physical sense but that he managed, by psychological methods, to instil so much terror into his pupils that they kept their naughtiness for some other teacher. If tested, however, the threat would be executed and Frank would have to pay the price of flouting the law. He never considered that this would happen. Such was his arrogance.

In practice, she had never been aware of any pupil misbehaving in Frank's lesson and so his array of tortures had never been put to the test. She had, as she had got to know him better, questioned why he had applied for a pastoral post. There was nothing to prevent his applying, that was his right, but what was the Headteacher thinking when he called him for interview to a post which required an interest in the welfare of the child? Frank had a cruel streak. She could not imagine children going to him for comfort, at any rate, not comfort of the appropriate kind.

The truth was that his application for the pastoral post had been a ruse to get closer to children in order to gain their confidence so that he could abuse and control them in some way. Children hated him for his overbearing attitude and his extraordinary demands for correctness in petty details. She would have wagered that children would never seek out Frank Hector willingly; they spent their schooldays endeavouring to avoid him.

Chris and Shirley brought the second starter to the table. Chris had acquired from her favourite greengrocer, Mr Norton, at Top o' th', some giant field mushrooms. He had collected them himself; a piece of information which she had not imparted to her guests. They were a meal in themselves. Frank shouted in glee when he saw them.

'Good God! They're bigger than that stink-horn fungus I saw growing in the hedgerow at Johnnie Arkwright's'.

Frank was referring to a local canal-side pub where he had been in rapture with this fungus. He had photographed it; he continued to describe it,

'A massive white protuberance thrusting upwards from the ground with the tip covered with a foul smelling slime...a truly, fascinating fungus.'

Chris was so disgusted she muttered to herself,

'How dare he compare my beautiful field mushrooms to that sleazy, stink-horn fungus...I hope he chokes on them'.

'Let's have another question', Hal suggested breezily. He could sense some tension in Chris from the look on her face. Frank selected another question at random. Without a moment's perusal of it, he read out,

'Do you believe that the size of a man's phallus affects his psychological state of mind?'

Frank's tic started up with a vengeance. He recognised this as Chris's question. There was that familiar handwriting again, not Shirley's nor Aitch's but that of the dreaded, relentless writer of memos to which he had never responded.

'Where's she going with this? What's she up to now?' he pondered as he tried to control his twitching cheek.

Chris had developed an obsessive, unnatural interest in Frank's psychological state of mind with regard to the phallus - his own and those of other males. This predilection of his had been quite evident from his trial, but she did not know whether he possessed a penis such as that portrayed by Min in the Egyptian temple or whether he had a weary, wee Willy Winkie. She suspected the latter. She would have to get the answer somehow. Not from Frank... but perhaps from Shirley. It would be a difficult question to broach but she would endeavour to get some response from her, otherwise, she would have to depend on Hal's ability to have a peek at the next available opportunity when they stood at a public urinal. She wondered what Hal would think about her obsession with Frank's male equipment considering her absolute dislike of the man.

She knew, because they had witnessed it in Bulgaria, whilst on holiday, that males with a pronounced phallus would advertise the fact by strutting around the nudist areas of the beach, or prolonging their nakedness in the pool changing room, or walking round and round the pool in their skimpy swim briefs. It was her opinion that a small phallus, like a small stature as in the 'Napoleon Complex' engendered in a man a bossy, aggressive, antagonistic attitude towards his fellows and a controlling nature towards his women, because they might find his phallus amusing and a symptom of sexual inadequacy.

Shirley had not had a lot of sexual experiences with men and so had no real knowledge about relative sizes of phalluses. But her belief was that both husbands were poorly endowed. She just knew that she favoured celibacy.

She had remained a virgin until the age of twenty four when she had had that life-changing encounter with Alfie Entwistle, a meeting which had resulted in Linus her son. Theirs had been a disastrous marriage. Alf and Frank were similar in many ways but Alf had never mistreated her. He had simply ignored her, preferring to go about his business which consisted mainly of dog racing, the betting shop and the Dun Cow. She conjured up in her mind's eye an image of each phallus and considered that each was similarly of inadequate dimension. She did not remember Alf's penis being scarred like Frank's pock-marked one. Her two relationships had been horrific in different ways. Perhaps the way Alf and Frank behaved resulted from either their early upbringing or a complex arising from their perception of sexual inadequacy. Shirley knew something of Frank's early life, but he had remained reticent about it. It had been a taboo area. So, she had left well alone. Her own experiences led her to believe that the answer to the question which they were debating currently was a definite *yes*...it was indubitably so!

Hal considered his own genitalia. He had never really thought about it until this very moment. It had served him well before and after marriage; it had never been the subject of ridicule and the women in his life had never complained about it. He had been blessed with a genial temperament and was considered to be a level-headed sort of guy but whether that had been caused by the size of his phallus, he was undecided.

'What do you think, Hec?' Chris took her opportunity to stick the knife in further as she posed the question. 'Do you think that the smaller the phallus the meaner and more malicious the personality of its owner?'

Shirley struggled to keep her composure. She knew, personally, what a puny, pathetic, little organ Frank possessed; she also knew his nature to be that of a cruel, controlling despot. She was rather surprised that all emphases and references had been concerning his fondness for the young, male body and nothing had ever been mentioned about his tyrannical treatment of women.

Chris persisted in her interrogation. She rattled off question after question. Frank hardly had the time to think let alone speak.

'You've been to Luxor, haven't you, Hec? You must have visited the temple there. Did you see the carving of Min? Everyone makes a bee-line for it. You're no exception. Did you touch it for good luck like the multitudes have done over the centuries? Did you feel pride or envy in your own cargo? Has your personality been affected by its size?'

Frank would not be drawn on this. He had suspected that Chris had been up to something when he read out her question. He puffed out his chest, tried unsuccessfully to control his facial tic and responded by saying that it was a good question for debate but he was to listen to them not for them to listen to him.

'I know why you won't answer, you pig, it's because we'll laugh at your answer', thought Chris to herself. She let the matter drop. She seemed to be the only one who was haranguing Frank. She would not have liked be thought of as a bully.

They finished eating and all, except for Frank, agreed that the stuffed mushrooms were delicious. Frank remained silent throughout. Chris asked Hal to put on some more music while she and Shirley disappeared together into the kitchen. Hal searched among their collection and rediscovered one of their all-time favourite pieces - a classic with which he felt Frank would find approval. Soon the gentle, soothing strains of Pachelbel's *Canon in D Major* were comforting to all those who could hear it and for five minutes or so all was at peace in the world.

CHAPTER FIVE

VIII

As he heard the first few bars of the melody played by the cello and organ, Frank's face assumed a beatific smile. He had closed his eyes and was faraway back in those halcyon days of his Academy.

He had grown tired of his work at the James Ratcliffe. He considered his immediate line manager to be an idiot and the Headteacher, Mr Probert, to be a fool, who interfered constantly in his modus operandi. That Day woman was as bad. He thought the pupils needed a good thrashing but he was not able, by law, to administer that level of punishment. He regarded his colleagues as mindless sheep all in thrall to that imbecile of a Headteacher. Well, he had had enough.

He informed his wife, Helen, that they would sell their very desirable house in the suburbs and use the money to fund his new scheme. Helen had not attempted to discuss the suggestion. She knew that Frank would ignore her anyway and she might end up with some hidden bruises. So she kept her thoughts to herself. He put in his letter of resignation which the Headteacher accepted with alacrity. He was glad that Frank Hector, a continual thorn in his flesh, would be leaving of his own volition. It would save him the bother of invoking a lengthy dismissal procedure. As far as Frank was concerned any job would be better than the one at the James Ratcliffe. In any case he had been appointed as leader of a local high profile brass band and it carried a salary.

He had been aware that a large country house kept reappearing on the property market. He researched his available funds, together with potential bank loans, personal loans and mortgage. He made an offer which was some twenty five percent lower than the asking price together with a letter containing his reasons for his insolence. He never doubted that he would be successful. Such was his arrogance.

He rather fancied going it alone, setting up a private school where he would pull all the strings and make all subordinates dance to his tune. He planned to install in this crumbling pile of masonry a new kind of institution in order to enforce good behaviour and discipline into that section of the youthful population who were heading in the wrong direction. He was of the opinion that this creeping liberalism as he phrased it would ultimately sound the death knell of an ordered, civilised society.

He would not have been concerned about Helen's opinions even if she had voiced them. He knew that he had her under his firm control and that she would obey him to the letter. She had, over the years, turned a blind eye to his relationship with his son, Colin, who seemed to have grown into a normal youth if somewhat introverted. Frank blamed Colin's boarding school for that.

At the end of the summer term, during the traditional staffroom party, he made his farewell speech to his colleagues, as was usual when a member of staff departed from the school for pastures new. He raised himself to his full height of five feet eight inches, his familiar green sweater hanging loosely on his weedy body, his deeply sunk, beady eyes, appearing to be blacker than usual and glittering with self-importance, he ended his short statement with a final announcement,

'I wish you all that which you wish me... only more so!'

There was a dramatic pause as he waited to see if his words had sunk into the dim brains of his colleagues, who were in elevated spirits to see him go. Delighted to observe their shocked faces, he leapt from the dais with a smirk and a flourish, his small snake-like eyes glittering with evil intent towards all those who sat before him. He was triumphant in the cleverness of his own wit.

He had been most fortunate to find Abercrombie Hall, a decaying but noble country house in a substantial acreage surrounded by a twelve foot high stone boundary wall with ornate but rusting iron gates at the entrance to the driveway. It was situated in the remote, rural geographical feature of the landscape named Scarp Edge Fold, a particularly isolated, windswept location. He had had great hopes for his new enterprise. The fact that he would be in sole charge of young, impressionable boys whom he could mould to his own design was beyond his wildest dream. He would ensure their absolute obedience to him by the coercive methods he had been subjected to as a boy himself and those he had learned and honed during his life thus far.

He remembered the sanctimonious Headteacher, Albert Probert, at the James Ratcliffe High School, afraid of his own shadow. Well, Frank Hector was not afraid of his own shadow or that of anyone else. He knew that his methods worked and if pupils obeyed him, then they would become educated and would develop into useful members of society. He was not a sadist but he believed that he had to be cruel to be kind. That had been his motto. He would not have to administer corporal punishment to any degree because he knew that from past experience, the mere threat of it was enough to ensure conformity. He had been delighted in the knowledge that he would be able to impart some of the lessons he had learned from the Pastor and from Leo, his two important mentors from the past.

He had been impatient to get started on his mission. Abercrombie Hall in its state of repair when purchased would not have instilled confidence in prospective clients. Refurbishment was essential if he were going to get parents to subscribe. He also had to reach his target audience. He needed to attract parents whose defiant, self-willed sons were an embarrassment to and a hindrance to them in their day-to-day affairs and in their other pursuits. He required parents who wanted to be rid of their unruly sons until such time that they could be relied upon to conform. They would be parents who were prepared to pay someone like Frank Hector to instil such conduct into them, that they would be able to improve their life chances. The parents attracted to his Academy would need sufficient funds to pay his rates. They were not unkind parents, just parents at the end of their tethers, needing some respite from their unruly sons. Frank knew that he was precisely that person. Not only would he convert those unruly hooligans into obedient, dutiful sons, he would inculcate in them the love of music. He would also ensure their literacy and numeracy. He knew that he had to achieve parental consent to his administration of corporal punishment should the need arise but he felt that this would be largely unnecessary as the fear of punishment was usually adequate in itself. Probably, as in the best public schools, he would instruct an older pupil, a prefect, to introduce Mr. Wallop to worthy miscreants. This action, he felt would be more acceptable to his critics, and he had been in no doubt, from earlier experience with the anonymous, lily-livered, permissive authorities in the education system, that he would have criticism from all quarters.

He had been exceedingly pleased with the purchase of Abercrombie Hall, a house that would eventually impress potential clientele, by its architecture, refurbishment and location, far away from the prying eyes of busy-bodies and the Local Authority who might not favour his methods. The location was very private and secluded and parents could be sure that their offspring were in a secure environment and unlikely to be able to get back home. There were sufficient, sizeable rooms to provide five dormitories, two classrooms, a dining hall, a common room, and associated offices and bathroom and showering facilities. The grounds were adequate for exercise. There was a derelict outdoor pool for refurbishment at some point in the future when funds permitted. A barn would provide ample space for the construction of a gymnasium.

His DIY skills were not to the same standard as his expertise on the cornet but when necessary, he could be a diligent worker. He had laboured in the past doing jobs for cash both in Ravensborough and in Philadelphia. He needed to mobilise a workforce to get a modicum of comfort for his incoming residents. It had been vital to get his dormitories and shower facilities in order. He had aimed to cater for ten to twelve pupils in the first instance so that he could teach the group himself. He would then prepare individual schemes-of-work for his pupils who would be of different ages and abilities. He had intended to employ another teacher when the need arose.

He had been able to purchase some substantial iron bedsteads from the defunct cottage hospital which was about to amalgamate with the main hospital in Broadclough. Thirty bedsteads had been available and although he had not needed them all at that moment, they had been such a good bargain and he had hopefully aspired to thirty pupils before too long had elapsed. He had acquired some sturdy, wooden tables which would have flexible usage, for academic classroom work, art and a variety of other tasks. The six main rooms on the ground floor furnished a substantial common Room, two classrooms, a dining hall, a kitchen and an office.

He had been able to furnish the Hall most economically. He had carried out extensive research into the second hand market and had found a wealth of useful items of furniture, soft furnishings and other useful paraphernalia all at rock bottom prices. The old saying that 'one man's rubbish is another man's treasure' was certainly true. Some of his purchases had been blemish-free. He had speculated about the reasons people had for ridding themselves of so many untarnished useful items. One of his proposed, necessary luxuries was the installation of a stereophonic sound system throughout the house so that he could play music anywhere and everywhere. He planned to bombard these uncultured layabouts with music morning, noon and night.

It had taken the rest of that year to get his property in order. The time had finally arrived for him to contact the local newspaper in order get some publicity so that enrolment of pupils could begin from January of the following year. He had worded the article carefully so that it would attract the kind of parent he wanted to target. Strict discipline had been emphasised. He had researched the going rate for fees and came up with the figure of £8000 per term, payable in advance. This would include all tuition fees, boarding fees, recreational activities, basic laundry, text and exercise books. A simple school uniform would be purchased through the Academy.

    Access to the telephone landline would be denied. Parental visits would be discouraged. There would be no half-term breaks, and if parents so wished, their sons would be allowed to stay in the Hall over the school holidays. Parents would be asked to complete a questionnaire regarding their child's behaviour at the end of home-visits so that he could assess the success of his methods. Parents would have to agree to the administering of corporal punishment where necessary. All boys would undergo a medical inspection at the commencement of each term. Parents wishing to withdraw their child would be obliged to give one term's written notice or be charged the full fee that term.

    Such was the wording that Frank believed that only people who could afford those fees and who were willing to pack off their perverse and wilful offspring would make further investigations. The kind of parent seeking his help did not want constant interruption from his child.

They would be paying him to act in 'loco parentis' and he would oblige. He had planned to concentrate on the academic and disciplinarian aspects of their education in the first two years in order to gain parental confidence in him as an educator. Later, he would introduce other physical elements to the curriculum. Frank's principles had been based on those of the typical, well-respected public school, such as had existed for centuries. Academic rigour, cold showers, physical exercise, and the inculcation of self-discipline would be the order of the day. Shirley Entwhistle had been the first parent to make an enquiry and to subsequently enrol her son, Linus.

The first cohort had been due to arrive on the first Sunday in January from two o'clock. Frank looked at his list and studied the names on it. He reckoned to be able to get a good idea of a boy's character simply from his name.

Linus Entwistle: Nine years old. The name, *Linus,* was rather unusual but the mother had appeared innocuous enough. Perhaps she had thought that such an unusual name would lead her son into a career on TV or in politics. It seemed to Frank not unusual for media celebrities to bear striking names. Linus had been the first to be enrolled. Frank remembered the mother, a soft, plump, placid well-dressed woman. She had been desperate to have her son accepted. There had appeared to be no father on the scene leading Frank to anticipate no problems from her.

Kevin Pratt: Nine years old. Frank grinned as he said the name out loud. He had always found the name *'Kevin'* amusing, and *'Pratt'* even more so. He struggled to remember what the parents' background was. He really did not care as long as Mr Pratt could afford the school fees. Frank made a note against the name to remind him to notice whether the boy would live up to his name. In any case, Frank was confident that Young Pratt would not cause him any grief.

James Ironside: Nine years old. *'A good strong name'*, chuckled Frank. *'We'll see about that.'*

The father of James was a well-known writer of TV comedy sitcoms and had requested that James be known by his mother's maiden name of *Ironside* so that potential bullying might be pre-empted.

Gary Achors: Nine years old.

Jason Willoughby: Nine years old.

Frank had taken an instant dislike to these two, even though he had never set eyes on them. He had had bad experiences with a Gary and a Jason in the past. He would take a special interest in them and probably punish them for the treatment he had received from their namesakes in his adolescent years in Little Scarp.

Steven Linscumbe: 10 years old. Frank recognised the name *Linscumbe* as being the same as that of 'Linscumbe's Bespoke Gent's Outfitters' in Ravensborough.

He made another note on his pad. He might make overtures about a bespoke suit if indeed the boy was the son of that tailor.

Francis Percival Timms: 10 years old. Frank could not imagine the bearer of this name being a boy, so naughty as to be expelled from the family home. He mused whether the boy was known as *Francis* or *Frank*.

Ludo Phoenix-Carter: 10 years old. His father had arrived driving a Rolls Royce.

'Interesting name…quite a mouthful…could be a quite a character…I'll keep my eye on him.' Frank thought, wondering about the background of the Phoenix-Carter family.

Kenneth Bourne: 10 years old. Frank could not glean any clues from his name. It was a straightforward, honest name

Leonard Holloway: 10 years old.

Edward Hardcastle: 10 years old.

These last two brought back memories of Leo from his 'Sally Army' days at Ravensborough and The Reverend Edward Pickering - 'the Pastor' and of course Eddie, the Pastor's legacy to him. He might favour these two.

Frederick Urban: 11 years old.

'Hmm...The oldest boy and possibly prefect material... We'll see,' pondered Frank, as he closed the folder containing the list of names.

These twelve boys formed his first cohort.

'That's a good start. Two dormitories' of flesh worth ninety-six thousand pounds in the bank,' Frank had thought with a self-congratulatory chuckle.

By four o'clock, all parents or their agents had vanished from the scene. Frank had watched them arrive and depart. There had been no long *good-byes*. He had observed with interest all the vehicles involved in the transportation of these villains. Frederick Urban had arrived in a chauffeur-driven Rolls Royce. Mr Phoenix-Carter had brought Ludo in a 'Rolls', driven by himself. Mrs Phoenix-Carter had not accompanied him. A Mercedes, soft top, had been driven by Mrs Holloway, step-mother to Leonard. Mr. Linscumbe, dressed impeccably, had driven Steven, in his immaculate, classic E-Type Jaguar. A BMW saloon, driven by his mother, had ferried James Ironside. An ancient Citroen 'deux chevaux' driven by the au pair, had delivered Kevin Pratt. Jason Willoughby arrived with his father in the latest Mitsubishi Pickup. Range Rovers transported Francis Timms and Kenneth Bourne. An ancient, well-used, battered, mud-spattered Land Rover, driven by a hired –hand, conveyed Edward Hardcastle, from the massive farming and stabling complex over at Broadclough. Finally, an immaculate but dated Renault Clio, driven by his mother, Shirley Entwhistle, had brought

Linus Entwhistle. She had given him a quick peck on the cheek before driving away. Frank had suspected from their first meeting that she had been probably the least well off. Her choice of vehicle confirmed his suspicion. From their modes of transport, it might have appeared that the Urbans were the most affluent but Frank was not taken in by such obvious displays of wealth and importance. He would watch closely the interactions between the boys to prove to himself that his initial judgements were correct. He had observed his clientele closely. They were members of the upper crust, nouveau riche or simply grafters He had already internalised their characteristic self-confidence which usually eluded the common man in the street.

Frank's philosophical theory was that the richer the parent the naughtier the offspring, similarly the poorest parents spawned potential miscreants; the rich brats misbehaved out of boredom, whilst the poor transgressed as a result of deprivation.

Whilst still in their civilian clothes, his charges had been informed of their orders for the remainder of the day. First, he would give them a conducted tour of the parts of the building to which they had access: the common room, the two classrooms, one of which housed the piano, the dormitories, the sick bay and the dining hall. After that, would come supper followed by one hour's free time in the common room and then bed and lights out. There would be an early start the following day.

Usually, the South-facing common room was well illuminated by natural sunlight for most of the daylight hours, but on a late Sunday afternoon in early January, when there had been little natural light, the room was dimly lit by four pendulous, pearl lightbulbs in their accompanying open shades. To the right of the door, the three walls had been lined with light oak bookshelves which had been discarded from the defunct public library. Frank had acquired these at a fair price from the local monthly auction in Broadclough. To have bought them new would have cost him a substantial sum. He had scoured second hand bookshops and jumble sales to find suitable reading matter for young adolescents, together with sufficient reference books and dictionaries.

The large rectangular room also boasted a table tennis table to the left of the door. Opposite that, the original marble fireplace dominated the room though it lacked cheerful, roaring flames; instead, it housed a paltry electric fire. In the space adjacent to the book shelves were three tables and a few stand chairs. A TV stood to the right of the fireplace. Frank had also provided an Xbox and an assortment of games for the pupils' entertainment.

The boys followed him like ducklings following their mother duck into the common room where they seemed suitably impressed with their facilities. Each classroom housed twelve individual tables, one for each boy. The music room- their classroom, boasted the piano. One wall was clad with two large-scale maps of the world, one political and the other physical. Both classrooms were equipped with a traditional blackboard.

After the tour, the boys filed into the dining hall in which a long refectory table had been furnished with twelve place settings and twelve identical white, linen napkins. Each boy had been asked to supply a unique napkin ring so that he could identify his personal napkin, which would be renewed each morning. Grand, wooden dressers occupied one wall.

Each boy was directed to his place by the authoritative Principal - Doctor Hector and supper commenced. Mrs Hector, who acted in the capacity of secretary, bursar, housekeeper and cook had prepared a light supper of scrambled eggs on wholemeal toast with fresh baby plum tomatoes followed by a pot of home-made, plain yogurt and a piece of fruit of their choice. They drank tap water.

Frank Hector watched the boys demolish their supper with typical schoolboy enthusiasm. He had been curious to observe their table manners and was impressed for the most part but had assumed that these boys were aware that this was their first meeting with new acquaintances and a new Principal and their behaviour had been influenced by this fact. Frank suspected that their true colours would be exposed within a day or two. Supper having been consumed, napkins were neatly folded and replaced in the napkin ring before being placed in the drawer in the dresser designated for that purpose. Three boys had been selected at random to go into the kitchen in order to wash up. The rest of the group were given the task of preparing a washing-up rota for the remainder of the week. Willoughby, Achors and Ironside had disappeared into the kitchen whilst some paper and a pen were given to Urban, the oldest, for him to organise the rota.

Doctor Hector led his brood up the staircase to 'Broadclough' dormitory which housed six iron bedsteads each with an accompanying locker. On each unmade bed, lay the name of its occupant, some bedding and a set of simple school uniform. The uniform had been purchased through Mrs Hector, the bursar, who had secured it for each boy using the measurements supplied by his family. It consisted of grey shorts, grey polo shirt, grey knee-length socks, a grey polo-necked sweater, a grey T-shirt, a pair of grey PE shorts, a pair of indoor shoes, a pair of black plimsolls and a pair of black outdoor shoes. The other six boys had entered 'Ravensborough' dormitory where an identical arrangement was to be found.

The Principal demonstrated how he required the boys to make up their beds. A bed-making lesson then took place. Doctor Hector gave a military-style lecture about the art of bed-making. Bottom sheet to be smoothed and without creases: pillow to be secure within pillow slip: top sheet to be tucked in neatly under the mattress. He demonstrated the hospital corner. They were asked to take particular note of the careful attention to tidiness in the finished bed.

'Now, go. Make your beds. I'll inspect them in five minutes'.

The boys scampered away to their task.

Then, the boys had been taken to the shower and bathroom enclave where they had been instructed to attend to their pre-bedtime ablutions. Doctor Hector had stated that *'Cleanliness was next to Godliness'*, and he had expected the regular brushing of teeth after meals and the regular washing of hands in order to prevent cross contamination of any infection between the boys. They had been allowed fifteen minutes to complete their ablutions which included a visit to 'George' - the WC, after which they had been instructed to get to bed. All lights would be switched off after five minutes. Conversation after lights out was forbidden.

Frank had been greatly gratified though surprised when his charges had carried out without demur all instructions to the letter. This was going to be easier than he had thought. He almost skipped to his office and closed the door. He felt pleased with the way the first day had gone. He reached for his bottle of whisky and gave a toast to himself and the future success of Abercrombie Academy. He took the opportunity to consort with Eddie before, finally, returning to the boys' common room to watch some TV prior to his retiring to bed. He had not known the whereabouts of his wife, Helen, neither had he cared.

At six thirty prompt the following morning, he blew a whistle. This was the signal that a new day had dawned; it was the first day of the rest of the boys' lives. Their days of lying in bed were over. Their future would be strictly regimented and determined by the clock and the sound of the Principal's whistle. There followed an instruction for all bedding to be folded over to expose the bottom sheet for airing purposes. The boys were informed that a dormitory inspection would take place every morning. They were instructed to don their PE kit for a brisk run round the field before showering after which breakfast would be served.

A typical January morning beckoned, cold, dark, frosty and unwelcoming. After ten minutes of brisk jogging, the boys dashed in to get their shower. At this time of day, the showers naturally ran cold and hence the morning shower would always be a cold one. Mrs Hector had prepared breakfast; a big bowl of thick, delicious, nutritious, steaming porridge, a banana and a glass of tap water awaited each boy.

The boys, all wearing the same grey uniform, sat down in their designated places with their particular napkin and ate their food, savouring every mouthful, after their gruelling first hour of the day. The boys underwent a uniform inspection. It was a simple uniform and not much could go awry. Doctor Hector, they would soon discover, liked things just so, not a button undone, not a hair out of place, shoes shiny. Miscreants on their first failure to comply merely received a fierce stare from their master, but they instinctively suspected that worse would follow for subsequent errors.

After breakfast, three boys headed to the kitchen to complete their dishwashing fatigues. This routine had always been a source of amusement for Frank. He was reminded of his favourite fictional character, Wackford Squeers, and his utilisation of the practical and regular modes of teaching.

Dish washing completed, all returned in silence to the music room. Frank had been astonished.

'Is this the calm, before the storm?' he wondered. Was he being assessed by them as they were by him?

The classroom contained the piano. Frank would have preferred a grand piano but he had regarded it as an unnecessary extravagance. He suspected that these under-performers would not appreciate such quality so he had decided to opt for a reconditioned upright. He addressed the class.

'Now, boys, let us start with a prayer'. It would be the same one every morning. 'Thank you, in advance, for the pleasures that await me and the trials that will test me. Make me into a willing, obedient worker.'

Soon they knew it off-by-heart.

Doctor Hector had an important announcement to make.

'Tomorrow, instead of your morning exercise, you will shower, dress in your PE kit and report to Sick Bay, where you will wait in an orderly queue for your termly medical inspection. I will start with the youngest, and work through the list. I'll give you, Urban, the list in the morning and it will be up to you to keep the lads in order. Understood?'

'Yes sir', Frederick Urban, had meekly replied, his gaze never leaving the floor. He was afraid to look into the glittering, snake-like eyes of the Principal lest he be turned into stone.

'Right, boys, let us get down to brass tacks. We all know why you are here in my Academy. Your behaviour over your short lives have driven your parents to the end of their tethers and they have put their trust into my tried and tested methods to get you back onto that straight and narrow path that will ensure that you develop into compliant sons, decent, civilised human beings and achieve your maximum potential academically. When you leave this Academy, you will be at the age ready to embark on your GCSE studies in a regular school. Until then you will be in my care and you will play by my rules.'

He lifted onto his desk his canvas bag of terror. First, he introduced them to Mr Wallop, the well-worn plimsoll. He described how Mr Wallop operated. The offender would be required to bare his buttocks and bend over a desk. Mr Wallop would come down hard on the buttocks once, twice or three times depending on the severity of the offence. Doctor Hector demonstrated the intensity of the wallop by thwacking the plimsoll on the edge of his desk. He replaced it in a prominent position on his desk. Willie Wagtongue then emerged from the bag. The boys guffawed at the antics and jerky movements of the marionette and the silly voices that were synchronised with its mouth-movements. Eventually, Doctor Hector addressed the doll,

'Oh, shut up your prattling, lad, otherwise this is what you'll get.' He took from the bag a roll of sticky tape. The marionette continued to babble and gabble in a high-pitched squeaky voice. 'This'll fix you,' the Doctor claimed. Sticky tape was stuck over its mouth and silence reigned.

The Doctor then held up his prickly mat and passed it round so the boys could get the feel of the spiky prickles.

'Naughty boys will be made to kneel on this for the duration of a lesson. That's three quarters of an hour'

He decided to keep the rest of his instruments of torture undisclosed for the time being. They had had plenty to digest already. There were four lessons in the morning: handwriting, spelling, dictionary work and finally multiplication tables which were chanted by the class in unison. The morning session ended without recalcitrance from any one of these labelled 'naughty' boys.

Mrs Hector had prepared for them a tasty lunch consisting of a hearty vegetable and pearl barley soup with chunks of crusty wholemeal bread, a salad of Romaine lettuce, slices of cucumber and pumpkin seeds with a slice of leek, cheese and broccoli quiche. A piece of fruit and a glass of tap water completed their meal.

Washing up fatigues completed, the boys were allowed some free time in the common room. Afternoon lessons commenced at half past one. Music appreciation followed lunch. They listened to music played by the most prestigious brass bands. Lessons in English comprehension and arithmetic preceded afternoon tea.

At the bell, every boy would troop off to the dining hall and collect his napkin from the drawer. Doctor Hector had already inspected the napkins before the arrival of the hungry boys and was appalled at the state of the napkin drawer. His cheek muscles had gone into spasm. Had these urchins already forgotten how to fold and roll a napkin after use before replacing it into its ring? There followed a lesson in which they were instructed how to complete the task in the manner desired by their Master. Each boy in turn, was made to fold and roll his napkin before his peers. The task was repeated until a perfect result was achieved. The boys were made aware of the penalties for future transgressions.

Mrs Hector had supplied bread and butter, strawberry jam, Marmite in a gigantic jar and a mug of Breakfast tea. The boys remained subdued until they received the signal that they could begin to eat. The Master then having left the room, the boys reverted to type; the rabble indulged in the sort of noisy, excited chattering, which was generally denied them, as they grabbed the bread, the jam and the Marmite. However, they were fastidious in the careful folding of their napkins when teatime was over. They all regarded this meal as a treat to be anticipated with relish.

The washing up done, lessons resumed... geography. Using the large map of the world on the classroom wall, they started to learn the names of the countries, their capital cities, their flags and their currencies. The day ended with another period of music appreciation. Doctor Hector introduced them to the piano melodies of Debussy, beginning with the lively *Passe-Pieds* and concluding with the calming *La Fille aux Cheveux de Lin* and *Clair de Lune.* Frank Hector had always been a fervent believer in the importance of music, in any form, in the curriculum.

They then had to wash before supper. Mrs Hector provided a light supper of a cheese and ham toastie, with a plain yogurt and a drink of tap water.

They were each allowed one treat a day in the evening, either a bag of crisps or a bar of chocolate. These they nibbled like squirrels with hazelnuts, to make the consumption of their tasty morsels as protracted as possible.

Once all labours were finished, a variety of activities to suit all tastes were on offer to the boys as they relaxed in their common room from the enforced academic rigour. The most energetic of them, their motion jerky with arms and legs flying in all directions, shouting with glee, or uttering rasping sounds as their breath ran short were batting the small, white, bouncing sphere to and fro over the net; others, more sedentarily inclined, were being entertained by *Mario and Sonic at the Olympic Games*, their high pitched squeals of delight competing with the *ping* and the *pong* of the table tennis ball. Meanwhile, the rest battled silently with each other in the amicable combat of Chess or Dominoes. The reading of a literary classic was the least popular pursuit.

Before bedtime, Doctor Hector would meet them in the common room in order to read out all the day's misdemeanours which would be punishable before prayers on the forthcoming day.

'Doctor' Hector donned his white coat and called in the first boy. It was Linus Entwhistle.

'Now, Linus drop your shorts and pants and off with your shirt and vest and let's have a look at you.'

He peered, intently, into Linus's face, then his chest and back looking for imperfections. He examined the backs of his knees and the elbow crease looking for signs of eczema. There were none. He scrutinised the boy's tiny organ.

'That's a funny little thing. What do you call it?'

Shocked and surprised at the question, Linus did not know where to look. He stared at his feet. He could feel the heat rising up his neck. Blushing to the roots of his ginger mop of hair, he admitted that he had never considered any such thing.

The Doctor instructed him,

'You must give it a name, and you'll always have a friend to play with. Now, get dressed quickly...Next!'

All the boys trooped in as called, one at a time, to be subjected to the Doctor's intensive, concentrated scrutiny. All were treated identically. After breakfast, they had an opportunity to share their experience of the medical inspection. All agreed that it had seemed rather odd; they had had an incomprehensible but universally common experience. The Doctor had not singled any one out for special treatment. As a consequence, they did not give it another thought. They assumed, in their innocence, therefore, that this was just another routine procedure in their new school.

The first week passed to Doctor Hector's great satisfaction. There had been no major problems. Punishments had been for untidy beds, untidy lockers, untidy napkins and untidy uniform. But the boys soon learned how to avoid the slipper. In class, the boys accepted his rules and Mr Wallop and Willie Wagtongue continued to sit on his desk without budging. The most recent punishment to have been invoked had been that for lateness at the morning jog. Offenders were made to run naked around the field. The importance of prompt attendance had been one of the speediest lessons they learned. Every Friday morning, during the English lesson, the boys were instructed to write a letter to their parents. Frank Hector did not want unexpurgated, misspelt and poorly punctuated letters leaving the establishment. He decided that he would compose the letter and the boys would merely have to copy it. This would have the benefits of his avoiding the reading, correcting and possible censoring every letter. He presented each boy with a piece of paper on which was typed a letter. Each boy had the same letter to copy.

Abercrombie Restorative Academy,

Abercrombie Hall,

Scarp Edge Fold,

Dear _____

I am enjoying my time at A.R.A. I jog every day. Mrs Hector gives us yummy meals. I am learning a lot with Doctor Hector. We get some time to play on the Xbox and we also play table tennis and chess. I am busy all day long. Doctor Hector is pleased with me.

Your loving son,

_____

'Now, boys, check that you have the correct spelling. See that you have crossed every *t* and dotted each *i*. Woe betide you if I spot a single mistake. Don't forget to write your name at the end'.

Frank Hector wished to convey to his clients that their offspring were being treated well, fed well, educated well and could write a grammatically correct letter. He knew that the boys would find copying the letter quite acceptable because it was all true. Their parents would be glad to receive such a missive and it would enable them to believe that they were not wasting their money.

Each day was much like the previous one. His undeniably, coercive methods were paying dividends. The boys, in truth terrified of his wrath should they displease him, adapted their conduct accordingly and they steered clear of his belittling punishments. With barely lifting a finger in chastisement, Doctor Hector had achieved the boys' complete subservience and his bank balance had never looked so healthy. Frank Hector had never been so content. By half past eight, all was quiet in Abercrombie Hall. Doctor Hector planned his lessons for the following day. Mrs Hector, exhausted, in her kitchen, planned the menus for the days ahead and lost herself in the fantasy which was her emancipated future should she ever escape from the purgatory in which she was imprisoned.

As the days turned into weeks, the term ended and the parents had the option of having their sons at home for the holidays or leaving them in the care of the Hectors who inevitably became their 'universal parents'.

Frank had been astounded by the number of his clients who had been selfish and uncaring enough to abandon their sons even at Christmas. It had been of no matter to Frank Hector. Abercrombie Hall was his home and there was enough room in his spacious establishment to cater for these enforced, reluctant refugees of whom a substantial number grew accustomed to residing full-time at Abercrombie Hall. Such perennial pupils were at the mercy of his control and domination throughout the festive season.

Frank Hector's clients spread the word among their friends and acquaintances who perceived the advantages of availing themselves of the appealing services of Abercrombie Restorative Academy. In time for the second term, the school population had grown to its maximum of thirty. Five dormitories and two full classrooms were in operation requiring another teacher for the second classroom, 'Crafts', and extra help in the catering and housekeeping departments.

Frank gloated at his success and rubbed his hands together like a latter-day Wackford Squeers in anticipation of his swelling bank accounts. Thirty pupils at twenty four thousand pounds per year amounted to seven hundred and twenty thousand pounds per annum, sufficient to pay off his mortgage on the Hall, clear all of his bank and personal loans and pay off all his bills. He decided that he had better squirrel some of the funds away to avoid paying tax unnecessarily. As his wife, Helen, could be described as an employee, he would set up an account in her name. She deserved some payment for her efforts as cook, bursar, secretary and housekeeper. However, he was not prepared to allow her to have access to it. He would remain guardian of these monies and the associated paperwork would remain secure in his safe. She would have to be content with the weekly cash allowance which he gave her for domestic expenditure. She might be able to save some of that for her own use.

He employed Andrej, a young refugee from Zagreb, to teach conversation in his own language and any other languages he knew. Frank was unconcerned about the actual languages being taught. His view had been,

'*Let them learn what the teacher knows.*'

Andrej was obviously fluent in his own language – Croatian, but also in English, German and Italian. Frank had made sure that he had given Andrej enough material to spoon-feed his charges should it be necessary. Frank kept a close eye on Andrej. He did not want his *special creation,* of which he was proud and possessive to be spoilt by this unavoidable addition to his staff. Similarly, Frank allowed Mrs Hector to employ a young migrant female to help with domestic chores. The girl, Anna, had been glad to receive a bed and pocket-money in exchange for her work in the kitchen.

Frank Hector's appearance altered; he grew from spindly to portly. His complexion had improved but yet he remained unkempt in his dress and his hair remained greasy and too long. He developed into a stout, flabby, bloated figure as a result of too much good wine and rich food. The expenditure of energy was not high on his agenda; he was no sportsman; he was a horn-blower. He had all the appearances of a wealthy man, for indeed, that is what he had become. Life had begun to treat him well. These so-called recalcitrant, truculent, little boys had been like putty in his hands and he was now in a state of complete complacency.

One of the principal sources of his pleasure arose from what he considered to have been his pièce de resistance - the extravagant stereo system whose musical sounds permeated the whole house. This had allowed his playing recorded music at any time of the day or night. Music was an essential ingredient to his well-being. He played brass band marches at reveille and the rest of the time, he switched to the calming, pacifying melody of Pachelbel's *Canon in D Major*.

'Hey, Hal, has your scintillating conversation caused Hec to drop off?'

Chris and Shirley were wheeling the main course from the kitchen through to the dining room and noticed that Frank seemed to be dozing. He opened one eye and scowled in their direction. He was unwilling to leave his dream-like trance just yet.

'Why can't they all go away and let me return to my dream?'

Reluctantly, Frank staggered to his feet. He had spent a few minutes reliving the good times at the Hall. But he realised that he had to come to terms with the fact that it was a fond, distant memory. It could never be repeated. He had overstepped the mark according to his critics and he had paid a heavy price. What he would have given to be able to go back in time to his wonderful Academy where the boys had thrived under his severe but not sadistic treatment and where he had been able to indulge in his voyeurism, in his opinion, not detrimental to the boys' well-being. If only he had never set eyes on that boy, Hardy. But it was too late…it was in the past…it was time to move on.

'Had a good snooze Hec?' Chris ventured, cheekily.

With heavily-hooded eyes, he glowered at her and replied testily,

'Just enjoying the music, my dear,' he mocked her.

'Don't you my dear me, you old goat', she said to herself. *'I hope these meat balls stick in your gullet'*.

They all took their seats at the table again and Hal served out the main course from the casserole.

'Not exactly haute cuisine, eh, Chris?' taunted Frank.

'It may not be, Hec… but it hasn't cost me the arm and the leg that you, or was it Shirley, paid out at the Palm Grove? I reckon you won't be stopping off for a fish supper on the way home.'

She could not resist reminding him of the paucity of food at his wedding breakfast.

Even though he would never have admitted it, Frank enjoyed the meat balls very much. Chris was an excellent cook of tasty meals but he would always maintain that she lacked the imagination of those cordon bleu trained cooks.

'Why don't yer improve yer skills on a cordon bleu course, Chris?' he suggested.

'What do you know about cordon bleu anyway? I don't suppose you've even boiled an egg in the last twenty years.

'Let's have another question,' Hal proposed. He could envisage the storm worsening between these two.

'Do you believe that the punishment should fit the crime?'

'What crimes are we talking about?'

'Let's put them into some kind of order from the most evil to the least evil.'

'Is murder at the top of the list?'

'There's a murder most days; it's not news any longer.'

'It's becoming normal behaviour. Our society has become desensitised to the crime.'

'Life's cheap. The government doesn't care otherwise it might devise a deterrent which works. They should take a more proactive approach to stopping it.'

'What about torture? Is that as evil as murder?'

'If people are murdered, they're dead. They don't get a second chance at living do they? With torture, at least, there's still life... of some sort'.

'I think that murder is the most evil and should carry the death penalty. This would be the most apt punishment; it would deter others and the murderer could not commit murder again. And another thing... the state, in other words, we the tax payers, would not have to support such scoundrels in the lap of luxury for the rest of their lives. I know they won't bring back capital punishment, but they should. Considering that all the latest technological developments in forensic science ensures that the murderer's DNA is invariably discovered at the scene of the crime, it would be virtually impossible to execute the wrong person.'

'A torturer should be punished according to the Hebrew *Law of Retaliation* –*'an eye for an eye'*...'

'What about violence towards another person? The punishment should be a flogging at the very least. Pain should be inflicted on the perpetrator in return.'

'What about the situation where there is a supposedly peaceful protest which gets out-of-hand, and the angry crowd start to vandalise the shops, break windows and steal the goods?'

'What about those ostensibly, normally, law-abiding people who loot evacuated property flooding and fire? Is this sort of violence acceptable?'

'Violence to another's property, whether state-owned or privately-owned is in my view unacceptable. That person is not harmed physically so it is not as evil as physical violence. People who offend should be hit hard in their pockets to pay restitution to the owner'.

'Fines should be deducted at source, and those on benefits should have them revoked until restitution is made. Imprisonment is too soft an option. The prisons ought to punish offenders according to their crimes – the harshest prison regimes for the most evil prisoners.'

'What about treason? Nobody's mentioned that. It seems to have become almost acceptable by the politically correct crowd we now have in charge.'

'If the death penalty were to be revived, then who would be the executioner? It's not everybody's cup of tea is it?

'Execution does not have to be a sadistic, unpleasant or painful affair like hanging, does it? We put our pets out of their misery by lethal injection. Doctors give their near-to-death patients an increasingly lethal dose of morphine. What's wrong with that? The state rids itself of the murderer painlessly.

'Drug addicts over-dose themselves, fatally, all the time don't they?'

'The last executioner in England ran a pub in Preston after he retired as public executioner. How weird is that? He sounds a most interesting fellow and would be a valuable addition to any dinner party!'

'Do you think that murderers should be punished with the fear of the noose or is death sufficient?'

'Well, none of us are sadists are we? Wouldn't death be sufficient?'

Shirley fantasised about what lay ahead later that night. She would enjoy being the executioner. She was positively looking forward to it.

'Rape is a violent crime. How would you punish the rapist?'

'Three successive treatments: first, surgically remove the rapist's genitals; secondly, render the rapist passive with chemical treatment, thirdly, lock the rapist away for a very long time. Personally I'd throw away the key.'

'What about the rape and molestation of children?'

'These criminals are of the lowest order and should be treated as the violent criminals they are - short of the death penalty.'

Most of the debate had been undertaken by Hal and Chris with the occasional interjection from Shirley. Frank had sat stony faced and silent throughout. He was pleased that provocative questions giving rise to debate were enhancing the otherwise deadly, dull conversation they would be otherwise having but at the same time, he suspected that Chris was trying her damnedest to provoke him into saying something he would regret. He would not give her any satisfaction if that had been her plan.

Whether he could develop it into a marketable game was questionable. Why would anybody want to spend their money on a fancy box containing questions which they could easily devise for themselves?

'What about you, Hec? Did your punishment fit your crime?'

Chris put Frank on the spot again. He had been correct in his assumption. Chris had been setting him up.

'Am I to be tried again?' he said. 'My conviction and punishment were serious miscarriages of justice. I did not hurt anyone physically except that Hardy boy who provoked me so much that I gave him a good hiding. That punishment would've been perfectly acceptable in the 1980s. He didn't suffer too badly. I never hurt the boys in my school. I liked to look at them, that's all... I never touched them. I might have administered some punishment for their misdeeds but it was harmless enough. The do-gooders in high places in this country have done a lot more harm to minors than ever I was convicted for...look at the Catholic institutions and the politicians for a start. There are a lot of evil bastards out there who get away with their atrocities because they close ranks; they're protected by the rest of their corrupt cronies.'

All this time, Shirley was desperate to speak but she remained silent, keeping her own counsel.

Frank's final comment was that, in his opinion, the actions taken by the state in molly-coddling villains achieved the very opposite of what it intended. Violent crime rates, manifestly, had been progressively on the increase since the suspension of corporal and capital punishment.

'Well we've got that off our chests. But talk's cheap; it's action that's needed'

'People need to stand up and be counted'

'You know what they say... either put up or shut up.'

'It was a good discussion,' Chris was congratulatory, forgetting for the moment that it had been she and Hal who had been doing most of the talking. Frank had contributed little apart from the pronouncement of his innocence. 'I'll bring in the trifles and the cheese. Put some more music on, will you please, Hal. Find that old LP, 'Second Wave', which we got from mum'. She was referring to a purchase her mother had made years before at The Star and Garter.

As she moved back towards the kitchen, she could hear that familiar melody, *The Ballad of the Five Continents*. She knew that Frank would be wriggling in his seat, so she suggested that Hal follow it with some brass band music to appease him.

Shirley followed Chris into the kitchen. She preferred to get away from the men and chat to Chris.

'What's Linus up to these days?' Chris had never met Linus, Shirley's son. She might have expected to have met him at his mother's marriage to Frank, but she and Hal had been the only guests. She knew that Shirley had met Frank through Linus's admission to Abercrombie Academy.

'He's back-packing in Vietnam. He planned to make the trip as soon as he turned sixteen. Those two years at Frank's school worked wonders for him. He lost all his truculent ways, settled down subsequently at Scarp Edge High School and got some good grades at GCSE. He likes the freedom back-packing gives him. He likes the freedom from the regimentation and the discipline of everyday life. He'd had enough of that at the Academy.'

'We noticed that he wasn't at the registry office.

'He just chose to stay away.

'He probably stayed away out of the embarrassment arising from his mother's marriage to a convicted paedophile,' Chris voiced silently to herself.

'How have you found Frank since he came out of prison? You were a great support to him.'

Chris was of the opinion that Frank did not deserve the long-suffering Shirley. She surely was too good for him. Chris noticed that there had been very little contact between them all evening. He had never even glanced in Shirley's direction let alone address her as a husband might be expected to speak to his wife.

Shirley had to be careful. She did not want to give Chris the impression that there was anything amiss between herself and Frank. Perhaps her appearance gave her away. She recognised that she had lost that sparkle she had had on her wedding day. She spoke cautiously,

'I supported Frank because I thought he'd done a good job with Linus. He, obviously, did a good job with the other boys or why would he get so much support from the parents during the trial? The Judge took all that into account when he passed sentence. He's suffered a lot… poor dear'. claimed Shirley, and left it at that.

She was not going to moan about the harsh treatment, both mental and physical that Frank had subjected her to. That was for her alone to know and to deal with in her own way.

They put the coffee on the hob then wheeled the trolley with the sundae dishes of trifle and the cheeseboard to the table. The liqueurs and truffles were already in the dining room. Chris lit her chef's candle and left it burning in the kitchen.

Hal had been playing some brass band music for Frank's entertainment. She could hear the strains of *Nimrod* whist still in the kitchen. Now as they entered the dining room, the strains of the cornet solo – *'Fairies on the Water'*, filled the air. Chris watched Frank's face as he listened, eyes closed, to the music. The cornet was his instrument. She scrutinised his expression, looking for some kind of reaction but there was none. He had gone far away into his memory and was intently reliving the past.

He had had such a long history with the cornet the instrument which he first encountered at Ravensborough Citadel. Leo had introduced him to the cornet and the various horns of his young band associates. When not playing in the band, they would disappear, carrying their instrument cases, of all sizes, into the woods at Ravensborough where Leo had renovated an old shack and there, they would open their instrument cases and carefully expose their horns to the sunshine-bright, refreshing air if the weather allowed it or to the dark, humid interior of the shack when the rain came pouring down. Sometimes, meeting in twos or threes, they would observe each other polish their instruments carefully, slowly at first and then finally, rubbing quickly to get the brass to shine lustrously in the warm, dappled sunshine. They would stay for an hour or two making music together. Although Frank was fascinated by their movements as they played together, he declined to join in their play, preferring to get his enjoyment by orchestrating their efforts. His preference was always for the quiet, gentle, melodies. He avoided the harsh, painfully, penetrating sounds of which some of their instruments were capable.

Finally, he left the Sally Army Band when Leo could teach him no more. He joined the Scarp Edge Brass Band, where he found young, willing participants whom he would teach in the same way as he had been taught by Leo. He would lead them to the foot of the mighty Beacon Scarp whose tip was frequently covered in snow in winter and by wispy white cloud in summer. There among the prickly gorse bushes at the base of the steep pathways to the summit, they would lovingly blow their horns of varying shapes and sizes to get the maximum performance from their instruments in the open air. Their improvisations would finally come to a climactic crescendo and they would all flop over, laughing, on to the ground where the springs of fresh, frothy water would gurgle forth all over them, He had enabled these youths' enjoyment of their instruments, whilst getting his own enjoyment by simply watching and listening to them.

It came as a great surprise to the members of the band, when this thin, diminutive, scaly-faced specimen, with his glittery, reptilian, deep-set, dark eyes was appointed to the leadership of the Great Scarp Brass Band...a prizewinning band of renown in the county. Who could have imagined that such an unattractive creature could be so talented a musician to possess the ability to conduct the band effectively at the highest competitive level? He was now a person of some importance and his fame spread not only by his talent but also by his own pronouncements of his great abilities as musician and maestro. His enemies described him as arrogant, making comments such as,

'Why does he continue to play the cornet when he can blow his own trumpet so loudly?'

As leader, he had full access to the band rooms for full-band practice sessions but, also, for individual sections' rehearsals. On other evenings, he would arrange meetings for young, aspiring individuals whom he had identified as being susceptible to manipulation into his ways. He would use all the tactics he had learned from Leo. He would stress to each of them the importance of playing his horn regularly to get the best effect, sometimes in the band room and sometimes in the countryside.

He would take them to a secluded spot well protected from view by an abundance of gorse at Beacon Scarp where they could practise without disturbing the rest of the community. Here, he would instruct them in their various instruments. Each would take his own instrument in turn and hold it for the others to watch as Frank showed each of them in turn how to finger the valves to get the perfect performance. He demonstrated how the trombonist could alter the effective length of his horn by making the slide move back and forth. He showed them how to place their lips on the smooth open tip of the mouthpiece and by causing their lips to vibrate they could achieve a vibration in the tubular resonator of their instrument. He would emphasise the importance of lip tension and air flow over the mouthpiece in order to achieve the desired pure tones required in an instrumentalist in this revered brass band. During these sessions with the youngest of the aspirant bandsmen, he basked in his own importance as a conductor of great renown and as a teacher in the art of playing the horn for personal pleasure.

Chris and Shirley deposited the final two courses on the table together with the bottle of Port. Chris knew that Frank preferred brandy.

'Hard cheese,' she thought to herself, whilst grinning at her unintended pun.

The dessert course had been made deliberately small because she had provided a full and varied selection of cheeses as Hal had an addiction to it; the fact that Frank also appreciated the cheese course was incidental. Frank appeared to be dozing by the fire. Both Shirley and Chris went over to him to rouse him. He had a look of self-satisfaction on his face and he was actually smiling.

'Obviously, having a good dream,' Chris thought as she touched his shoulder.

'Wake up, Hec, come and get some pudding and some cheese.'

Frank stretched, and came back to life. He had been in Heaven for a short while.

The effect of the Zymkase was wearing off so he decided that he would take some more with the cheese. He was getting through this pack very quickly and he wondered whether the doctor would give him another prescription so soon after the last one. He needed to make another appointment for the forthcoming week. He felt quite wide awake. That little interlude among the band boys had given him a burst of energy in spite of the pain in his leg.

'I'll pass on the trifle but I'll tuck into the cheese and port. Got any goat's cheese?'

'*You would want goat's cheese, you old goat!*' she thought, but, instead, said,

'Sorry, no. Hal's not a fan of that, but I'm sure we can accommodate your tastes. All our cheeses tonight are Scottish. We've got some Caboc; that contains cream and is best eaten with oatcakes, also Lanark Blue; you'll like that. It's made from sheep's milk. There's Isle of Mull Cheddar and Crowdie. You'd better eat plenty of Crowdie; it's said to alleviate the effects of the whisky and you've had plenty of that tonight. There's also some Dunlop. That's a mild one…a bit like soft Cheddar in texture.'

Shirley thought she would steer Frank away from the Crowdie if she could, but she need not have worried. Frank rather liked the effect that whisky had on him.

'How come you've got all those? I've never 'eard of 'em?'

'It's called mail order…have you heard of that?'

He ignored her.

'I'll just use the little boys' room if yer don't mind.' Frank stumbled down the hallway to their newly installed wet-room. It had a perfumed, feminine-inspired quality about it. He felt the nausea rise in his throat but he gulped it back. He looked in at the kitchen where Chris was making the coffee. He went in and noted the messy, untidy worktops.

'I've just been inspecting the plumbing in yer new wet-room.'

'Oh, yes?' She waited for the punch-line.

'Showers 'ave their place, I s'pose, but a sauna cleanses yer body far more efficiently. Of course, yer 'ave t' keep sauna scrupulously clean otherwise yer get mould forming all over t' place 'cause of the damp conditions. I supervise Shirley while she scrubs and polishes ours after every use.'

'*I bet you do*', Chris thought.

'Does it cleanse the mind as well?' she answered.

'There's nowt dirty about my mind', he spat back adding, '*bitch*' under his breath.

'Just watch you don't get overheated in your sauna, Hec, Too much heat can have serious effects on the body.'

She remembered the occasion, on a cruise ship, when she had spent too long in the deck Jacuzzi enjoying the company of her friends; her reddened face and overheated body had caused her discomfort for a full day.

'There's no chance of that; the temperature is easily controlled'. He went on, 'Yer like working amongst mess, do yer? I wouldn't tolerate this mess in my kitchen; I mek Shirley keep our kitchen spotless and there's nowt out of place. I'm surprised Aitch lets yer get away with it.'

She looked up slowly from the worktop and stared at his back as he wandered out of her sight. *'Drop dead, Hec,'* she mouthed at him.

Hal's cheery voice could be heard from the adjacent room,

'Do we want another question to debate at this time of night?'

The clock had chimed the hour some minutes before. It was past one o'clock.

'Yes. Why not? We've still got coffee and liqueurs and every one seems wide awake…… even Hec'.

Frank spoke,

'What's the difference between Truth and Belief?'

Once again Chris rolled her eyes and gave a deep sigh as this perennial question in Frank's repertoire emanated from between his thin lips. He liked to debate the sort of questions for which there are no correct answers; they were dependent on the point of view held by the debaters.

Frank had used to arrive at their house, unexpectedly, at the most inconvenient times...usually just as they were about to eat. Chris would become irritated and would make it plain to all that he was not welcome. Her response was like fuel to his fire and he would try to goad and mock her even more. She was not prepared to enter into any philosophical argument with him because it was so time-consuming and there was always something else more useful that she could be getting on with. She had never liked him anyway, so to debate with him was an anathema to her. Yet Hal relished this sort of debate because he, naturally, wanted to persuade his opponent to his point of view and he never seemed to mind Frank's intruding on their meal time. This response of Hal's would infuriate Chris even more; she would stalk off, in fury, and leave the men to their debate.

Chris and Hal were like Jack Spratt and his wife in many ways. Perhaps that is why they had remained happily married to each other when many of their contemporaries had fallen by the wayside.

Chris recognised that Frank was taking another opportunity to upset her composure. She was determined that he would not get the better of her.

Frank was becoming increasingly animated. He had filled himself with varieties of cheese with which he was unfamiliar and had made in-roads into the port, and he began puffing on a cigar. He was awash with the various liqueurs on offer and could not drink them fast enough. He was appreciating all these questions and the ensuing debate and he considered that his game might become a viable proposition if marketed correctly. In view of all the alcohol and painkillers he had consumed, Chris was amazed that he was still able to speak cogently.

Hal immediately joked, 'You're born, you live, you pay taxes and then you die…that's the truth.'

Chris decided to stick the knife in further.

'You believe in what you think to be true. Whether or not it is true, is another matter. For instance, I believe that you, Hec, are a vile, predatory paedophile. I also have confidence that you were convicted and imprisoned because the jury believed it too. Now is that the truth or not?'

Frank's facial tic became more obvious as his agitation accelerated. Starting to fidget on his seat and gazing wildly around at each of their faces, his face darkening and his deeply-sunk, beady eyes becoming a dull black, his reaction was as fast as that of a lunging rattlesnake.

'The trial was a total fiasco. The judgement constituted a flagrant miscarriage of justice. I was maligned totally. Look how the parents supported me - sending letters and attending court in sympathy. My friends, so-called, weren't there… I might add.'

He looked at Hal for a few significant moments before he resumed speaking.

'I wish I could fathom out who'd contacted the newspaper. That new boy is the only one I can think of, but even he seemed unlikely. Hardy had seemed to revel in the 'cut and thrust' with me. He had been trouble from the start. The other lads had been no problem at all. Kids do not like to be punished. That kid, Hardy, was a real tough nut, not as likely to be intimidated by the strictness of my regime. The parents of the rest of the boys were grateful to me for the help I'd given to them and to their sons. If there was proper control in the home and in the state schools then a school like mine would have been unnecessary. In this ridiculous liberal society in which we live, the yobs and criminals will ultimately inherit the earth… so much for the meek.'

Chris retaliated,

'You really are a cruel, controlling bastard, Hec, in the sorts of punishments you gave, not only in your own school but at the James Ratcliffe before that. JR was glad to see the back of you. Don't you imagine for one second that I don't know the sort of things you did'.

She was astonished by the ferocity of her attack and the potency of the venom which she spat in Frank's direction. It had been fomenting psychologically for many years and, at that moment, the tight control over her behaviour which she had maintained, hitherto, snapped and Frank felt the full fury of her antagonism towards him.

Frank leapt out of his chair. In the blinking of an eye, he was in her face, close up and dangerous. With furious gestures and a raised voice, he snarled and growled at her, triumphantly, reverting to the vernacular, which, habitually, he did whenever he was angered.

'Just get yer facts right, woman. Yer can call me what yer like but *bastard* aint one of 'em. Just read mi birth certificate. Mi conception was legal not like that of most of the sprogs in your hi-falutin school. Think back t't last question; yer seemed quite keen on severe punishments then, Madam. Have yer forgot that?'

His face flushed, he moved animatedly, from foot to foot, as if he were dancing manically on hot coals. He was obviously impressed by his own incandescent eloquence. He was intensely breathless, decidedly drunk but remarkably lucid.

'For God's sake, Hec, don't have a heart attack', Chris retaliated in a quiet tones, the absolute opposite of Frank's frenetic outburst.

It was at this point that Shirley, her nerves jangling and her body aroused by the thrill of this exchange, noticed the lateness of the hour.

CHAPTER FIVE

IX

'It's a quarter to three', announced Shirley.

'Oh, thank goodness,' thought Chris, *'they're going at last'*.

She stifled a yawn. She felt worn out. Although weary, both physically and mentally, she had to admit that it had been a lively evening with no shred of boredom. She had thought that it might have been a complete disaster with all those home truths being aired, but as far as she was concerned, the evening had been a success. It was Hec who had wanted to test drive his game so he should not have taken all her foul comments to heart.

'At least, he's got some feedback, if he's sober enough to appreciate it,' she said to herself,

'Hey, Hec, don't think of leaving yet. The fun's only just starting. I thought since it's got so late, I'd get us all an early breakfast. What d' you fancy, Hec? What about some succulent sausages from some tender young porkers?'

Frank sat down with a thud onto his chair. He was exhausted after the incessant, ugly exchanges between himself and Chris. His head had become unbearably fuzzy with the strong alcohol and Zymkase in his system and he lacked the necessary energy to physically throttle her. He could do nothing but sit and inwardly seethe at this woman who continually argued with him and would not be silenced. The other women in his life had succumbed to his control but Chris was an exception and there was nothing he could do about it. His face began to twitch uncontrollably in his panic at his inability to assume dominance over her.

Shirley, all this time, apparently subdued and looking down at the floor in embarrassment, but secretly enjoying this penultimate act of the drama in which she was a principal player said,

'Thank you so much for everything. I'll be in touch when I've consulted the diary about a day when we can get together for a serious female pampering session'.

Chris beamed at her.

Frank lumbered over to Chris; he was well plastered.

'How's the leg?' She asked.

Ignoring the question, he attempted to hug her. He was sharp enough to summon sufficient strength in order to make the intended hug more painful than would be obvious to either Hal or Shirley. But Chris, alert to his wily ways, out manoeuvred him. Neatly, she sidestepped his open arms. He grimaced as he lost his balance, so jolting his leg. His utterances were incomprehensible. He yelped in pain as they edged, nervously, towards their car.

Chris and Hal stood together, her arm around his waist and his around her shoulders as they watched the pair depart. Shirley made no attempt to help the drunken, staggering Frank as he slipped and slithered over the slippery, snow-covered ground towards the passenger door. The car stood quietly for a few moments then finally, the engine turned over, and it chugged out of view down the winding driveway, disturbing the silence of the cold, black night as it did so.

'Thank God that's over. Let's hope we don't see them again for a long time. The pig never even thanked us for all the help we gave him.'

'How could he?' said Hal. 'He was totally blotto - P as an N. It's a wonder he made it to the car without falling over. I pity Shirley. He'll have it in for her. He'll treat her as a substitute for you.'

CHAPTER FIVE

X

Shirley commented, as she drove, carefully but with speed,

'Well, that was jolly wasn't it Frank? You couldn't have wished for a better discussion about your game, could you?'

'Stop yer blatherin' woman. Yer as bad as 'er,' was his only comment.

He had little more to say during the journey home. He was too drunk and too drugged. He had only himself to blame since he had consumed so many of those liqueurs, all of which must have been at least twenty per cent proof...whisky, wine, liqueur and pain killers. It was a wonder he could stand. Drunk as he was, he was remarkably lucid in his thinking. He was not interested in talking to Shirley. He made out that he was asleep but he was thinking about what Hal had said to him concerning writing about his imprisonment. He took the opportunity, on the drive back to Scarp Edge, to consider what he might include in some sort of auto-biography.

His mind went back to the last days of Abercrombie Restorative Academy. All had been going so swimmingly well for two school years. He had paid off much of his debt; he had stowed away, in a secret bank account, quite a few thousands of pounds. He had refurbished the old swimming pool and had converted the old barn into a respectably equipped gymnasium.

He had maintained his practice of a termly medical inspection, ostensibly searching for lice, eczema and bodily rashes, but in reality he had enjoyed looking at the naked male body on every occasion he could engender. Swimming naked had been a new sport for the boys as had naked wrestling. He had researched and introduced Ancient Olympian wrestling. For the Greeks, it was the ultimate in the training of young men. They covered their bodies with olive oil and sand to protect them from the sun's harmful ultra-violet rays. After combat, they would scrape the oil and sand mixture with a *strigil* and wash in cold water. Frank had considered that if this sort of sport was acceptable to the ancient Greeks, then it would be quite suitable for his boys. He had read the novel by D.H. Lawrence and watched the subsequent movie, *Women in Love,* in which the two main characters, Gerald Crich and Rupert Birkin had indulged in the sport on a Persian rug in front of an open fire. Frank had always found this scene with the flickering light from the flames highly sexually charged. He had never experienced such emotion personally but had hoped to get some second hand thrill from watching the adolescent boys perform.

During the two years of his Academy's existence, he had alleged that he had not had to chastise any boy on more than the odd occasion. They had known his rules. They had known what the consequences would have been for disobedience and so their behaviour had been exemplary. That these boys had fallen foul of the state system, said much about the woolly, liberal, ineffectual thinking and practices of the majority of schools, causing teachers to suffer nervous breakdowns and ultimately to leave the teaching profession because of their incapability, through no fault of their own, to control the pandemonium occurring in their classrooms. Frank had never had the slightest problem in this area. He had had total control. He had never touched the boys except to corporally punish them for their misdemeanours, but there had been that unique, deadly occurrence.

    He had been at a loss to explain how and why complaints had been made about him. He had racked his brains over and over again. He had been accused of a number of misdeeds, including the conducting of medical examinations for which he had no medical training, the encouragement of lewd behaviour among the boys by the introduction of naked swimming and wrestling, the observation of naked boys in the pool and in the showers, the punishment, meted out for lateness to the morning jog, of running naked round the field. When he had cogitated on his alleged misdemeanours, he had had to acknowledge that seeing the naked, young, male body had given him pleasure. He did not understand why he should be chastised for that. What had been his crime?

He could identify a specific occasion when it could be argued that he had been at fault. It concerned a new pupil, Timin Hardy. This boy had joined the Academy at the beginning of the autumn term of the Academy's third year of existence. He was the adopted son of white parents but he had appeared to be of mixed race. Black hair and a dark, olive complexion with obvious sprouting of beard and moustache were clearly visible. The Hardys had been led to believe him to have an eastern European ancestry. The boy had been enrolled at the Academy for the usual reason of being problematic at his comprehensive school. He was a young Adonis and an obvious *cock of the walk*. Although only thirteen years of age, he already had the muscularity associated with an eighteen-year-old. Obviously, he was postpubescent with unusually wide shoulders and large hands, When stripped naked for the medical inspection, the advanced growth of black, curly hair on his testosterone-infused body had thrilled Frank whose greatest surge of excitement came as he had gazed in awe at the enormity of the boy's phallus which grew in length and girth as Frank had watched open mouthed and wide eyed. He was so unaccustomed to witnessing such a vision in one so young that he had had an erection himself and had reached an orgasm in consequence. He had become so agitated by the whole experience that he had felt the need to touch the boy's massive organ, an action he had not performed formerly on any other pupil. The boy, Hardy, had appeared to be well-accustomed to this sort of adulation. Frank had suspected that it had been the primary reason for Timin Hardy's enrolment at his

Academy. The boy, gaining even more confidence under Frank's admiring eyes, had begun to strut around the sick bay, thrusting back his head revealing his protuberant Adam's apple and his dark, puce-coloured phallus, massively erect, protruding from his lower region like an engorged, rigid, mud snake.

Frank had been reminded of his similar, acute excitement on seeing for the first time the stinkhorn fungus, *Phallus impudicus*, the photograph of which had adorned the wall of his study.

The boy seemed to recognise a flaw in Frank's personality and Timin pursued a regime to unsettle Frank and so to destroy the power Frank had held over the thirty boys in his care. He had taken great delight in testing Frank's patience with all manner of perverse infringements of the disciplinary policies. This had led to some insecurity in Frank and he had become fearful. He had considered thrashing the boy. He was not a tall man and the boy was bigger and stronger than he and so Timin had refused to accept the threatened corporal punishment. Hitherto, Frank's domination of his prey had not been by superior strength but by the instillation of terror. However, young Hardy patently had not been terrified. The tables had been turned.

Frank had desperately tried all his formerly successful means of control but to no avail. What other action might he have taken? If he had retained the boy, the school ethos would have been destroyed by Timin's mere presence. The boy had to be expelled. This failure of Frank's methods had led to some slight erosion of his self-confidence, but he had been determined to take a positive outlook. He had hoped that this hiccup in his hitherto smooth-running rule of power would soon have blown over. Before he departed, the brazen, audacious, young, Hardy insolently defiled the walls and any other surface with graffiti... ... ... *'Doctor Hector: dick detector'*: *'Doctor Hector: prick inspector'*: *'Doctor Hector: fear injector '*... ... ...

    The graffiti had been written in blackboard chalk and was easily washed away but not before it had been seen and internalised by the other boys. Evidentially, the genie had escaped from the bottle; Frank's bubble had been burst; his fate had been sealed; he was the biter bit.

    Frank's impending, downward demise had gathered pace. News of the alleged, salacious, scandalous activities at the Academy had been leaked maliciously by some mischief-maker to the *Broadclough Daily News* which had scooped up the ordure with alacrity. Frank had been scuppered. He was in a state of disbelief, and despair. So lovingly, he had built his perfect, private autocratic domain and then it had come crashing down about his ears. He had decided to carry on as best he could. There was always the chance that once the dust had settled, the whole unseemly affair would have been regarded as a nine days' wonder and business would resume as before.

Frank had been roused, rudely, from his sleep on that bleak, February morning. It had been the sort of day that never gets truly light with a dark, grey, overcast sky and a painfully cutting east wind together with a fine drizzle. The house was being subjected to a deep climatic depression which boded ill. All the signs had been unfavourable. There had been a loud rapping on the solid oak front door and a bleary-eyed Frank Hector had staggered to his feet and had felt his way down the stairs for it was not yet light and in his stupor he had neglected to switch on the light. Who could have been rapping on his front door in the middle of the night? The boys were still sleeping in their dormitories. It was too early for the reveille whistle. That would not sound at its normal time any more. He had opened the door. Two, tall, broad police officers were standing in the open porch, their dark uniforms glistening with millions of sparkling, droplets of rain.

'Frank Hector?'

'Yes.'

'We are here to arrest you for the alleged crimes of sexual misconduct with various juveniles at your school. You will be taken to Ravensborough Police Station where you will be questioned about these allegations.'

Frank was stricken with a feeling of panic. Feeling faint and sick with disbelief, he had gone first hot then cold. The first beads of perspiration appeared on his forehead then as the visibly dripping sweat became excessive, he had used the back of his quivering hand in a frantic attempt to mop it away. Sweat, oozing from every pore then had drenched his whole body, producing a cold, clammy condition which he had found desperately terrifying. How had he allowed this catastrophe to happen? His mind had run haphazardly from one recent event to the next. Suddenly, his legs had felt weak. He had thought he would faint. His throat had become dry; his mouth had developed a bitter taste and his voice cracked as he spoke,

'What time is it? ... I don't understand.'

The first police officer repeated his statement and then he requested that they might enter the building whilst Frank dressed. Frank had been in no state to argue. He was not a violent man and was not obstructive and in any case he was too debilitated by the shock of this intrusion to be on the offensive. He became powerless and sapped of all his usual energy. His legs felt as if they would crumple under his weight.

In Abercrombie Hall, at six o'clock, darkness reigned apart from the light from the single, low wattage light bulb dangling from the ceiling in the hallway. Normally, at that time, boys would have been scurrying hither and thither getting ready for their morning exercise but the house had remained ominously cold and silent. The warm, nutty aroma of porridge, bubbling on the range, which normally would have been wafting through from the kitchen was not and never again would be available to his senses. The reveille whistle had not been blown and consequently, oblivious to the events taking place at the front door, all innocent souls had slumbered on.

'I must inform my wife,' spluttered Frank.

One of the officers who had escorted him to his bedroom noticed that Mrs Hector was not in his bed. The aura in the room had demonstrated plainly that this was not a shared bedroom. There was no inkling of femininity about it. Furthermore, he had been aware of the astounding order and tidiness of the space. *'Was this a former military man?'* the police officer had wondered. Frank collected his cornet, some clean underwear, his electric razor and his wallet.

Helen Hector, being summoned by her husband, immediately had jumped to attention in her usual manner. She had been stunned to see the events unfolding before her eyes. Frank had always been in charge. Now, he was bent over, his head hanging and having to take orders instead of issuing them. Frank had been handcuffed before being taken away to a waiting police car, and had been whisked away to the police station now based in Ravensborough, the one in Scarp Edge, having closed down some years previously.

After a drive of roughly thirty minutes, Frank had found himself in Ravensborough Police Station in an interview room where he was informed of his alleged crimes. There had been four charges - sexual activity with a child under fourteen years of age: causing or inciting a child to engage in sexual activity: sexual communication with a child and voyeurism. He had been advised of his legal rights and his right to a solicitor. He had been cautioned by the interrogating officer,

'You do not have to say anything, but it may harm your defence if you do not mention, when questioned, something which you may, later, rely on in court. Anything you say may be given in evidence.'

He had been questioned about his alleged offences and his answers had been recorded. He had denied all charges.

Frank was detained in a police cell for twenty-four hours whilst the police attempted to collect evidence to support the charges. This meant the setting up of interviews with the thirty pupils and three adults back at Abercrombie Hall. His personal belongings were confiscated. Frank was taken through a creaking, rusting iron-barred gate, which was unlocked to admit him and afterwards locked again. A raucous, discordant noise emanating from the jangling of keys caused his musically sensitive eardrums to vibrate violently. He had been obliged to enter a stark, cheerless corridor where the walls were shedding flaky, pale, green paint reminiscent of the parings of a discarded Granny Smith apple. There was a series of windowless doors. The police officer directed him to enter a cell through one of them. This would be his straitjacket for the following twenty-four hours. At a height of nine feet, the wall housed a small, grime-encrusted, spider-web festooned window, heavily barred, but admitting sparse daylight. The six-foot wide cell was bounded by walls which were tiled from floor to ceiling, white originally but now yellowed from age and the accumulated odour and sweat of its various and numerous occupants. The grouting was no longer white but a grubby grey. His cell was just long enough to accommodate a solid, concrete platform on which lay a thin mattress and a pillow, each of which was covered with dark green plastic, uncomfortable for the detainee but easily cleaned when deemed necessary for subsequent users, together with a thin, green *shoddy* blanket Against one wall stood an unlidded lavatory and a wash hand-basin both manufactured of stainless steel A roll of lavatory paper was provided. The door, although windowless, had a small aperture through which the prisoner could be summoned or observed by his captors. Frank approved of order but this was a fearfully bare, bleak space. He had nothing else to do but to sit on the bunk, to think, to wait and listen to those jangling keys as they bounced stridently against the knees of his unsympathetic captors during their heavy-footed marching up and down the corridor outside his cell.

    He was detained in this restrictive man-hole of a place for a further twelve hours after which he was informed that his alleged crimes were of such gravity that he would remain in custody until his court appearance before a magistrate. He was given a date in the following week.

The Magistrate, on hearing the charges, Frank's denial of them and the evidence collected by the police from the twenty-nine children and three adults at Abercrombie Hall and the expelled Timin Hardy at his home, announced that Frank would be referred on to the Crown Court. He was denied bail. Frank was remanded in custody for three months in Castleton Prison, after which he returned to Ravensborough Crown Court to attend his trial.

He had three long months to consider his plight. He was so convinced of his innocence that the initial feelings of panic subsided and he became calm and rational. It was obvious to him that his modus operandi, as reported to the investigating officers by the witnesses, had been considered to be criminal by the authorities. He remained adamant that he had done only good work; he had been in the process of rehabilitating his pupils back into acceptable patterns of behaviour which was what their parents were paying him to do. The fact that he took pleasure in observing their progress seemed to be his crime. He considered the alleged harm which he had inflicted on his charges. In his opinion, there had been no damage to them physically or mentally. He considered himself to have been unjustly imprisoned for his one action involving the boy, Timin Hardy.

Later, when interrogated in the calm, ancient, highly ornate, awe-inspiring Crown Court with its shiny, polished, mahogany benches and rails and the plush, red velvet, upholstered seats for the Judiciary, he had remained composed. He denied fervently the allegations of child molestation, but had to admit to the truth of the allegations regarding nakedness in swimming, wrestling and running, the medical inspections, the observation of the showering process, and the inadvertent touching of the Hardy boy's genitals. He had justified himself using the guise of being in loco parentis.

He was also accused of harsh treatment and the threatening of harsh treatment. He could not deny this, but hotly insisted that only offences had been punished. Given the nature of his school and the outcomes desired by the parents who paid his fees, he had acted in accordance to their wishes. In his summing up, the Judge took notice of the vast number of letters, received in support of Frank Hector from parents and their subsequent support by their attendance at the court hearing.

The jury took very little time to reach their verdict. Frank was found to be guilty on all charges.

Frank Hector who had been educating these cohorts of misguided adolescents into becoming model, obedient sons who were literate, numerate and musically aware had felt that the justice system had let him down. It was true that he had observed these boys indulging in their naked frolics but where had been the harm in that?

The Judge sentenced Frank to: six years detention in Pinchfold Castle Prison, the invalidation of his teaching qualification, the denial of access to and contact with minors and placement on the sex offenders' register. His sentence might quite well have been longer but the Judge took cognisance of the vast number of letters in Frank's support written by parents who claimed that he had worked wonders with their naughty offspring. Not only had they offered support in writing but they had appeared in large numbers at the court hearing. Frank had much to thank them for. He had noticed the presence of his wife, Helen. He had been aware of her stony facial expression throughout the hearing. She had ignored him and she gave no indication of her state of mind. He realised that he had become persona non grata amongst those who knew him.

He was taken below the court room to a cold, stark cell where he waited for most of the day. He would get used to waiting. That was all there was for him to do for the forthcoming three years or so that he would have to serve assuming that he would earn maximum remission for good behaviour. He had no intention of behaving otherwise. He would get plenty of time for reflections on the past and for visions for the future. He would no longer be in control of others. It would be they who would control his every move. He had no idea what would be in store for him. He was heading into unknown territory. He had anticipated with anxiety his arrival at his destination and the sort of reception he would receive at the hands of the hardened criminals with whom he might come into contact. He had not relished the notion of being viciously targeted by them and he suspected that the guards would turn a blind eye to such bullying and other perverted actions. He believed that the criminal types at the top of the 'food chain' could literally get away with murder. He anticipated with dread his future with the dregs of society.

The waiting continued, until, finally, he was escorted outside with seven other felons to the transfer vehicle which was standing by. This huge, white vehicle, with the logo, *SPECTAMUS,* resembled a vast, refrigerated, meat-delivery van designed to transport living human flesh. It had five small windows along each side, each one representing a lost soul on his way to Hell. Still hand-cuffed, he was motioned by a broad shouldered, grim-faced officer into a small, human-sized compartment into which he was locked. He had no idea for how long he would be subjected to the close confines of this cold, impersonal transfer-vehicle. His watch had been confiscated along with all of his personal possessions. He had been given no food or water. Surely, that provision was his human right? Was he going to be starved as well as banged up? He had resolved that, in future, he would consume all forms of nourishment which were offered to him in order to protect himself from any future incidence of food shortage. His toilet-sized cubicle offered no comfort as the prison van rattled noisily along. At least, he could not be thrown about much as the van manoeuvred around bends in the road since there was so little space for to and fro movement. The monotony had been relieved, to some extent, by fellow passengers, familiar with the routine from their previous journeys, indulging in incessant, rowdy banter, each one attempting to bolster up his own spirits by his vociferous participation in the chorus.

Such cacophony had been painful to Frank's ears, and in endeavouring to exclude it, he remembered his beloved cornet and hoped that it was safe.

CHAPTER FIVE

XI

After his protracted reverie in the prison transport vehicle, Frank, momentarily, returned to reality. The car, carrying Frank and Shirley home, skidded on the slippery, snowy surface of the road. He yelled,

'Watch what yer doing yer useless berk. Yer'll get us both killed.'

Shirley slowed right down. Taking her eyes off the road, she turned and looked in his direction. His eyes were closed. With narrowed eyes, staring and piercing, she spoke, silently, to him,

'You drunken, gluttonous sod! Little did you know, but you have just eaten your last supper as the condemned man.'

The drive home, although tedious and tiring at that time of day, after that incident, was mostly uneventful. Owing to the paucity of traffic and the sound-deadening effect of the newly-precipitated snow, the roads in the rural area were silent for the most part during the journey. Theirs was the sole vehicle travelling in the direction from

Great Barrow to Scarp Edge. The fresh snow lay undisturbed on the road ahead and under her tyres, making the slightest error of judgement on her part possibly fatal. A few taxis most likely ferrying inebriated passengers, just as she was doing, were travelling in the opposite direction, their headlights on full beam being particularly glaring at such an ungodly hour. They might have blinded her at any other time, but she remained unaffected, so fixed was she on the final, climactic act in the drama that was about to played out.

As they approached Scarp Edge, she was suddenly distracted by the flashing blue light of an oncoming police car followed almost immediately by an ambulance. Someone was in trouble. Perhaps it was an accident on the road on which she had just driven. She felt quite safe in the knowledge, in the unlikely event of her being stopped by police for being on the road at that time of night, that she would not fail a breathalyser test. In any case, the local police, no doubt, were probably enjoying a hot cuppa in the warmth of the surroundings of one of their regular *do-drop-ins*.

Shirley had been most diligent in not exceeding her intake of alcohol at the Days'. She had rationed herself, deliberately, to two drinks only and hence she had remained sober...well within the legal limits for driving. The rest of the journey was spent in silence apart for the sounds of intermittent snoring and grunting noises from

Frank, who appeared to be back in a deep sleep. His mind had drifted back to the past and his nightmare continued.

The prison van had arrived at its destination, Pinchfold Castle Prison, a handsome landmark in the town. Immediately, he had recognised the familiar façade which he had driven past on many occasions. Its appearance was typical of so many prisons of its generation, boasting a great, Roman-arched gateway with solid, double doors, in a central plane wall, flanked by two tall cylindrical towers topped by slated, conical roofs, reminiscent of illustrations of castles found in books of children's fairy tales. The walls were reputed to be fifteen feet thick and impenetrable. Like many Victorian buildings, the prison was constructed from a warm red brick with decorative, horizontal bands, arches and quoins in Portland Stone. The windows were surrounded by stone sills, jambs and lintels. In another world and another time, it might have been a castle administered by the National Trust.

    The vehicle had entered the prison yard through the vast, double oak doors, powerfully constructed, yet surprisingly ornate. Then, looming menacingly, were two more sets of forty foot high, leaden-grey, heavy, steel, locked gates, each surmounted by coils of razor wire. The gate-keepers had required the prison van to halt before admittance so that the obligatory paperwork accompanying the prisoners could be checked by the guardians of the gates. With a deafening, intimidating clamour, symbolising the prisoners' relentless incarceration, the massive gates had swung shut, slowly engulfing the prison van. As he had nervously scratched a seeping scab on his wrist, Frank, his facial tic much in evidence, had the fearsome feeling in his bowels that this was a place which permitted no escape. Urgent messages which were transmitted repeatedly from his desperate bowels to his brain had gone unheeded as there were no facilities in the van for their evacuation. He had to sit, buttocks clenched, in the hope that he could reach a lavatory before his body refused to wait any longer for its release from the nagging ache it was enduring. He had endeavoured to take his mind off the problem by studying the prison architecture. He had viewed, incredulously, the enormity of the prison-yard beyond the gates and the massive expanses of undecorated red brick with a multitude of tiny, barred-windows, behind which a single or perhaps two trapped, tortured souls were pacing the floor like rats in a cage, anxious for their release. Having arrived at the main door of the prison, there had begun the slow, conveyor-belt-like admissions process. With only his thoughts for company, confined in his icy-cold cubicle, Frank had lost all sense of time. He had to wait his turn as each felon underwent the seemingly, never-ending formalities of admission. Waiting had become his major occupation. At last, his slow transfer had gathered some momentum as he had been shunted from reception area to holding cell, then on to another holding cell. At each stage, some sort of interrogation had taken place and information had been given. At this particular point in the proceedings, the group of newly-admitted inmates had been able to view and assess each other from their appearances. All ages, shapes, sizes and criminality had been represented. To Frank's eyes, they all had a lean, hungry, wolfish quality to their demeanour, so characteristic of the criminal type. It was as if they shared the same genome. He had wondered whether he fitted the pattern. A good many of the most cynical and cruel of his fellow prisoners most certainly had noticed something odd about him, specifically the spasmodic contractions of his cheek muscle. Their mutual mimicry of his malady had not passed his notice, warning him to take care lest he became an object of contemptuous ridicule and mockery which would have been certain to lead to bullying. He had wondered what they had thought about him. Now, he could hazard a guess. He had wondered if these people ever had an intelligent thought. He had wondered if they ever thought at all.

He had been directed to the next conveyor belt. Thus began the next section of his admission procedure. It had started with a strip search. He had been made to sit on the Body Orifice Security Scanner, the so-called *BOSS* chair which detected whether or not any electrical or telephonic equipment had been thrust up his anal passage or any other orifice in order to avoid detection. So nauseated had Frank been by the mere thought of this possibility that he had begun to retch, but there had been nothing forthcoming but bile. An inspection of his hands and nails, head and hair, teeth, armpits, groin and genitals would reveal his general state of health. Here was the biter bit! Had the boys at his Academy undergone the same emotions as he was experiencing at that moment? He had considered that possibility. It had provided him with food for thought during those interminable waiting periods as no other form of food would be forthcoming for a long while.

A photograph bearing his name, date of birth and prison number had been presented to him with the instruction that it should be carried on his person at all times. The prison official had referred to it as his 'mugshot'. It was a most dreadful image and Frank appreciated that he looked the very epitome of evil. He had been issued with bedding and plastic cutlery and some prison clothing which he had hoped would be of the correct size. The banter on the prison van had led him to doubt the inevitability of this. The grey prison uniform with which he had been issued reminded him of that worn by his *prisoners* at Abercrombie Academy. The irony of the situation had not been lost on him.

Then, onwards to the wing, his final destination, where his cell was situated, Hector, FH4791 passed through the strong, iron door, unlocked for his benefit, into a vast arena, four storeys high consisting of a lot of naked, shiny steel in the form of stairs and walkways off which there were fifteen doors. There was a mass of bare, green-painted pipework and cast iron roof supports. The iron balustrades, which prevented accidental falling from the narrow walkways, were universally painted depressingly in green. This largely empty space had been full of noise resulting from the reflection and reverberation of every sound from the primarily metal surfaces. A large safety-net was strung between the walkways on the first landing, intended to be a life-saver for any inmate intent on suicide by jumping off, or being murdered by being pushed off, the walkway. His wing, B wing, like the others, contained one hundred and twenty cells. As he had stomped up the metal staircase to the third storey, he had become aware of the stench that he would always in the future associate with that day - that malodour with occasional overtones of bleach and pine disinfectant redolent of a gents' public lavatory.

During the protracted admissions process, Frank had a great deal of time on his hands in which to think about what might lie before him. He had not wanted to be targeted as a sex offender. He continued to believe in his innocence and the injustice meted out to him. He was aware that in the prison hierarchy, his alleged crimes were at the bottom of the heap and if broadcast, he would be likely to be attacked and injured by heavyweight jail-birds and possibly by the guards. He was not the tough guy he had always appeared to be when handing out punishments and putting the fear of God into little boys. He wanted to remain anonymous as far as he was able. He realised that this aim was probably unachievable. He needed a strategy. What crime might he have committed realistically? He gave some serious thought to crimes which were more acceptable to the bullies who ran the wing. Offences which required physical power and strength such as armed robbery, burglary, rape or murder had seemed to him as unlikely. Eventually, he had decided that fraud would be the best option. The authorities always had seemed to punish perpetrators of fraud more heavily than crimes against another person and that might be acceptable to those at the top of the food chain - the chief villains who controlled the prisons.

'Tell people nothing and they will be none the wiser; tell people what you know and they will be as wise as you.' That would be his strategy.

Silence would be the best policy but it would not be achievable. He would play the game so as to achieve his own ends which were, as short and as safe an incarceration as was possible. He would go along with what would be meted out to him and bide his time. He would make it known, somehow, that he could be of some use in the literary and the musical education of his associates-in-crime and that might become a feasible route to an easy stretch.

He had been taken to cell five on the third landing in B Wing, nudged into his new residence where a smoky atmosphere and the fetid stench of a sweaty body predominated. His companion, an obese, flabby fifty-something, with a grey stubbly chin and a shaven head, lay on the top bunk, smoking.

'I'm Hector', announced Frank.

'And I'm Zsa Zsa the frog,' chuckled his gap-toothed, stable companion, 'otherwise known as Felix the cat. Wotcha in fer ?'

'Tax evasion', replied Frank, hoping that there would be no further probing.

CHAPTER FIVE

XII

BEEEEP BEEEEP!

The loud sound of a car horn instantly awoke Frank from his dream-like trance. He got up from his half lying position in the front passenger seat.

'What the bloody 'ell...?' he yelled.

It was an impatient taxi driver, sounding his horn loudly in an attempt to get Shirley, who was driving in a deliberately cautious manner, to either speed up or pull over in order to allow him to overtake. She braked suddenly in panic and as the taxi sped past, the aggravated driver made a rude gesture to her by holding up two fingers.

'Are yer trying to kill mi or summat?' Frank complained as he nursed demonstrably his painful leg.

'Stupid pillock... scaring the wits out of me like that!' Shirley shouted at the rear end of the fast moving taxi as it sped at high speed away from her. 'Now, get back to sleep, ratface,' she spat at Frank, whilst harbouring the fantasy of his impending doom.

Frank was already asleep and ignorant of her instruction.

Each day in prison had been like all others but that particular one had been memorable.

Hector, FH4791, had stood naked in his cell, looking down at his pink, bloated, pock-marked body. If he sucked in his belly, he would just be able to glimpse his pale, flaccid, pockmarked penis. He had always abhorred the sound of that word, penis. Years before, his friend and mentor, the Pastor, had recommended to him that he name it. He had called it Eddie. He and Eddie had experienced some interesting escapades together but Eddie was now a part of his past. He had re- christened this part of his body, St John, so named after the arrogant St John Smythe of TV chat show fame. He had a low opinion of St John Smythe whom he had dubbed a 'Big Prick'. However, the truth was that although he shared that quality of arrogance with St John Smythe, his own equipment would hardly be described as big. Conceivably, that inadequacy had contributed to his psyche. He had read in some magazine or newspaper article, he could not recall precisely which, that a small penis, being the cause of dissatisfaction in women, frequently turned men into tyrants, control freaks and woman-haters. The 'Short man Syndrome' was similar. Short men and he was also one of those, as were Hitler and Bonaparte, apparently became tyrannical, as a result of this syndrome, in their interactions with others in their everyday life and in the wider society.

As he studied his body and St John especially, he had been reminded of those occasions many years before, when that particular instrument had been of considerable interest, on a good many occasions, to an elder of the Pentecostal Mission – the Reverend Edward Pickering.

Frank experienced an acute pain in his left leg. The motor cycle accident scarring from years before was very evident. Invariably, the pain became more intense in low temperatures. He had wished for some of those strong painkillers his doctor had prescribed for him at the time of the operation on his leg. He had resolved to request, at the earliest opportunity, a plentiful supply of Zymkase from the prison doctor.

He had then been behind bars for two full years and ninety days. With luck be might be out in another two hundred and seventy five days. He would start to count the days.

His cell in Pinchfold Castle Prison had the appearance of the inner chamber of a diminutive, depleted cold store. The painted walls were coloured in green, akin to the hue of the male mallard's head. The floor was overlaid with cold quarry tiles, in a shade of yellow ochre speckled with brown. In this primitive prison, the cell lacked personal toilet facilities. On the wall was a call button to be pressed when an inmate required the use of the communal washing facility. A concrete construction in the corner served as a bed on top of which lay a thin, green, meagre, plastic-covered, mattress with a duvet, already folded neatly at the end of the bed. He supposed that plastic covered mattresses must have been bought in bulk by the HMP, as it was the same sort that he had slept on in Ravensborough Police Station.

A small chest with three drawers completed the furnishings. Such was his habitation, a far cry from the luxury surroundings he had enjoyed before his admission to this hellhole. He had been fortunate. He had his own cell. He had tolerated his first cellie – Felix the cat, for over a year. Considering their positions at either end of the spectrum in terms of age, culture and intellect, they had bonded well. Felix had been in and out of prison many times in his burglary career and, consequently, he was a mine of information about prison life. He had passed on invaluable advice about survival in Pinchfold Castle to Frank,

'Show respect, don't be nosey, keep your mouth shut, stay clear of drugs and gambling, keep yourself fit and don't get cosy with the staff.'

Felix the cat had been a humorous cell-mate and had kept Frank sane during the early days, but Frank needed some solitude so that he could play his cornet and prepare his lessons for his work in the Education Department. In due course, he had been granted a single cell. Here, his personal safety was guaranteed. Inmates, such as he, were often targeted by the hardened convicts on the block. His crime of abusive behaviour was not a passport to a comfortable existence. He had to keep his wits about him in the early days when he had to use the walkways, whilst using the library and outside when exercising. Although, not weedy in stature, he was short. He considered himself to be strong in character but he was physically unfit and somewhat intimidated by his current companions, who, in comparison with himself, he described as *brick shithouses* in stature and *shithouses* in nature. These bruisers did not care for his type of crime. They were the bank-robbing brigade and for them child abuse was off limits. Not that Frank considered himself to be a criminal. He had never hurt anyone. He had tried to give a good leathering to the creep Hardy, but Hardy was bigger and stronger and had refused to take the punishment. Frank was not a violent fellow like these burly types. He might have slapped his wives a bit but, in all likelihood, so had they. Fortunately for him, his injuries at the hand of unforgiving fellow convicts were slight in comparison to some he had read about, and in anecdotal accounts he had heard. His concocted, acknowledged crime of fraud had not caused him any trouble; his real crime had stayed a closely guarded secret. He had been most astute in keeping information, about himself, to himself.

    Probably, his talent for playing the cornet was his saving grace. On entering prison, his cornet - his most valuable and prized possession, had been taken from him. He had felt lost without it. He asked the warders how long they would keep it. They told him that if he behaved himself, perhaps it would be returned to him before long. He did not plan to make matters worse for himself. He would play their game. All he wanted was his cornet. There was no guarantee but if he got it back, he wanted it to be sooner rather than later.

    Finally, his skills had been recognised by the prison authorities; he was being utilised as a teacher of Music and English. The prison management had been progressive in dealing with its population and had come to the realisation that music, both the appreciation of it by listening and the learning to make music, could be a valuable tool in the rehabilitation of inmates from the least to the most violent.

    He did not know for how long he had been standing naked alone with his thoughts. Too long, he had reflected. The time had come for him to cover up. He had thrown on some clothes for his walk down to the bathroom. It was six o'clock. The loud rap on the door had been made by the officer on duty demanding that he got out of bed. He had picked up his cornet, and lovingly polished it until it gleamed. He had begun quietly to play an old Sally Army favourite, *Healing Waters*. The world stood still during such occasions and made his life there more tolerable. He replaced it lovingly on the chest of drawers. He shaved hastily, then carefully cleaned the razor and replaced it with precision into the right hand corner of the top drawer. He picked up his toothbrush and toothpaste which also lay in the same drawer.

    He rang the call bell so that he could get his ablutions over before others stirred. The facilities were basic. The overpowering odour of carbolic disinfectant was much in evidence. It was an old prison built in the 1860s and he had concluded that nothing much had been updated since then. He had used the W.C first then had turned on the shower so that it could run for a while in order to achieve a decent flow. In his former existence, before being locked away, he had enjoyed hot, power showers but all that emerged from the plumbing was the paltry dribbling and spurting of cold water. He had undressed quickly in the cold atmosphere and took a swift shower; he had applied similarly cold showers at the Hall. The boys had come to no harm… so why should he?

In no time at all, he was back in his cell. Opening the top drawer of the chest, he replaced his toothpaste and brush into the space allocated to them. He had located his watch in the second drawer and fastened it on to his left wrist. He took his diary, also, from the second drawer and opened it ready to record the contents of his breakfast pack. Opening the third drawer of his chest, he took out his prison uniform which he had put there, neatly-folded the previous night. A few handkerchiefs had been placed meticulously in that same drawer. He had taken one, carefully avoiding disturbing the ones remaining. And so he had dressed, in standard issue prison uniform - grey jogging bottoms, grey sweatshirt… grey everything.

He proceeded to prepare his breakfast. He opened his breakfast pack which had been delivered to his cell the previous evening. It had contained a small box of cornflakes, some bread, margarine, jam, and a carton of milk - barely enough to feed a mouse and he had the appetite of a weasel. He had eaten it deliberately slowly, endeavouring to extract the last atom of nourishment from his scant serving, savouring the flavour of the cornflakes, then the bread and jam. Even so, breakfast had ended in a trice and he had been left still hungry.

He sniffed the air recognising the whiff of bleach. The fumes had diffused under his door; he could almost taste the stench of the chlorine. He heard the clanking of the heavy-duty mop bucket as it was dragged along his corridor and the sound of the mop head as it hit his door.

He picked up his cornet again and reminisced about days gone by in Ravensborough where, in the Salvation Army, he had learned to play the instrument; in Scarp Edge where he had been a regular member of Scarp Edge Band and finally in Great Scarp where he had been the conductor of the town's esteemed brass band. Those had been good times. He had sighed deeply as he remembered his times with the bandsmen. He had spent the following hour in his cell with his cornet for company, being glad to be in the possession of melodies that he knew without musical notation. Playing familiar tunes had been his salvation.

At eight o'clock, precisely, he had presented himself for roll call. Perhaps his cell would be searched. He had nothing hidden, nothing illegal. He had been intent on making his imprisonment as brief as was possible so he had paid great attention to ensuring that he observed prison protocol to the letter in order that all of his actions were impeccable, thus earning him maximum remission.

He had anticipated a positive day ahead. He had an English skills class later in the morning. He had been gratified that his efforts were bearing fruit. To give illiterate fellow human beings the ability to read and write and to observe their delight in their achievements was considerably satisfying. Later that day, he would be involved in a music appreciation session with some visiting instrumentalists. The prisoners' faces would light up at the pleasure they derived from the mixture of classical, modern and brass band music which was where his musical prowess had lain. At the end of the session they would applaud and stamp their feet to show their appreciation.

He had started to hum a tune to himself in anticipation.

Much later, as lockdown approached, surprisingly he had received a letter from Helen. Helen had never written to him. He had never expected her to. He had received a letter from her solicitor in the month after his conviction stating that she was seeking a divorce from him on the grounds of unreasonable behaviour. He had thrown it in the trash bin. Occasionally, there had been one from a former teaching colleague, Henry Day who was merely responding to the letters which Frank had sent to him. He had seemed to have been forgotten by most. His correspondence for the most part had been with Shirley Entwhistle, the mother of a former pupil who also made the occasional visit when Her Majesty's Prison allowed it.

The letter was from Helen, his wife of nineteen years. The divorce she had been seeking was finalised.

'It's took yer long enuf', he spoke out loud to the letter which he still held in his hand.

He felt bitter about the rapidity with which Helen had closed down his school. He had lovingly built it into a successful business over eighteen months and within a week of his conviction; she had set the wheels in motion for its destruction.

The remainder of his time behind bars had been spent in much the same way as the first two years. Visits from Shirley Entwhistle had been as regular as had been permitted by the rules and regulations of Her Majesty's Prison. She had written to him every week, mostly women's drivel. Rarely, had he completed reading her letters. He had cultivated her, however, believing that she might be a useful ally or even an appendage on his release. Certainly, she had seemed to have been a successful business woman with cash to spend and so he saw no reason why she should not spend it on him. Shirley certainly had the sort of personality he preferred in a woman - quiet, docile, deferential and submissive, seemingly keen on him. He had wondered what it was about him which had attracted her. He had drooled at the thought of having her under his thumb and at his beck and call.

  Eventually, he had been called to the Governor's office and given the news that he had been waiting for since the day he walked in through those massive locked doors. The date of his release would be a month from that day. His would afford him sufficient time to write to Shirley and request that she collect him on that release date. He had been so glad that he had kept her address when he had thrown her letters into the trash bin.

CHAPTER FIVE

XIII

Intent on getting home without an accident on such slippery roads, Shirley was glad of the lack of conversation. She concentrated her thoughts upon what lay ahead. She had already gathered all the items needed and had secreted them away. The most difficult task had been getting hold of the packs of Zymkase. Frank was so meticulous; he would know if some were missing. She had needed only to ensure that the packets, so carefully stacked in the corner of the cabinet, were of equal height to escape possible detection. She had had to be constantly alert to any opportunity to raid Frank's cabinet to gather her supplies of Zymkase, relying on times when he had been drinking heavily and dosing himself on the painkillers. She had kept her fingers crossed, continuously hoping to avoid detection.

Shirley had been driving on 'automatic pilot' for the final ten minutes or so of the journey. She was lost in her subconscious, her brain going over and over all the fine detail of her murderous intent, constantly searching for potential hiccups which might crop up during the final act.

In a flash, her mind switched back to reality as she realised that she was approaching the street on which they lived. With great care and stealth on her part, the car glided to a silent halt. Slowly opening the door, making no sound, she cautiously stepped out into the fresh slippery snow, anxiously avoiding losing her balance in her dressy shoes which were quite unsuitable for the prevailing conditions underfoot. She removed them and ran up to the front door, her feet tingling in the cold, wet snow. She found her key and slipped it into the lock and opened the door. It was desperately cold inside as she had anticipated. Before departing the house some seven hours or so earlier, she had turned down the thermostat deliberately in order to engineer a low temperature on their return. She had guessed what Frank's reaction to the low temperature would be and so she would then encourage Frank to make use of the comforting sauna. She turned on the light and turned the dial on the thermostat to its regular setting. She slipped her feet into her boots and stomped back to where Frank slouched, waiting in the car.

'Wonder if he'd freeze to death if I left him here?' she pondered.

Frank had not been asleep after all. As soon as she got hold of him, he made a move to exit the car. His random, haphazard movements confirmed his state of drunkenness.

'Oh God, he's awake. Was he watching me just then?' she thought, suddenly panicking. *'He's got a colossal capacity for the booze. But he's so drunk. What if he's not drunk enough? He made sure there was nothing*

left in Hal's liqueur bottles. First a glass of Advocaat, then a refill of cherry brandy, followed by a refill of Cointreau, and so he continued to systematically drink them dry. How can he still be standing?'

He grunted and complained as she tried to help him through the treacherous conditions to the front door.

'Desist, Woman!' was his sole comment. On entering the house, he snarled. 'It's bloody cold in 'ere. What's to do wi' t' bloody heating? It's like a bleeding cold-store.' He peered at the thermostat. 'Bleeding heating's packed up…typical!'

'Never mind, luv, let's turn on the sauna. That'll soon warm you up.'

He nodded as he staggered up the stairs and headed for his bedroom. Shirley was right on his tail, marvelling at how compos mentis he appeared to have remained. She followed him in.

'Yer needn't wait here. Get t'sauna going'. He barked out his order. He swallowed more painkillers.

'OK luv,' she replied, striding purposefully out of the door.

The four-person sauna occupied the smallest of the three bedrooms which had been lined for best effect with Canadian hemlock. The sauna cabin which was electrically powered occupied most of the room. It contained slatted timber benches on which to recline, and was entered via a smoked-glass door. The *loyola* - the steam shock - was caused by sprinkling water over the heat-retaining, volcanic rocks. The sauna was of the highest quality and had been supplied with lengthy instructions, particularly recommending that its use should be avoided after alcohol, a heavy meal or drug-taking and sufficient water should be imbibed to prevent dehydration. It had been imported from Finland and had been professionally installed at great expense in their terraced house on Sylvan Way, in down-town Scarp Edge.

It was an ostentatious acquisition of which Frank was exceedingly proud. It had been something of a showstopper and a jaw-dropper which Frank had boastfully displayed to Hal and Chris on an earlier occasion. They had viewed it as a sleazy, inappropriate addition, with its *vihta* - a bunch of birch twigs - whose use was strictly for beating oneself to stimulate, the circulation , but which they suspected he used for more basic practices. Their view was that it discredited this once respectable terrace.

Having donned the plasma-coloured, latex gloves, which she had placed earlier in a prominent position so that she would remember to wear them, Shirley basked in self-indulgent pleasure for a quiet moment as she recollected that Frank's present physical condition did not satisfy any of the manufacturer's recommendations. Until that moment, she had displayed signs of nervous tension but miraculously they had dissipated, never to resurface, into the ether as she realised that she was in control…absolute control, at last. Her face having adopted a severe expression, Shirley switched the sauna controls, with fierce determination, to the maximum. In order to maintain her newly acquired self-confidence, she walked back, taking long, deep breaths and deliberately slow strides towards Frank's bedroom. She found him ridding himself of his final pieces of underwear and she delighted in the knowledge that never again would he wear clothes designed for a living body. She took his towelling robe and offered it to him in a final act of disingenuousness. Still muttering about the lack of heat in the house and totally ignoring her, he grabbed the robe and stumbled past her onto the landing. She did not take any offence at his ungrateful response to her apparently helpful gesture. It merely confirmed, in her mind, the correctness and natural justice of her plan and her resolute determination to carry it out to the letter.

Lurching into his sauna, he flopped onto a slatted bench. The amount of alcohol and drugs in his system were beginning to exert their deadly effect.

> He would never again regain total consciousness.

Shirley considered what might be the vilest act she could perform as she anticipated watching Frank die. She stared long and hard at him as he lay draped on the boards of the sauna, his naked, measly, Lilliputian external sexual organs modestly covered by a towel. Her latex-gloved hand sprinkled some eucalyptus-infused water onto the rocks. An immediate burst of a minty, honeyed aroma filled the air. Since he hated women with a vengeance, Shirley knew that the sweet scented atmosphere would have been unbearable to him.

The mere idea of sexual contact with a woman had always filled Frank with revulsion. Whether it was a result of his early fumbling with the local village girls or an inborn feature of his personality, it was impossible to know. However unpleasant he had found the experience, he had, nevertheless, managed to sire a son with Helen. Shirley had never been intimate with him. The arrangement had suited them both equally. Sexual contact with a man had never been one of her priorities, probably as a result of her having suffered disappointing experiences with Alf Entwistle, her disappointing, disingenuous, drink-dependent first husband.

Frank had subjected her to psychological torment for reasons she failed to comprehend. She could not understand why he had behaved in this way when she had been so caring towards him. Shirley had given him her approval when Linus had been at the Academy. She had been satisfied that Linus's conduct had improved as a result of Frank's methods. Consequently, her support had been unstintingly granted during his trial. After his first wife's intended desertion, Shirley dispatched letters to him every week and made visits to Pinchfold Castle Prison when protocol permitted. Furthermore, she had lavished money on him when he had alleged that all of his savings had been spent on solicitors' and barristers' fees and on his divorce settlement. Payment for that wildly extravagant wedding breakfast at the iconic Palm Grove restaurant and for the hire of the Silver Ghost to ferry them there had been from her account. Hers had been the exorbitant purchase of the Bechstein grand piano; she had included his name on the deeds of their house and the gift which had given Frank most pleasure was her purchase of the Finnish sauna which became his pride and joy. What she deliberated, had he done in return but treated her like the dirt on his shoe? It was true that he had been attentive at first, but it was all a ploy; she had been fooled; he had regarded her as an easy touch; all her caring, sympathetic acts of kindness towards him had been viewed as signs of weakness and he had exploited them.

He had subjected her to a life of subservient drudgery by perpetually insisting on her repeating her cleaning and tidying; he continually checked her bedroom so that he could find reasons to complain; he constantly checked that items of every description were in an ultra-state of absolute cleanliness and order. She had existed through this living nightmare for long enough. It was time to take action. It was Shirley's opinion that his coming to an unpleasant end would constitute a just punishment. She had had evil fantasies about procuring his death for most of their marriage, but she had never had the courage or the opportunity to take action until that heaven- sent invitation to the Days' dinner party landed on the doormat, enabling all of her fantasies concerning his demise at her hand to resurface.

She still wore her gloves and would continue to do so. With the unaccustomed confidence of the practised assassin, she left the sauna when an appropriately high temperature had been reached and closed the door. She returned with a packet of Zymkase capsules, two tumblers, one of which contained water, so essential to the maintenance of the body's hydration, and the other contained the amber-coloured single malt Scotch of which he was so fond. She had filled both of them almost to the brim. She placed the painkillers and both glasses within easy reach of his hand.

'Here you are, Frank, this whisky will warm you up.'

Frank was in a semi-comatose state. He had already drunk a copious volume of alcohol and had taken painkillers to excess but in his drugged and drunken state, he was beyond caring. He accepted her offer of more capsules and the whisky readily with the wild abandon that often accompanies the consumption of too much alcohol. Meticulous in the extreme, she had left no finger prints on any of the glasses or the ladle she had used to add water to the rocks. She had been fastidious in her attention to detail. The packet of painkillers which had been placed next to him, she had also been scrupulous to handle with her gloved hands. There would probably be some evidence of her having been in the sauna but, after all, she had used it in the past, so, inevitably, there would be traces of her DNA.

Shirley opened her iPad and tapped the screen a few times. The sound of music could be heard issuing from the tablet. She adjusted the volume to a level which Frank would be able to hear but which would not be so loud as to disturb the neighbours on the other side of the party wall.

'What about this? Frank. Here's some music to die for, you miserable git!'

The strains of *I will survive,* were clearly audible inside the sauna.

Frank had drifted into a nightmare-like trance in which he witnessed a naked woman, her legs spread wide before his gaze, penetrate her vagina using a dildo which consisted of a bright orange, substantially-sized, carrot. He was mesmerised as he watched in disgust as she gyrated in front of him. He listened to her groaning with apparent pleasure as she stroked her clitoris slowly at first and then rapidly as she approached orgasm triumphantly. It was as if she were taunting him about his own inadequacies. The nightmare scenario seemed to be never-ending. His head was becoming even fuzzier as he lost consciousness for a moment. Shirley was fully aware of his drifting in and out of consciousness. She rose, matter-of-factly from the bench from whence she had been performing for his entertainment; she removed the towel from the bench, and as she was leaving the cubicle, she added more water to the hot rocks. The steam which emerged was scalding hot. He was feeling deliciously warm inside because of the whisky and wonderfully warm on the outside because of the heat from the sauna. He was able to have a final congratulatory thought on the good idea he had had, to use the sauna to warm up his body before retiring.

Shirley closed the door, put on her bathrobe and headed for his bedroom. She laid out, on the chest of drawers, some pieces of toilet paper to serve as a disposable retaining napkin. She placed an empty glass on to her specially-prepared area and carefully emptied several capsules of Zymkase into it. She was careful not to exaggerate the amount of drug; she did not want to fall foul of the inevitable post-mortem on his body. She topped up the glass with more whisky from the bottle he kept by his bed.

'Surely, if the heat of the sauna and the Zymkase doesn't kill him, the amount of whisky I'm pouring down his gullet will', she predicted.

She wrapped all the emptied capsules tightly within the toilet paper napkin and flushed them away. She checked the surface where she had been working for any evidence of her deed. All seemed to be in order. She had deliberately avoided wearing perfume whose lingering aroma might have alerted some bright, young, perspicacious detective to her possible implication in Frank's demise. She returned to the sauna with the now deadly drink and the half-empty bottle. She approached him and encouraged him to drain the glass and to swallow more capsules. He did so willingly.

'This'll ease your pain,' she whispered to him and to herself she added, *'you cock-sucking blood sucker'.*

More water was added to the rocks and Shirley resumed her position opposite him. It was really sizzling in there. Not much alcohol had passed her lips at the Days'- a gin and tonic on their arrival and a small glass of red wine with the main course. Feeling perfectly sober and enjoying this spectacular if somewhat macabre situation, she resumed with melodramatic gusto the thrusting of the carrot into her bruised innermost part. Her voice adopting a theatrical whisper as in the archetypal stage aside, Shirley delivered the final line of her encore.

'Die! Die! You scabby scrote!'

Shirley looked at her watch and surveyed the scene. It was now four-thirty, the most deadly time of night and she was still wide awake, invigorated by her daring escapade. The temperature in the sauna was high…too hot for her, so she departed the crime-scene having left the whisky bottle, a tumbler of Scotch, a tumbler of water and a half-empty packet of Zymkase pain killers within Frank's reach. She put more water on the rocks and looked at the temperature in the sauna; it was at its maximum.

Feeling over the moon, and bursting with excitement, Shirley almost danced down the stairs towards the kitchen where she removed and subsequently discarded the cling film wrapping from the carrot. With smug self-satisfaction, she would devour the carrot as a memorable part of her lunch later that day. She relished the notion that it would represent a cannibalistic act, a final act of fulfilment derived from the ecstatic dispatch of the serially monstrous husband. She took the tumbler that had contained the overdose of powdered Zymkase and washed it carefully to remove all remaining traces of the drug and then having dried the tumbler, she replaced it in the cupboard behind the other glasses. Finally, she washed her gloves ultra-carefully, returning them to the box which still contained virgin gloves and replaced it in the wall-cupboard in the small utility room. She retraced her steps upstairs with a tot of whisky and ginger wine and entering her own room, placed it on her bedside table. She took a sip and felt the warmth of the Whisky Mac in her stomach.

She revisited the third bedroom and opened the door of the sauna. Immediately, it became evident that the heat was stifling in there. It would have been a miracle if Frank could have survived these conditions. In spite of being hardly able to breathe, Shirley sprinkled more water onto the rocks, sufficiently to obtain a further steam shock. A huge blast of super-heated steam billowed from the stove towards him.

'If you can survive this, my darling husband, you deserve to live,' she muttered with cynical sarcasm.

Shirley continued her mission for a further two hours in order to see it through to its conclusion. She did not require sleep. That would come later.

Ultimately, when she was satisfied that there was a cessation of his breathing, the assassin checked again for any careless errors which might have occurred during her state of euphoric excitement. She turned down the temperature control to the one suggested in the manual and made her exit to the sitting room where she kept her collection of antiques. Shirley faced her prized Harlequin and Columbine miniature manikins and spoke out loud to them,

'There, there, my lovelies, he'll never threaten you again'

EPILOGUE

April

After an early breakfast, encouraged by the warmth of the spring sunshine, they were busy in their garden; Hal was giving the lawn its first cut of the year and Chris was pottering among the flower beds carrying out much needed gardening chores, the worst of which was the weeding out of the tenacious, ground-hugging perennial grasses which had established themselves the previous summer during which their stealthy growth had been camouflaged by the leaves of the 'Big Daddy' Hosta, and the clumps of agapanthus. Now fully exposed in all their ragged, untidy state, they appeared to be provoking her into action. She hated that thankless task because the weeds, by their very nature, usually returned. They were the great survivors in the world of plants. She always took her grandfather's advice and carried the hoe with her. It saved a lot of back-breaking work, but it was not a useful weapon against such weeds as horsetails and couch grass. The phone rang. It was a miracle that they had heard the bell, owing to the bellowing of their new petrol-driven lawnmower, such a pleasant sound, on a summer's day when heard from a distance, but a cacophonous din when in its immediate vicinity.

Chris dropped everything, mentally thanking the caller for allowing her some respite from her back-breaking activities and rushed to the land-line which was located on the window sill in the kitchen. It was Shirley ringing to inform them of the date given for the inquest into Frank's death on the night of their dinner party one month previously. She presumed that they would be receiving a letter themselves directly from the authorities.

They had not set eyes on Shirley since the Monday after the unusual circumstances of Frank's death when they had called at the house on Sylvan Way in order to give their condolences and she to receive them. She had described to them how, on that Saturday morning after sleeping late, she had discovered Frank, dead in the sauna. Within his reach had been a tumbler of water, a half-empty whisky bottle, a half-full tumbler of single malt whisky and a half-empty packet of his Zymkase pain killers. She had dialled 999. The doctor and an ambulance had been summoned; the police had arrived too. Hal confirmed that he had seen a police car outside their terrace. She had obviously been asleep when Hal had put the mobile phone through the letter box. She did not know, she alleged, whether he had taken an overdose, deliberately or accidentally, or whether the heat of the sauna together with the alcohol and the drugs in his system had caused a heart attack. An inquest was inevitable. Shirley had made the assumption that the coroner would demand a post-mortem in order to discover the cause of death. She explained her need to escape all the publicity surrounding his death and his previous history which she anticipated would be sifted through by the local newspaper. It was the sort of sleazy story they were fond of printing for the titillation of their readers.

She had been at the hospital and then at the police station for the remainder of the Saturday. Then she had stayed alone in the house, incommunicado, on the Sunday. After their visit on the Monday, she had fled, incognito, with her sister, into deepest Wales, whilst maintaining contact with the local police in Ravensborough. It had been necessary to put her business on hold for the duration of her absence, much to the annoyance and inconvenience of her clients.

As they had departed from Sylvan Way, Chris could not help having an unsympathetic thought about the incongruity of such an idyllic name for such an undistinguished row of terraced dwellings.

They knew from the date she gave them that they would be able to attend the inquest in person as it was scheduled to be on the last Thursday of the Easter holiday. They must have driven past the Coroner's Court in Broadclough on numerous occasions because it was on the route which they had taken delivering Max to the KGV junior department. However, they had not noticed it; probably, they had been too engrossed in testing Max on his multiplication tables and spellings.

They decided to do a dummy run to find the exact location of the court building and the whereabouts of convenient parking places. They had grown unaccustomed to driving in the busy centres of towns and cities, but such legal edifices were typically situated in those urban hubs. On the approach to Broadclough, they became aware of the growing intensity of traffic and its accompanying toxic fumes which were able to percolate into their personal space inside the car obliging them to inhale the poisonous effluent spewing forth from surrounding vehicular emission systems even though all windows had been closed and the fan switched off. The acrid stench of other people's exhaust fumes stung their nostrils and left a dry, bitter taste on their tongues. They remarked to each other how fortunate they were to live in the rural hinterlands.

Chris spied the imposing nineteenth century courthouse, flanked by a modern, multi-storey car park and an office block on the left of the dual carriageway at a junction, complicated by traffic lights and iron barriers to restrict the careless meanderings of the jaywalker. The nearest and therefore most convenient parking area for pedestrian access to the courthouse was in George Street, in the multi-storey car park accessible from a side street just one minute's walk away at a cost of three pounds for a two hour period.

Two weeks later, the day of the inquest dawned. Chris woke early as usual, and left the sleeping Hal. She had the urge to do some baking. Whenever she was anxious or worried, she felt the need to find some way of allaying her unease. Making a batch of pastry or baking a cake usually did the trick. She decided to make a large, carrot cake which would be consumed later that day after the coroner's inquest.

Chris's recipe was very simple. She turned on the oven to the required temperature. Having mixed her dry ingredients in a large bowl, she poured into the mix, sunflower oil, apple juice and beaten eggs and combined them thoroughly, ridding herself of her malaise as she did so. Finally, she added the grated ingredients, apple, carrot, and sultanas and gently stirred the resulting batter which she carefully poured into her cake-tin and baked it for an hour. Her simple topping consisted of a mixture of mascarpone cheese, natural yogurt and a dash of vanilla essence. The bake was completed before they set off for the inquest.

The early mist had not cleared as might have been expected in mid-April. The weather, having settled into a soft drizzle, was more like low cloud making driving difficult. The darkness and gloominess of the day intensified the impending gravity of their ordeal in the coroner's court.

The hearing was timed for half-past one on Thursday, 19th April. The official invitation had advised them to arrive in good time. Hal had presumed that theirs would be the first case after lunch. He had wondered how long the proceedings would last; he did not want to pay any more than three pounds to park their car. If they arrived at the car park at one o'clock for a one-thirty hearing, even if there were to be a late start, surely the coroner would get the job done and dusted before his ticket had expired. He resolved to take a chance.

Hal had arranged with his parents to come in order to child-mind for them. Grandpa Day had made a good recovery from his heart attack but he had been advised to take care. He should not get involved with any more heavy work such as snow clearing which no doubt had been the trigger for his condition. It had been arranged that they should pick up Helen from Great Ridge and Shirley from Sylvan Way on the way to Broadclough. These two wives of the late Frank Hector had a lot in common with each other but on the journey, they did not share much conversation. They were too much involved with their own private thoughts. As their journey progressed, the weather improved and by the time they arrived in Broadclough, the sun was beating down, the earlier, damp gloom having been replaced by sunny stuffiness.

The traffic was very heavy due to the time of day. The lunch-time traffic had not yet abated because of family outings on such a lovely day in the Easter holiday. Having parked their car in the multi-storey car park, they had to walk down the side-street to access the court building by the central front door. The imposing three-storey building was magnificent in its construction and was typical of the beautiful, intricate workmanship of the

Victorian period. It was constructed mainly of a warm, orange-red brick with ornate sills and lintels of Portland stone. There was a central, canopied entrance flanked with two arched windows. The first floor bore a row of three large windows, the middle one of which was in the form of a semi-circular bay and was situated immediately above the main entrance. On the façade at the third floor level, there were four, smaller windows. All windows were multi-paned. Two large, varnished timber signs on either side of the front door announced, in gold leaf, CORONER'S COURT. Two narrow flower beds containing easy-care shrubs softened the severity of the edifice and separated the brick walls of the courthouse from the iron railings at the boundary with the pavement.

As Chris walked up to the central front door, she pitied the unfortunate window cleaner whose task it was to keep clean and shiny all those tiny panes of glass. They entered and made themselves known to the court usher who asked whether they wished to be sworn in or to give an affirmation. They all chose the latter. They entered the austere and unwelcoming court room, containing a mass of highly polished dark oak woodwork. The pungent, lemony aroma of furniture polish was much in evidence. Facing the door was the high bench behind which stood a central, grand, well-upholstered throne-like carver for the coroner's use. This was flanked by two lesser chairs for other officials. The witness box stood before the bench, to the right, so that it was in full view of the coroner, the other participants and the viewing public. Helen looked across at the former, *Broadclough Daily News* reporter, John Sutton, and they exchanged glances in acknowledgement. He had recently been promoted to Deputy-Editor; she wondered whether he was enjoying his new job.

There were several witnesses to be called to give their evidence: the wife, Shirley, who had discovered the body: the friends, the Days, who had held the dinner party: the police officer: the doctor and finally the paramedics.

Shirley, was first to be called into the witness box. She was asked about the circumstances in which she had found Frank. Had she known that he was dead; what action had she taken; why had he been in the sauna; at what time had he gone into the sauna. The final question concerned the reason for his using the sauna at that time of the night.

She spoke very calmly explaining that she had slept late because they had had a late night after a dinner party with friends, the Days, in Great Barrow, arriving home at approximately a quarter past three in the morning. She had gone straight to bed and had assumed that Frank had done the same. She explained that they did not share a bedroom. She had found his body, late the following morning, in the sauna with a tumbler of water, a half-empty bottle of single malt whisky, a tumbler half-full of whisky and a half-used packet of Zymkase strong painkillers, all of which were within reach of his hand. He had obtained the Zymkase from the doctor a few days before. He had been naked apart from a towel. When he had not responded to her calling and shaking him, she had immediately rung for an ambulance and had called the doctor. The police had arrived soon after the arrival of the ambulance. The paramedics, after a rapid assessment of his condition, had taken him straight to the hospital at Broadclough. She had accompanied them in the ambulance. She said that she did not know why he had decided to take a sauna at that time of night but that he had complained about the low temperature in the hall when they had arrived home. She explained that he had been drinking heavily during the evening and had not followed the dosage instructions on the packet. He had known himself that he had exceeded the stated dose but the pain in his leg from an accident years before had been unbearable. He had seemed not to care.

Hal was questioned next. He, too, showed no signs of nerves, but Chris knew what a good actor he was. He was asked what his relationship with Frank had been. Hal explained that they had been teaching colleagues some years before. He had maintained a superficial friendship with him because they had liked to debate with each other, abstract thoughts and topics currently in the news. They had occasionally met socially. There had been a certain amount of contact during his imprisonment in Pinchfold Castle Prison, largely as a result of Frank's initial letter to him and thus an intermittent correspondence had ensued. A chance meeting in the supermarket had resulted in the Hectors being invited to a dinner party at the Days as Frank had an issue to discuss with him concerning Frank's devisal of an adult party game which he wanted to test out at the dinner party. During the test run of his game, 'Truth or Belief', questions of an ethical nature had been discussed, and the air had been somewhat heated at times, as a result of home-truths having been told. Hal also described that Frank had been exceedingly drunk, having consumed most of three bottles of liqueur virtually single-handed. But he had not been incapacitated. He had been lucid enough to thank the host and hostess and could walk to the car though with difficulty because of the snowy conditions and the pain in his leg.

Chris was the next to be called to the witness box. She felt slightly dizzy in the heat of the afternoon sun which was filtering in through all those multi-paned windows. She had not felt like eating earlier but now felt faint with hunger and wished she had had some porridge at breakfast to sustain her. Her hands were clammy and she could not wipe them dry as much as she tried. Chris heard her own squeaky tones as she started to give her evidence. She had, to hand, the statement which she had made at the police station in Ravensborough, back in early March, on the Monday following Frank's death. She corroborated Hal's evidence. Frank had consumed a lot of whisky and liqueurs and he had swallowed several strong pain-killers. He had appeared to be in a lot of pain. She added that there had been no love lost between Frank and herself. They had been former colleagues at the James Ratcliffe High School but had been frequently at loggerheads with each other over his treatment of the children in his care and his total disregard for authority. He had had a lot of interesting feedback regarding his adult party game but had had to listen to a great many facts about himself which would not have pleased him.

The doctor was the final witness to be questioned. He confirmed that Frank had visited the surgery within the previous week prior to his death, in order to obtain further supplies of the opiate pain killer, Zymkase. The doctor confirmed that he had emphasised to Frank the necessity of adhering to the correct dose and to avoid the consumption of alcohol. He had not been aware of the stockpiles in Frank's medicine cabinet.

The coroner, after a brief discussion with the attending police officer and the paramedics and after considering the doctor's and the post mortem reports, soon came to his judgement. There was no absolute proof, from the post mortem, that the fatal heart attack suffered by the deceased was deliberate or accidental. The massive heart attack would have followed from the amount of opiate pain killer and the amount of strong alcohol he had taken, exacerbated by the high temperatures produced in the sauna. The coroner delivered a verdict of accidental death.

'What a remarkably apt conclusion and what a creepy coincidence,' Shirley thought, hiding a broad grin

from the assembled personnel, at the same time delighting in the tingling sensation which was running up and down her spine. *'How Frank would have enjoyed this whole investigation. Everyone has the 'belief' that his was an accidental death whereas the 'truth' of the matter is that I murdered him. This subject was, after all, his favourite topic for debate.'*

As the announcement was made for the court to rise, all four looked at each other with some kind of relief that the proceedings finally were over. Shirley would now be able to obtain the death certificate and get the organisation of the funeral underway. Hal hurried them along; he needed to get them back to the car; he was within his time limit, but only just.

On the return journey to Great Barrow, there had been substantially more conversation than on the outward journey. Helen and Shirley, talked to each other all the way home and discovered that although they had both hated Frank for the despicable ways in which he had tormented them, they had found, in each other, a firm basis for friendship.

Helen had left her tea shop in the safe hands of Anna and Andrej for the day and was very happy to join them all for afternoon tea at Luxor Lodge.

Grandma Day had been notified by phone that their return had been imminent and so she had put on the kettle to boil and was in the process of brewing the tea as the car came into the driveway. She had laid out plates, napkins, cups and saucers in readiness on the capacious table in the family room. Finally, a platter of assorted malted-brown sandwiches of egg mayonnaise, cheese and pickle and ham and mustard was produced, together with the frosted carrot cake that Chris had baked that morning.

They all were feeling ravenous after their nervous ordeal in the unfamiliar surroundings and practices of the Coroner's Court. The platter of sandwiches was soon demolished.

'Anyone for carrot cake?' Chris asked. 'I got some absolute whoppers from Norton's, chunky and juicy- top quality- the best I've had for a long time'.

Shirley positively squealed with delight. She confessed that she had not eaten carrots in a cake before.

Chris served a large slice of carrot cake to everyone and they all agreed that it was the best cake ever. For Shirley, there was an added piquancy in the carrot content at which she had a secret, inward smile to herself.

For Helen, an exciting, new life was hers for the taking with her business venture –'Helen's Haven'. Also, her social life was waxing bright. The snippet of information concerning her dinner-date, later in the week with John Sutton, Deputy-Editor of the *Broadclough Daily News,* she would keep to herself for the time being. She would also keep secret her whistle-blowing disclosure to John Sutton about the dubious, depraved behaviour of

Frank Hector at Abercrombie Restorative Academy and she could be sure of John's confidentiality because she knew that a reporter never divulges the source of his information.

END